THE ORDER OF WALERA

A.M. DYER

MISTY HOUSE PRESS

To request permissions, contact the publisher at Mistyhousepress@gmail.com

Paperback: 978-0-6454629-2-0

Audiobook: 978-0-6454629-4-4

Ebook: 978-0-6454629-3-7

This is the first edition of this publication

Printed in Australia and Internationally.

Published by Misty House Press

Mistyhousepress@gmail.com

MISTY HOUSE
PRESS

THE ORDER OF WALERA

A.M. DYER

MISTY HOUSE PRESS

This book is dedicated to my loving wife,

Lizzie Dyer.

Thank you for all of your love and support.

CHAPTER ONE

The sails flapped, held hostage by the mast against the wrath of the impending winds. The chills crept to the tip of the captain's fingers and toes as the last group of passengers boarded, and the eeriness of the trip sank into his bones as he turned to his boatswain. If there was ever a time the seaman could sense the inevitability of a storm looming, this was it. But the captain couldn't tell why the sea's acrimony did not feel wholly like the worst was yet to come.

"Whatever is not on board this ship in five minutes gets left behind!" the captain of the Flea yelled, strained urgency in his voice.

The boatswain, a thin man with a scraggly, mud-coloured hair matted against his skull, looked back at him, perplexed. Then he looked at the faces of the dozen people that were still trying to board and at the men still rolling the barrels onto the ship.

"They still got 'bout ten barrels left!" he replied, pointing in the direction of the cargo.

The captain did not afford the direction of the boatswain's outstretched arm the courtesy of a glance. "I told you, if it's not onboard in the next five minutes, it gets left behind in Duken. I don't care who or what it is. I'm not waiting here a moment longer than that. If you want to know how serious I am, you keep your skinny legs in Duken waters by the time the last sail is drawn," he said, as he gave the call for his seamen to prepare the ship to set sail.

His message travelled quickly and the men rushed the barrels and the rest of the cargo on board as the sounds of the hands on the ship readying to set sail played in the background. The people waiting to board were anxious to catch the last ship leaving for Edenborough as they began to shove their fares in the face of the boatswain.

At the end of the line, which had quickly turned into a hoard, stood a figure who was not disturbed by the announcement. The face was hidden from daylight, buried beneath the cover of a wide black scarf that formed a hood over his head. He wore a grey rumpled shirt underneath his black leather vest, and the ends of his trousers were buried in his boots that were laced high up to his shin. His only baggage was a small satchel strapped across his chest. He stepped swiftly to the side as the bodies in front of him jostled each other, arms outstretched so the boatswain wouldn't miss them, each determined to secure their place before the final sail was drawn.

Through the chorus of "here" and "take mine" among the plethora of calls and other languages, he watched with eyes that snapped at every movement as he barely moved his head. The boatswain sounded like he was drowning as he took each person's money and struggled to scribble down something that looked like names while complaining to the rest of the crew about the consequences of the captain's decision to have the ship leave immediately.

The man in the scarf took a step forward and stuck his left foot out ever so subtly behind an old man that smelled of ale. The old man stepped back and tripped. Trying to save himself from the fall, the old man grabbed another man in front of him, who threw himself against the back of the crowd to compensate. The crowd struggled for balance, bodies pressed against each other while they carved enough space for the man in the scarf to step forward.

The man in the scarf walked to the front of the line, past those who had been distracted by the crash, and dropped his coins into the hands of the mouth-breathing boatswain, from whom he took the charcoal and wrote down something that would pass as his name before walking on. Eyes trailed after him, starting with the perplexed boatswain and the passengers he left behind in the stir.

When the ship finally pulled away from port not a second past the captain's time, the anxiousness settled as the passengers found themselves places to pass the journey. The Flea was not a particularly large ship, and luxury was far from its task, but it got those passengers and cargo that managed to get onboard across the sea to the other side of the continent. Extravagance on the Flea was getting one of the three private staterooms to oneself while the rest of the passengers crowded a large cabin, sharing each other's stench for the duration of the trip.

In the corner of the deck, the man in the scarf sat on a small box with his head down. He rolled a copper medallion etched with a black star slowly across his knuckles. Around him, conversations bubbled up as strangers with different accents began talking in anticipation of the journey. He could tell without looking which part of the deck held the easterners – Ravinshore spoke like each syllable burnt their mouths. And he'd guessed it from their clothes already, but four of the passengers sounded like they were from Queen's Hill. The foreigners who'd only had a taste of the three kingdoms looked too reserved to speak at their table. Three of them were merchants, with one looking less fazed than the rest about the trip.

He clapped the medallion into his fist as he turned his gaze to his right to a pair of tiny sandal-clad feet standing a yard away from him. He slowly raised his head to the bright eyes of a small child in a dull blue dress. They locked eyes for a moment, the girl's gaze burrowing into his before it turned to curiosity. She was perhaps the only one on the entire ship who'd caught a glimpse of his face beneath the scarf. He watched as she looked down at his closed fist, then back to his face before the voice of a mother snapped at her and the child slowly moved away, eyes still looking at his hands.

The man in the scarf wandered into the cabin and sat in silence as, one after the other, the passengers succumbed to exhaustion. The tide wasn't troubling enough to have any of them too concerned to sleep. Soon he was the only one awake, listening to the various gears and snorts of the snoring around him. On the deck above, the sounds of the crew dropped away. The flame of the lanterns in the cabin burned bright and undisturbed. It danced as the man fingered the medallion in his hand and rolled it to a rhythm similar to the ship's movements.

In a different cabin, four men were coming down off their exploits of ale with the captain and crew. They had passed the time with drinks over stories of concubines, conquests, and controversies. At the mercy of his inebriation, one merchant with a chip out of his right ear used the chance to rant, saying he had brought his crates of special tobacco from Edenborough to Duken for some particularly noble men and they had had accepted it like common gluttons, showing their gratitude generously enough that it bordered on worship. But then, he said, the gratefulness had expired when he brought up the fact that Duken did not seem to be interested in following its sister kingdoms in expanding and progressing.

He made it clear that he'd given them a piece of his mind about how Duken was being held back by not adopting the new traditions and remaining unyielding about its thoughts on magic. The merchant had not mentioned it specifically, but he implied that the kingdom was being held back by its own lack of flexibility and the paranoia of a king reminiscent of another from a certain war. Some of the voices at the table had fallen less ebullient as he spoke, and others had toasted and banged mugs in agreement.

The captain had been part of the group who had gone quiet. The taste of ale soured in his mouth as he stepped out on deck to see what mood the sea was in. The eeriness persisted, but the sea was calm and the fog hadn't worsened since they had set sail from Duken.

The captain's mind, consumed by the trip, paid little attention to the merchant and his drunken words. The fact that he had made it out of Duken alive was evidence that all he had done was upset a few nobles. There didn't seem to be anything to be concerned about as the man was hours away from the other side of the continent, though left to him, the captain would ask the merchant to keep his mouth shut if he cared about keeping his head on his neck. Despite being in the middle of the sea, the kingdom had ever-open ears and a reach that extended far beyond its walls.

There were some thoughts that people of Duken knew better than to air in the open, opinions that had the potential to disrupt the peace of the kingdom. The captain would have asked the merchant why he didn't use wisdom when speaking about a certain king and the war, because there was something that had followed the reign of that king and had ended that war. A shadowy cloud of doom that hunted those perceived to represent disorder. One he was not prepared to experience. Getting his ship across the sea to Edenborough was about all of the chaos he needed to deal with.

Not long after the captain retreated into his own cabin for the evening, a surreptitious calm washed over the ship as it inched closer to its destination. The boards of the deck were silent as a presence drifted through the shadows to the cabin where the intoxicated merchant and his men had moved for the night. In the cabin, two men had their heads on the table against the half-empty jugs of ale, and another rested his head against the ship, sitting on a box and drooling out the side of his mouth. The chipped-ear merchant was on his back with his hat over his face, one leg on a bed, and the other on the floor as he snored the loudest. None of the men so much as twitched at the presence in the room. But the tumult that followed broke the ship's slumber and had all of them pouring out across the deck. Voices yelled against the thrashing waves. The ship lurched forward and back as the merchants struggled to keep upright.

The captain screamed orders at his men as the sail struggled against the heavy winds; he looked down to see the merchants and a few other men spill out of the cabin like ants from a hole that had been stomped on.

"How can we help?!" a voice yelled from below despite the pelting rain and the rumbling of the clouds.

"Make your bloody hands useful with those ropes if you can, keep your eyes on the sail, offer your hands to the man that needs it. Get anything that's not tied to the floor either tied down or down below! And you, with the wide eyes," he said to a man who was futilely holding his hat on his head, "go around and make sure water isn't finding its way anywhere inside the ship. If you see anything get up here as fast as you can and tell me! The rest of you, keep whatever's flying loose in those cabins strapped down, then join the crew in keeping the cargo intact!" the captain screamed his orders, hoping they heard them. He assumed they did when they all scattered, some across the deck and others below. The eeriness he had been feeling all through launch was coming to life.

In the fight for survival, no one found the chaos on the ship lacking as everyone ran back and forth. Two men were with the cargo, trying to keep it in place, when suddenly one of the lights went black. One of the men left to replace it. The chipped-ear merchant was left alone to watch the cargo. The unrest on the deck as the ship moved violently with the storm blocked the chipped-ear merchant's senses and, with his back turned to fix the cargo, he felt a sharp pinch in the back of his neck. He flinched and turned, but saw nothing in the dim light of the room. He spun again, many times while gripping his neck. He hardly felt any pain by the time his partner returned with light.

A figure had passed by in the ship's darkness. And the warmth rattled against the skin of his neck. "It was like a needle," he told his partner, touching the sting in the back of his neck. He was sure that he had seen something in the shadow.

"It's the storm, surely! The madness reaches everyone and yours has come early!" the other man said to him.

For a brief moment that night it had looked hopeless, but the storm quieted eventually and the Flea made it to Edenborough before dawn, and one after the other, the grateful passengers disembarked. On the harbor, the little girl with small sandals held a medallion inscribed with a star in her hand as her mother led her away from the ship. The star glinted against the light as the girl took one more curious glance at it before grasping it tightly.

And as the Flea docked, the boatswain walked to the cabin and woke the merchants; all but one responded. The boatswain called for the captain, who arrived at the cabin to find a dead merchant with a web of black veins along the side of his neck.

Wide-eyed, a chill strangled the captain's heart. What were the odds that the merchant's death was a coincidence, mere hours from speaking ill against the kingdom?

In the middle of the streets in Edenborough, a man in a black scarf sauntered away from the docks towards the center of town with a needle hidden in his leather gauntlet. He touched his arm where a trident brand lay hidden beneath the material of his shirt as the cold breeze from the sea descended.

CHAPTER TWO

To the north of Duken, across the Black River and surrounded by hills, was Queen's Hill, a kingdom that allowed the practice of free magic and had more mages than anywhere else on the continent. And to the east was Ravinshore, the largest of the three sister kingdoms. Ravinshore had more land than Duken and half of Queen's Hill combined.

Duken had its waters – the Black River and sea at its beckon; the majority of its people were fishermen, harbor men, and seamen. Duken put great effort into its harbor, which allowed goods from the other side of the continent to pass through its kingdom before they made their way to either Queen's Hill or Ravinshore. Merchants and foreigners planted their roots in the kingdom and made it so that its fortune would rival Queen's Hill.

For the north, Queen's Hill had the best hunters and livestock, and the best structures amongst the three kingdoms were located in Queen's Hill, including the highest point in the three territories – the Queen's Hill Castle, where the king and the royal family lived.

Ravinshore had the best builders amongst the three – the best metal work was done by a blacksmith of Ravinshore who created everything from weapons to armors, to wheels, to jewelry. A person from Ravinshore was naturally handy and skillful. The men of Ravinshore were also known for being the tallest of the three kingdoms and having long hair; King William of Ravinshore was a man who had a particularly imposing look, quite the opposite of his counterpart from Duken.

King Mathea had taken reign over Duken after his father's demise, becoming the youngest king on the continent at the age of fourteen. While he had still been the heir to the Duken Kingdom, Mathea had been obsessed with the need to remind people who he was, an attribute that came partly because of his diminutive size. Mathea was small for his age, smaller than the rest of his younger siblings. The moment he had realized his power, he began punishing anyone who dared make a spectacle of him. Before he took the throne, Mathea had ordered people whipped in the middle of markets for not showing him enough respect. In the years since his father's death, he had not changed.

King Gerard of Queen's Hill's celebration of his daughter's marriage had seen the kings of the three kingdoms sitting at the same table for the first time since William had ascended the throne. Mathea's golden seat had been brought special all the way from Duken; adorned with gold, it was unmistakable. It had a step and was fitted with a raised red velvet cushion and a mechanism that allowed him to raise it whenever he desired; it was meant to bring him to a reasonable level to his peers when he was at the table, but it barely made a difference in regards to King William. Mathea looked like a child between the other two kings, even though he was the oldest.

Mathea's insecurity worsened at the party as he felt mocked and overlooked. But despite everything that had occurred at the celebration, it was at the private meeting between kings where Mathea found his bane.

When Mathea stepped away from the company of kings to take a leak, he heard Gerard and William's loud snickering. He was sure that they were mocking him and his detest for both of them grew as he heard them talking about Duken. King Mathea returned to his land with the certainty that King William and King Gerard had been conspiring to usurp him.

For months, Mathea kept his eyes peeled. Fearing imminent attack, he ordered his generals to set up strongholds and move troops to the borders, the shore, and Black River for when the attack came. But nothing did. King Mathea's anxiety about his supposed enemies led him to a solution that came to him in a dream. Mathea, trusting no one in any of the three kingdoms, hired two assassins from overseas. When they arrived, he pretended they were advisers, and gave them the task of getting rid of his problems.

Of the two assassins, the one sent to the Queen's Hill killed King Gerard. Along with killing the king, the assassin also murdered his crown prince. As screams of horror spread through the kingdom across the Black River, the assassin that had been sent after King William failed when he struck the king's brother instead and was captured.

Mathea's madness came true in the combined fury of Ravinshore and Queen's Hill, and the war he had so feared finally arrived.

The War of Black River lasted four years, even after Mathea's death. Duken's tyrant had finally been killed by one of his own generals, who took the mad king's head after Mathea had lunged at him with a sword when he refused to send more of Duken's young boys to die in his war.

Three months after Mathea's death, the three kingdoms finally agreed to lay down arms in a White Indulgence. King William of Ravinshore, Queen Lyra of Queen's Hill and Mathea's exiled brother, who had returned, agreed that in order to avoid a future war, each kingdom would create an Order that would serve and protect it. Each Order would be entrusted with the power to stop anyone that might pose a threat to the peace of the kingdoms. It was also decreed that no Order from another kingdom was allowed to occupy a territory outside its own.

Duken formed the Order of the Three. In Queen's Hill, Queen Lyra created the Order of the Red Flame. And in Ravinshore, the Order of Walrea became the silent and unseen defenders of the kingdom.

***

Olin pushed the door open as gently as he could, peering in until he was sure it was indeed empty. He stepped through, eyes wide as the silence of the room greeted him. He had been there just once after his arrival and since then he had not been able to stop thinking about what he had seen.

Olin gently nudged the door closed and stepped further in. The room was large – it wasn't the largest one he had ever seen, but it was definitely close, and looked more memorable than the last one. In the center was a large table with twelve seats, and on the walls hung unique portraits. The portraits were unique because they had no face; he had never seen anything like that before. He walked to one of the portraits and stared at it; the figure was dressed in a black leather doublet with laces and had brass gauntlets on each of his wrists. Olin assumed that the faceless figure in the portrait was a man, given the look of his chest beneath his vest.

As Olin stared at the image, he noticed a mark on the back of the man's forearm almost hidden by his gauntlet. It piqued his interest, but he couldn't see it clearly, so he moved to the next portrait. On this one, he could see only half of the mark but nothing more, so Olin moved to the third faceless painting, hoping he would be able to see the full mark. The man in this painting had a roll of cloth bandage over his arm underneath the gauntlet.

Olin spun in a circle and counted twenty portraits hanging on the walls, all of them faceless. He suddenly realized why the men in the paintings had no faces. They were watchers, Lord Watchers of the Order to be precise, and the identity of any of the past or present watchers could only be known by the king, members of the Order, and a handful of others.

Olin moved around the room, awe in his eyes as he gazed at the semblances of the men that had led the Order of Walrea and kept peace in Ravinshore. He might not be able to see what they looked like, but he knew that they were the protectors of the kingdom. He had heard stories of Watchers of the Order ever since he was a child, and he had always hoped that he would one day become one of them. Most of his childhood, he had anticipated the day he would be summoned. Now, it had come.

It had come, only it wasn't for what he had hoped. Olin had dreamt of becoming a watcher someday, to protect the people and the kingdom, but when he'd realized that he had been summoned to become a sciff, it had sunk his heart. Though he had been disappointed by the realization, his only bit of hope was that he was going to be in Walrea, the Watcher's Den, and close to his childhood dream.

Olin ran his hands over the tallest chair at the head of the table, imagining the Lord Watcher addressing his men about how to deal with the threats looming over Ravinshore. He crossed to the other side of the room and continued to peer at the rest of the paintings. These looked brighter than the ones on the other wall, and Olin assumed they were from the most recent century. The way the watchers had posed for the paintings remained the same, and their faces remained blank on the canvas.

Olin stopped in front of one portrait where he noticed the watcher was missing a finger – the pinky finger on the watcher's right hand. Olin drew closer. He stared at the painting and, for the first time since he'd been in the room, he ran his fingertips across the canvas, feeling the texture of the hand where the finger should have been.

The painting tilted slightly at his touch and he gasped as the room creaked.

He turned around to make sure that he was still alone. Once again calm, Olin stepped up to reposition the portrait on the wall, but was surprised when it tilted to the right even further. A wall to his right creaked open.

He took a hurried step back. All of Olin's reservations lasted but a moment as his curiosity took charge and he stepped towards the newly opened wall. As Olin drew closer, he realized that the opening was a door rather than a wooden wall serving as a background to more paintings. Olin peered in through into a small room, not as small as a cell, but much smaller than the painting room. He stepped in. If there were any windows, he couldn't see them, but there looked to be small holes at the top of the walls, just about the size of half a brick to keep air coming into the room. The holes allowed some light, just about enough that, if the door was closed, he would be able to tell what time of the day it was.

Olin could see in the secret room because of the two lit wall-torches hanging on either side of the chamber. He couldn't tell whether the flames burned from a spell, or normal fire. There was a table in the room, much smaller than the one outside, and this one had just a single chair attached to it. On the table sat a pile of scrolls, with a single scroll laid open, and Olin stepped around the table to reach it. He passed two smaller doors, each seemingly part of a cabinet. Olin tried the first but it didn't budge, so he tried just a little harder, with the effort of a young man who was nothing if not curious but couldn't afford to break anything in his attempt. Admitting defeat, he left the door and its hidden contents and moved to the next, casually, nothing like a young man cautious of where he was wandering.

The young sciff tried the next door and let out a gasp when it opened and he saw what was behind it. He had always wondered what one might look like in person, and the paintings he had been staring at since had only made him more curious. Olin ran his eyes from the long-laced boots up the trousers to the vest with its laces. Gauntlets hung on each side. His eyes moved to the mask covering the lower half of the wooden mannequin head. Chills run through his body as he slowly reached out to feel the doublet. But he stopped short, remembering some of the myths he'd heard when he'd been younger about how a watcher could always tell when his vest had been touched and how some watchers had poisoned their own clothes. Olin withdrew his hand and settled for merely taking in the attire with his eyes.

After having his fill, Olin closed the door and finally made his way around the table to the scrolls. He picked up one of the unopened ones and examined it, but set it back down just as quickly. Olin then sat in the chair and stared at the open scroll in front of him. At first, he saw nothing – the scroll looked blank – and the sciff leaned in and stared at it for a moment, intrigued and almost disappointed. Then he picked it up and Olin's eyes widened as he could suddenly see what was on it. He couldn't tell for sure what it was – the language wasn't one he recognized. The only thing that he could tell was that it looked like a map, with the sea to one side and a line running from it through a landmass. Olin could recognize mountains on a map – he had seen some before on pages of scrolls with his uncle.

Olin jerked when he heard creaks followed by footsteps. He dropped the scroll, got up slowly, and inched towards the door with his lips pressed into a thin line. His mind spun, trying to piece together an excuse for his presence here. There was none. As a mere hand servant of the

Order, the sciff could not afford to leave the safety of the hidden room, not when he wasn't sure what was waiting for him besides a premature end to only his second week at Walrea.

Olin pressed himself against the wall and reached for the door to close it; he left a slit open as he was sure that the sound of the door closing would be just as loud as when he'd accidentally opened it. If whoever was in the room wasn't deaf, they would definitely hear it, just like he had. Olin held his breath, frozen where he stood, hoping to the gods that the crooked painting wasn't noticed. He swallowed when he heard voices that hinted he might be doomed after all.

CHAPTER THREE

"I know it's only been a matter of days, but can we be sure that there won't be some kind of intervention that could work against this?" the first voice asked.

There was a brief pause before the response came; the second voice sounded deeper and much calmer than the first. "You sound like you have suddenly forgotten what we have used and what he's suffering from. There's a reason why what has befallen him is hardly ever used, and it's because there is absolutely nothing that can be done to stop it. There's also no way to trace it, even if it's suspected. Why do I need to remind you of this?"

"Because this is different," the first voice hissed. "We have taken care of obstacles that have had wealth and connections at their disposal. But none of them have been like this."

"It doesn't matter if all of the mages, sorcerers, or healers in the kingdom are summoned, he's not getting out of this alive."

"Still, I would have preferred if we had done it quicker. Why couldn't it have been done quicker?"

Another pause, then a response came from the decisive voice, "Because, L, Edmond succumbing to his death in anything less than three days was going to start a crusade of investigations we couldn't afford to deal with. Not with everything we have planned."

"We could have dealt with the questions ourselves. It would have been our job after all. Would it not?" came the second voice after another step and scuff echoed in the room.

"Tell me again why you seem panicked? You have never doubted any of your other assignments. You have done what was asked of you. All you need to do is be patient now."

"Patience is easy when you don't have it all on the line."

"Enough!"

Olin gasped and the door he held creaked against his grip. He pursed his lips and held his breath. The pause that followed didn't help his anxiety.

"Every moment that you and every other watcher is out there doing what needs to be done, everything is on the line. You do not become what you are by not sacrificing everything. You did that from the moment your blood and your sweat dropped on Walrea and you swore everything to become what you are. The only reason I am indulging you in this conversation is because you have the grace of your past achievements to fall on, and that is a one-time grace you get, nothing more. Do not take it too far and risk sinking your motivation into shaky ground. I need to know that you have not suddenly grown feeble and common."

"Of course, I haven't."

"Then let that be the last I hear of your questions. Your attention should be on what's next. Things have already begun to move now that he is seen as frail. Once it is done for good, there will be even more to deal with for the plan to succeed and everything will move quickly. Check on everyone and let them be reminded that once they receive the signal, there can be no room for hesitation or failure."

"You don't have to remind anyone. You have never had to."

"Yet here I am, reminding you. For your own sake, watcher, I am going to pretend that it never happened. Do as you have been told," the daunting voice answered.

Olin struggled to keep still as he listened to yet another bout of silence. The reality of the conversation began to sink in, replacing the fear of survival that had gripped him moments before. Eventually, two sets of footsteps faded and a door closed. He waited for a moment before he slowly widened the door, peeking out before stepping from the secret room.

It was then that he noticed a pillar against the wall by the crooked painting that obscured the painting's position from most of the room. Olin closed the door and watched the painting fall back into place. He looked around the room; he was alone again. Olin swallowed hard before quickly hurrying towards the exit, opening the door slowly. He stepped out of the room and glanced down the hall to see two figures walking away several yards to his right.

He started to follow them, only to realize how suspicious that would be, and turned to go the opposite direction. Then Olin stopped short, and his eyes widened as he realized what he had just seen. He turned in time to catch sight of the masked face of one of the men looking at him. The other soon joined him. Olin's heart dropped, then started thumping in his chest as he turned and started walking away as fast as he could. If there was ever a moment he had felt dread in his life, this was it.

Olin didn't bother looking back as he left the passage, making his way down the stairs and hurrying in the direction of his room. After reaching it, Olin slammed the door shut, leaning against it. It took him another moment to come to terms with what he had heard and where he had been.

The Den of Walrea. If all of the bells ringing in his head were right, then there was a fair chance his curiosity might have fetched him something worse than Wylie's scolding. He stepped away from the door, keeping his eyes on it as he stepped backward towards the window. There was a chance – if he chose to be hopeful – that it was all in his head and he hadn't even heard right, and the figures staring at him weren't worth panicking about. If that was true, then there would be need for overreacting, because no one probably cared.

But then he heard footsteps, and Olin saw a shadow move underneath the door and he shook his head.

He turned and looked out the window; there was a wagon attached to a horse parked a few yards away. Olin looked back one more time, weighing the odds that he was imagining it all. It was easy to imagine a life in the fields, safe with friends, telling stories to scare the children. He would even take an actual nightmare haunting him ... anything but what he was facing now. Olin watched in horror as the handle of the door moved slightly. Before he could change his mind, he climbed out of the window and jumped.

***

Thorne opened the door to the room and glanced around, expression serious. Nothing in the furniture or the paintings seemed out of place. He swept his gaze behind the door around to each corner of the room as he searched for anything that looked off. Nothing.

Thorne moved towards the painting with missing finger and stared at it. It looked like nothing had been disturbed and he was about to walk away, but then he turned back again. He glanced at the wall behind the next painting, but still found nothing amiss. Thorne touched the hand in the portrait and moved the frame in a way only he would know. The hidden door opened and Thorne walked into the room. It looked no different than how he'd left it. The scrolls were still on the table and nothing seemed disturbed. At least until the watcher reached for his belt and pulled out his dagger. He nicked himself in the palm and as the blood beaded, he closed his fist in the air.

"Commostro ad ostedio!" Thorne said as his blood dropped to the ground.

A series of glowing red threads emerged from the blood, twining around every part of the room that had been touched since his absence. Thorne followed the threads to the handles of the cabinet door and eventually to the table and the scrolls. He picked up the scroll he had left open and the Lord Watcher ground his jaw as the thread burned around it.

***

Olin landed on his feet like it was nothing and ran to the wagon waiting a few yards away from the stable. He leapt into the back and threw the empty sacks that smelled just as bad as horse manure over his legs and the rest of the body, keeping as still as he could, but there were no bells, no hurried footsteps or voices clamoring for him.

For a moment, the silence gave the illusion that nothing was happening. But then again, Olin thought, he was in the one place in the whole of Ravinshore where a ruckus didn't need to be created before doom found him.

Olin made sure the sack covered his hair properly, then pulled it aside to peek through. Everything still seemed ominously normal. Then Olin froze as a half-masked face appeared in the window he'd jumped from. The watcher turned in the direction of the wagon just in time for Olin to feel the weight of a bundle of hay thrown over him. A basket followed and soon Olin heard the sound of the driver climbing onto the seat of the wagon before they started to move. His heart was barreling in his chest, and Olin wasn't eager to question where they were going as they left the Watcher's Den, he just prayed that the wagon didn't stop.

CHAPTER FOUR

Queen Ariana rose from the bedside and walked to the window, peering down at the field below. Her eyes caught first on the little redhead and she watched as he threw his head back to laugh; next to him, a girl's shoulders shook as she joined him in laughing at the older boy who was peeling himself off the ground, dusting his behind with a shocked expression. He looked at the dirt in his hands and showed it to them and they laughed even harder. He took off after both of them, chasing them around the field, his long strides carefully measured to give their smaller legs a chance against him. She watched as he stopped the chase abruptly and grabbed the redhead, who all but ran into his arms while the girl fell into another laughing fit.

Silently watching from the window, the muscles of Ariana's face tightened and the corner of her mouth twitched, trying to force a smile she could not permit. She looked away from the children towards the stable where a servant was trying to get a grey stallion to step out and her heart ached again.

"Your Grace."

Queen Ariana turned slowly to Ole, who bowed. Beside the Court's Counsel was a young woman dressed in a black robe with a satchel strapped across her body. The young woman pulled the hood of her cloak down and bowed just like Ole had.

"This is Isabelle, the sorceress from Maedro," Ole said.

Ariana straightened as she stared at the woman in front of her. Isabelle looked back at the queen. Ariana couldn't have cared less how daunting and tanned Isabelle looked, how she was dressed, or where she was from.

Only one thing mattered to her: "Can she heal him?" the queen asked, uncharacteristically curt.

Ole glanced at the sorceress and then back at the queen. "She comes highly recommended, Your Grace. She specializes in strange situations like His Majesty's."

Ariana still stared at the foreigner, as if she could judge skill from sight alone. The Maedrian sorceress was the fourth healer that had been brought into her husband's chamber in the last four days and her predecessors, who had all supposedly been highly skilled, had each failed. Nothing they had done had as much as made the king twitch. Since his last collapse, he had only been getting worse, paler with each day that passed.

The queen nodded at Ole who gestured for the sorceress to move towards the king's bed. The queen stood by, hands crossed over her chest as she watched the mage examine her husband. The chamberlain stood by to assist.

Isabelle dropped her satchel and took the king's hand for a whole minute, saying nothing. A moment later, the mage opened her eyes and turned to Ariana.

"I need to cut him," she said.

"Excuse me?"

The sorceress looked from the queen to Ole and back. "I will need to see the king's blood, just a little drop of it. Will you let me do that?" she asked.

Ole looked in surprise at the queen, waiting. As much as Ariana wanted to question the reason behind the request, she wanted her husband to open his eyes more. She nodded, then watched with Ole and the chamberlain as the sorceress reached for a satchel and produced a long needle from inside a small tube. Ariana clenched her fists as Isabelle took her husband's hand and pricked the tip of his finger gently to draw a bead of blood. The sorceress then began to mutter words that the queen couldn't understand, casting a spell with the blood. A glowing thread swirled from Isabelle's right hand as she worked, seemingly drawing the essence from the king's blood.

Ariana switched her gaze from her husband to the sorceress and back, waiting for something to change. Isabelle finally stopped and wiped away the blood, then turned to faced the Ole and the queen.

"So?" Ariana asked. "Do you know what's wrong with him? Can you wake him?"

"I will be very honest, Your Grace. It's not good. Let me say it this way: if His Majesty gets well, it will be nothing short of a great miracle."

Ariana clenched her fist and her face pinched. "Were you brought here to talk about how impossible it is to heal the king? If you are clueless about what is wrong you can say that, you won't be the first one to pretend as if they knew something that they did not!" she retorted.

"Apologies, Your Grace, I don't think the sorceress meant any upset," Ole said, stepping forward and bowing his head.

"I do not mean to upset the queen," Isabelle said. "I apologize if it appears that I may have. But for me to say this, you must understand that I saw something, or should I say, I did *not* see something. When I touched the king, I could not feel his life force. It was as if it was no longer there. That is very terrifying. Ole has told me what happened and it didn't sound like anything I know of that could bring a man down like this."

"And what do you know that could bring a man down like this?" the queen followed quickly.

"Magic," Isabelle answered, drawing a gasp from Ole. "And not just any kind of magic, it is the *Egro*, dark and powerful magic not practiced by ordinary people, or good people. But even for that kind of magic to have been used on the king, the sorcerer would have needed to have the king alone long enough to draw out his life force. That does not sound like what happened."

Ariana shook her head. "No," she confirmed. "It isn't."

Isabelle looked back at the king, then returned her gaze to Ariana. "Which is why I cut him to see his blood myself. And what I sensed is the reason I said it will be a great miracle if the king can be saved. You see, Your Grace, the only other explanation for the mysterious illness and fading life force is that the attack is coming very slowly. Instead of happening at once, it is taking its time till ... till it is done."

"What are you saying?" Ole asked.

"I am saying that the king's blood is the very thing that is now draining his life force. I think the king has been poisoned," Ariana answered.

The chamberlain stiffened where he stood a few paces away from the king's bed; he could feel the pores of his forehead threaten to break out with sweat.

"What?" Ole's eyes widened. "That's impossible! No one would dare do that! The king's meals are all tasted beforehand. He is watched by guards at all times. There's no way anyone could have gotten to him. There's no way anyone could have managed it!"

Isabelle stared at him, holding back the words: *yet here he is.*

"How could ... how could it have happened?" Queen Ariana asked. The trembling apparent in her voice.

"I'm afraid I cannot say for sure. But if the king has not faced a dark sorcerer who drained his life force, the only other way it could have been done is through his blood. His blood is very dark, corrupted. If it had been noticed when he was first poisoned, there may have been a better chance to save him. But now, it will take the impossible to save His Majesty," the sorceress said.

"What is it?" Ariana stepped closer, desperation in her eyes. "What impossibility could bring this miracle? What will it take? Ask whatever you want, whatever you need. What will it take?"

Isabelle shook her head and sighed. "I'm not talking about material things, Your Grace. I talk of magic, a kind of skill that has not been seen for centuries. A kind of power I do not have because it is so rare it is almost impossible to find."

Ariana's hands dropped as she stared at the sorceress. She had feared the possibility that nothing would come of this, but she had also hoped because she could not afford to think of what it would mean for there to be no way to save her husband. Ariana walked to the bedside. His short brown hair seemed to have thinned since he had fallen ill and his skin continued to pale, with dark shadows around his eyes.

"Is he ... in pain?" Ariana asked. She hoped he wasn't. With the horror of what the sorceress had revealed, she hoped at least he was being spared the torture of the agony.

The sorceress looked to Ole before she turned to the queen. "He feels nothing," she answered. Isabelle took a few steps closer, seeing clearly the pain Ariana was feeling at her husband's illness. "I am sorry ..." she began to say.

"Why?" Ariana asked, somewhat curt. "It's not as if you had something to do with what has happened to him. Now," the queen said, looking at Isabelle, who had hardly blinked at her response, "I was of the impression that your visit would be different from the other healers who'd come and mouth-breathed all over my husband." As she spoke her face was almost stern as her gaze.

Immediately after she said the words, Ariana knew they were unfair; the previous healers had all come, filled with pride that would be the ones to figure out what was ailing the king, and heal him. They had used magic, just like Isabelle, and Ariana had watched as none of the so-called greatest healers in Ravinshore had been able to figure out why her husband had collapsed in the middle of the palace. Each of them gave nothing but myriad excuses and it-could-bes. Despite her morbid news, Isabelle had known something, had been sure of something. Had told her something.

Queen Ariana knew her words were far from fair.

"Well, I apologize that I have not healed your husband as you expected me to, but I have been honest with you. Hope remains, however small," Isabelle said.

Ole's brows rose at the sorceress's words. "What are you saying, Isabelle? You mean there's something you can try?" He looked anxiously from her to Queen Ariana, whose gaze was locked on the Maedrian woman, unwilling to miss how she would answer.

"The kind of skill this will take is not something I alone have." The sorceress glanced at the king before meeting the queen's stare. "But it doesn't mean I cannot seek who has it," she said. "If I'm able to find a Grand Sorcerer who is powerful enough, together, we might just be able to try the impossible and—"

"Give Ravinshore a miracle," Ariana finished and Isabelle nodded. "Isabelle," Ariana said the sorceress's name for the first time, curtness gone from her voice. "I have asked you before, but perhaps in words that were too ignorant and in a manner that was deaf to everything except what I wanted to hear. What will it take for you find this person who can help you help my husband?"

"A horse and two days. So much power is very rare, as I've said, but there is someone I used to know, and if he cannot help, he may know who can. I need to go to Duken."

Ariana glanced at Ole, then back at Isabelle. "You will have a convoy accompany you," she said.

"No—" Isabelle caught herself before she spoke again, "I am sorry, Your Grace." She bowed. "I mean, I do not need a convoy. I just need a horse that is well-fed and in good shape. I cannot go looking for who I need with an army of guards behind me. I do not mean to speak small of your offer or your guards, Your Grace, but you must know that a convoy will only slow me down and draw unnecessary attention. A horse and some water will be just enough, Your Grace."

The queen exhaled. "Fine. Two horses, one for you and the other for the escort that will accompany you. Not because you need the help or that I doubt you can handle it on your own, but because you *might* need it and, considering what is on the line, there is no way I can allow you to go on a quest to another kingdom, a place like Duken, for that matter, without at least an escort, one you can be assured will not slow you down and will not attract attention. I am leaving nothing to chance."

Isabelle looked content with the queen's decision. "Very well, Your Grace. I will set out on the journey as soon as I can."

"Yes, of course," Ariana said. Before Isabelle turned, the queen placed a hand on her shoulder. Their eyes locked.

"I haven't known you before today, but I'm entrusting you to find help for my husband."

"And I will do everything I can to bring His Majesty that help."

"Thank you." Ariana glanced at Ole, remembering something equally as important as the mission. "And can I trust that you will keep the true reason for your visit to Duken to yourself? No one else can know, absolutely no one." The queen stared into Isabelle's green eyes to impart how intimate the conversation was, and how the trust she was being given was a power greater than her magic – to hold the burning secret of an entire kingdom as she rode into another land, a very different land despite the fact that they were sister kingdoms.

"You have my word, Your Grace. Not a single breath of His Majesty's situation will come out of my mouth to anyone except the one person I'm going to find," Isabelle promised.

Ariana nodded and removed her hand from the woman's shoulder. Isabelle turned to leave and Ole called for her to wait for him outside the room with the chamberlain. The queen watched them leave before returning to the window, where the youngest of her children were still playing mindlessly in the field, safe in the belief that their father was fine and only taking some time to himself.

"Do you trust her?" she asked.

Ole considered his words carefully, aware that either answer could have unintended consequences. "I do, Your Grace," he said. "I knew her father, who was also a sorcerer. He was a good friend of mine before he passed. The truth is, I have known Isabelle since she was a child, and though it has been over a decade since I last saw her,

I trust her enough to do what she has promised and to keep it to herself."

"Nevertheless, find her an escort that you trust with your own life, perhaps one from the King's Guards. I know she's said that she won't need the help, but have two more follow them from a distance, just so nothing happens."

"Of course, Your Grace," Ole answered. "What she said, about His Majesty's—"

"I am quiet now because I want her to be far from the palace before I begin to raise hell. Someone did this to my husband, and someone in this palace knows about it. I will find every single secret. I will have their head on spikes in the middle of the kingdom before she returns," Ariana answered, fury laced through her voice.

Ole blinked hard at the queen's words. He knew there was no stopping what was to come, and he would be lucky if he were to survive the wrath himself. It had been under his watch that this had happened, that someone had managed to get at the king.

But the queen going on a vengeful tirade while the king was still dying wouldn't be the wisest course. "If I may, Your Grace. It is unacceptable, what has happened, and we will find who is responsible for this, but perhaps it would be a more calculated move to continue to pretend ignorant while you fish out the imposter?"

"And give whoever it is the chance to make their move? Poison the king even more? Or come for me or my children?" Ariana glanced from her children in the field back at Ole, the rage in her eyes that of a mother.

"No, Your Grace, of course not. That will never happen—"

"Edmond losing his life force was never supposed to happen either!" The queen's voice quaked with anger. "Whoever has done this will answer for it. I will not let them take any more from me. I will end them before they get close to my children," Ariana said and instinctively looked through the window, tracking anyone walking near her children in the field. *What if they already were?*

"So will I. But, Your Grace, I beg that you see things the way I do right now – we have the chance to play ignorant while we watch and wait. You could have all of the servants questioned, as well as the guards, but that would risk letting whoever it is know we're coming for them. Instead, I would advise that we work in silence and hope that Isabelle is able to find the power His Majesty needs. An attack on King Edmond is not something to be taken lightly. Whoever is responsible has a motive that may mean they don't fear their own demise, making them unpredictable if cornered. And I know this may not be as comforting as it is intended, but I doubt they would want to risk suspicion by coming after you or the princes and the princesses."

"I am comforted, Ole."

Ole bowed. "Give us two days, let us send Isabelle on her way, and give me till she returns. I promise I will have something. Until then, I will have eyes on the princes and the princesses, and you, too, Your Grace," he said. There was silence for a moment as he contemplated his next words. "Perhaps we should inform Walrea about this?"

Ariana shook her head. "No. The Order can have whoever it is after I'm done with them," she said, rage still in her voice. She knew that informing the Order of Walrea of an attack on the king would have the entire kingdom silently sacked in a matter of hours as they tried to find who it was. Ariana chose Ole's own words. "No one else can know," she said.

Ole bowed again before he turned and walked out of the room.

Ariana looked back to the stable and the stallion below, then turned to her husband. The horse was his favorite and would never let anyone else ride him. The animal's rebellion as its master lay dying was hard for the queen to understand.

"You have to wake up or that horse will die without ever getting out of that stable," she said.

CHAPTER FIVE

H iding for dear life, Olin remained as still as he could in the back of the wagon. Every time he felt it slow down, his heart thumped in his chest. But he grew more hopeful the longer he rode unseen in the hay and the sacks, and the wagon continued on, undisturbed. There was no doubt that if the watchers knew of his escape, then he would have been caught, along with the poor merchant who was helping him unknowingly.

Olin peered through the layers of sacks covering him to see the clouds and the sky above as they moved. He inched up slightly to see that they were still in the middle of the road leading away from Walrea, heading towards the town and Black River. Olin could no longer see the hill that served as a maker for Walrea and his mind settled a little. He turned around and saw the driver of the wagon, an older man with a balding head who was holding the rope of the horse's harness, bouncing to the motion of the wagon on the stony road. Olin considered getting the man's attention, but then thought the man's oblivion was a good thing. Instead, he sat quietly as he was driven into town.

The wagon soon stopped at the edge of town near a shoemaker's shop and Olin leapt out of the back before he could come face to face with his helper. But he was loud enough that it caught the driver's attention, and he turned just in time to see Olin as he landed on the ground and set off in a sprint.

"He – hey!" was all Olin heard as he quickly turned left across the street behind a blacksmith's forge and disappeared.

The confused driver looked back at his wagon, got down and ruffled the sacks as if to find out if the boy had taken something or left something behind. He looked back in the direction of the road he had driven from, took his hand to his head and scratched with the quizzical look on his face as he wondered when and how he could have picked up a stray, a whole human, and not know he had been there all the while.

Olin did not stop as he navigated through the streets. He was more than familiar with every nook and cranny of the town he'd grown up in. Thinking of his pursuers, he chose a roundabout path home, cutting behind buildings, through alleys, and a few times through stables and pens just to avoid the main route. Every twenty or so paces Olin would pause long enough to glance back before hurrying on again. A few times he'd heard yells that sounded like they were directed at him, from people he knew, but Olin couldn't spare any small talk as he snaked through the town.

Olin almost broke through the door when he reached home. After getting inside, he looked out to be sure yet again that he hadn't been followed. When he saw nothing but the emptiness of the street, he closed the door.

"Uncle!" he called out. "Wylie!"

He moved from the living room through the two other chambers with no luck. He did, of course, have an idea where Wylie could be: either out helping build the frame of someone's new house or hunting in the forest with Old Ron. Olin considered going back out and looking for his uncle at the most likely of those places – his carpenter shop – but the thought of being back in the open made him reject the idea quickly.

Olin sat on a chair in the room, head in his hands, curly black hair falling over his lowered face as he replayed events in his mind, remembering how he had managed to get himself into this mess. He should never have been in that room. But had he really done anything wrong? Besides being in the wrong place at the worst possible time and hearing a conversation he had absolutely no business being part of, a conversation that had the potential to change Ravinshore entirely, throw the entire kingdom into disarray if it ever came out. *If* it was true.

Had he really heard right? Had he really seen right?

Olin stood, questions swirling in his head, and walked to the bowl of water in the corner of the room, dipping his hands in the cold water and splashing his face. The cold sent chills through the rest of his body, waking him up, but doing nothing for the agitation. The words. The voice. The message.

Had he really heard right?

The hand. Had he seen what he'd thought he'd seen?

Olin could not make himself sit back down. Despite his decision to wait for his uncle, he continued to look out the window after every few paces. Finally, he went to his uncle's chamber and found his sword resting against the wall. Hoping he wouldn't need to use it, Olin took the sword and returned to the living room to continue waiting. Not long after he'd armed himself, Olin's head jerked to the door at the sound of footsteps outside. He gripped the weapon harder and his breathing hastened as he stared at the door and whoever was behind it.

The door opened and Olin lifted the sword, only to find it pointing at his uncle, who had frozen with a confused look on his face. Wylie glanced from his nephew to the sword in his hand.

"If you're pointing that at me, you had better be ready to use it, son," Wylie said.

Olin exhaled deeply. "Oh, Uncle." He lowered the sword. "Thank heavens it's you! Where have you been?"

Wylie pointed outside the house to the dead duck on the floor. "Hunting, Olin," he answered. "Like I do for my own meat, sometimes. Now, what has you standing inside the house waiting for me with a bloody sword? Have you been possessed or something?"

"No, Wylie."

"Did you take something from someone possessed?" Wylie asked with a serious look on his face.

Olin scoffed. "No! I didn't. I'm not here because anyone is possessed."

"Why the bloody hell were you waiting for me with a sword?" Wylie asked.

Olin huffed, frustrated. "I wasn't waiting for *you*. I mean, I was, but the sword wasn't for you, it was for someone else. I didn't know who was going to come through the door," he answered. He stepped towards his uncle, pulling the older man inside the house, with a glance outside to make sure there weren't any masked men on the street before he pulled his head back and in and closed the door.

Wylie was still frowning. It made his face seem even more lopsided, with one brow set higher than the other due to an old scar. "What happened, Olin. What did you do?"

Olin took his hands to his head, raking his hair back. "I didn't do anything! Why would you assume that I did something wrong?"

Wylie glanced at the sword for an answer. "Because I know that look, and that is the look of someone who has managed to find himself in some horseshit and is now waving a weapon around. I know the look you have when you've done something, Olin, so what is it? What happened?" Wylie stepped towards his nephew, staring him in the eye, forcing Olin to focus on him in return.

"I swear I didn't do anything wrong. I was just walking about, minding my duties for the day, when I wandered into this room. It had all these paintings of what I think were old Lord Watchers, but I couldn't see their faces – the paintings were made that way. I swear I was just admiring them, and then I accidently unlocked a hidden door that led to secret room."

"And was that when you decided to leave?" Wylie asked, tone hopeful.

"N – no. So I wanted to see what was in the room and I went in, I only saw a cabinet with watcher's attire, and a few scrolls. One of them looked like a map but I couldn't quite tell what it was. Before I could leave the room, I realized that there were footsteps and voices so I hid inside. But while I was there, I heard the voices of the people in the room and what they were saying and ..."

"And what, Olin? What did you hear?"

"I don't know. I might have heard wrong. I might have been confused. Maybe it wasn't what I heard."

"Olin!" Wylie called his nephew's name to snap him out of his usual state of second-guessing himself when he was overwhelmed. "Focus, Olin, what did you hear?"

"I think I might have heard something about King Edmond being sick and someone in Walrea is responsible. There seems to be a plan, and that plan involves the king getting sick ... and not surviving it. I think someone in the Order has poisoned the king, Wylie. I heard them talk about it."

"What?" Wylie's face pinched as he stared at Olin, unsure if the boy was in his right mind. This was by far the most ridiculous and dangerous story the boy could have come up with. Wylie needed more information. "Son, have you found yourself some immoral stash of hooch or dipped your beak in ale today?"

"I'm not drunk, Wylie! I know what I'm saying!"

"Then you know that what you're saying is just about the craziest thing that anyone might have said in Ravinshore in over a century," Wylie answered.

Olin shook his head. "And don't you think I know that? I know how it sounds, Wylie, and I've been asking myself if I heard right, because I know what this could mean. And perhaps I would still be doubting myself if I hadn't been followed."

Wylie's eyes widened. "You were followed?"

"Yes, at least I think I was. I'm sure I was. At Walrea. When I left the room and returned to my chamber, someone was at the door. I panicked and escaped through the window. I knew if I was caught and couldn't prove that I'd heard nothing, I ... It's the Order, Wylie. The Watchers of Walrea, I couldn't have fought them."

"So how could you have possibly escaped if they were after you? Son, you wouldn't be standing here if the Order thinks you're a threat."

"I ... I know!"

"So, is there a chance that you weren't seen? That maybe all of this could just be a big overreaction?"

Olin went to the window. He looked out and saw nothing – the entire neighborhood was completely undisturbed. He turned to Wylie, who was waiting for an answer.

"I want to believe that. Nothing would calm me more than knowing that all of this is just in my head, Wylie. I don't mind being called crazy if it means I'm wrong and the king isn't ill and dying, and that the Order of Walrea isn't behind it. I want to be wrong, but the watcher that appeared in my room at my window after I jumped doesn't give me hope that it was nothing. And they saw me leaving the room. The watchers. The look in their eyes makes me doubt very much that I might have heard wrong. And above everything, the mark I saw on one of the watcher's hands tells me it could very well all be true." He planted himself on a small wooden chair.

"What mark did you see?" Wylie asked, tone much calmer, and curious.

"I'd seen some part of it in the portraits on the walls. Even though I couldn't see their faces, the marks were there, on the back of their left arm. It looked something like a circle with three lines leading out of it. The paintings on the wall belonged to the past Lord Watchers of Walrea, Wylie, and one of the two watchers that were in that room had that same mark. The one that saw me afterwards," Olin answered.

Wylie's face twisted in concern at his nephew's words. A circle and three lines. There was no denying, he knew what it meant. If Olin had seen that, and the man with that mark had been one of the watchers that had been talking about poisoning the king, then it was real. Because Olin was right, the mark belonged to the Lord Watcher and only a handful of people outside Walrea knew that. But if Olin had been followed by the watchers and they knew who he was, he would have disappeared, or his body would have been found somewhere in the forest with a hole in it. He wouldn't have made it home to utter a word of what he's seen.

"How did you say you managed to escape?" Wylie asked.

"A merchant's wagon. I got in and buried myself in sacks and hay so the first watcher didn't see me. The wagon left Walrea almost immediately and the merchant had no idea I was in the back as he drove all the way to town. No one saw me. I got lucky, I guess."

Wylie considered the odds of Olin managing to escape arguably the most dangerous place in Ravinshore unnoticed in the back of a wagon. Possibly he had been followed and he just didn't know it. But then again, Wylie knew that if there was a chance that they knew who Olin was and where he would flee, he wouldn't have seen his nephew alive again.

Wylie nodded. "Okay. Let's hope your luck holds until we figure out the best thing to do."

Olin frowned. "What about what I heard? That the king is sick and the Order might be responsible? Shouldn't we tell someone? Shouldn't we go to the palace or something?"

"No! Absolutely not, son! Are you crazy? Do you have a death wish? Why would you want to do that?"

"Why wouldn't I?" Olin asked, confused. "I've just learned that the King of Ravinshore might have been poisoned by the same Order that is meant to protect the kingdom, and you think I should keep quiet?"

"Olin, if what you've stumbled onto is true, then you absolutely do not want to get in the middle of it. It's much bigger than you, it's much bigger than the both of us, and all you will do is get yourself killed if you decide to blab about it. You cannot tell a soul. You've managed to survive, stay here and don't go anywhere, don't talk to anyone. Come dawn, we'll set out for Black Castle and you can stay there for a while."

Olin shook his head. "I cannot believe this, Wylie! You would have me keep something like this to myself when it could affect all of Ravinshore?" He stood up and his uncle spun to face him.

"I would have you be safe, goddammit!" Wylie snapped. "I would have you alive and breathing, grow old and rotten like your father and mother never did. I would have our bloodline not end somewhere in the dirt in the middle of the forest in Ravinshore or in the Black River. I would have you live to find a woman and have fat babies and never remember this again! Because there is no way a word of this comes out of your mouth to anyone on this continent that it doesn't spell the end for you, for me, for our family. So, for once, Olin, son, for once, just trust me and erase everything from that head of yours."

Olin fell quiet.

The look in his uncle's eyes was unlike anything he had ever seen before. Wylie was not the kind of man to ever fear anything. His uncle stood in the face of every challenge, never cowering. Wylie had been a swordsman; he'd been part of the king's personal guards in his earlier life before he left to settle into the quieter role of a carpenter. While many considered this life to be less worthy for a man knighted by the past king, Olin knew there was a lot more to his uncle. Wylie was the reason Olin had desired to become part of the Order; he was the one who had showed him that being courageous was something innate, something Olin could be too.

To hear Wylie saying that he should remain quiet and run didn't sound right. Even if his safety was the only reason.

"Do I not owe it to the kingdom and the people of Ravinshore to let the King's Court know?"

"And who do you think makes up the King's Court, Olin? The Order is much more than what you might have glimpsed in Walrea, son. A lot more. The moment you open your mouth, it ends for us." Wylie stepped towards his nephew and placed his hands on his shoulder. "I know you think you need to defend and protect the kingdom, but you can only fight an enemy that you can see coming. Whatever you think you owe the kingdom, you cannot pay it if you are dead. Do you understand that?"

"So, I do nothing?" Olin asked, staring in his uncle's eyes. Wylie's face looked older than he'd ever seen it. The wrinkles on his forehead seemed to have multiplied, and his grey mustache and beard looked thinner around his stern mouth.

Silence fell as Wylie dropped his hands from his nephew's shoulder and looked at the sword in Olin's hand. He didn't need the flood of memories to remind him of the stories held in that steel. He looked up, beyond Olin to the open window, stepping towards it. The only thing he saw was the arriving dusk; it was quiet, not that Wylie would expect to hear it if troops of the Order of Walrea were coming for them.

Wylie knew, as much as he might fault his nephew for failing to keep his curiosity in check, that Olin's heart was in the right place and all he wanted was to do the right thing. Wylie's argument to keep quiet and run was because Olin was his brother's son and his only family, and his life was worth more than the king's as far as he was concerned. He couldn't deny the truth – he couldn't refuse the question in the boy's eyes. The urge to act when everything went to shit was something that ran in his blood.

"No," Wylie said, "You wouldn't be doing nothing. You would be taking a wiser path of action, one that would involve less chances of you facing the Order's wrath and becoming a target. You will not be going to the palace. We'll stay till dawn and then set out for Black Castle. When we get there, you will stay, and I'll take care of the rest."

"I was the one that heard it. I'm the witness."

"The witness who was poking his nose where he shouldn't have been in the first place, a sciff. You might not have realized what this means, but it's bigger than you, and you and I might not be the only ones facing the consequences if this gets out. All of Ravinshore will, but some will be flayed first. So, no, Olin. When we reach Black Castle, you will stay there, keep your head down, do whatever is asked of you, and speak no word of this to anyone."

Olin scoffed. "And how exactly do you plan on dealing with it? What'll you do?"

"That's for me to figure out, young man. You have enough to worry about. Now go and pack," Wylie said with a glance back at the window.

"Why don't leave now?" Olin asked.

"Because there's something I need to get before we leave, and by the time I'm done it will be too dark," Wylie answered.

He looked at the sword in Olin's hand and the way the young man gripped it. Wylie was comforted by the thought that Olin knew how to handle his weapon. He'd taught him how to hold his own in a fight. Wylie's only wish was that Olin had magic. Because a sword was only good enough for an enemy that one could see. And the Watchers of the Order of Walrea were hardly ever caught trading blows with an enemy.

Wylie walked to the door and slipped out. "Stay inside, I'll be back soon," he promised.

CHAPTER SIX

"**W**ho is he?" Thorne asked the watcher standing behind him in one of the sciff's small rooms. The Lord Watcher glanced around the chamber; the table pressed against a wall had a candlestick, a cup, a soup bowl, and a few scrolls sitting on top of each other. Nothing stood out. Thorne raised his hand towards the half-burnt candle and a gentle breeze whistled from his fingers, setting the wick aflame and lighting the room more brightly.

"He's a sciff, a new one," L answered from behind him.

Throne picked up the topmost scroll on the table, gazing at a drawing of a creature like a horse but with two heads; he picked up the second scroll and found another creature that looked a bird, an eagle with four wings and a tail. All of the scrolls looked the same, many with creatures that didn't exist in Ravinshore or anywhere else on the continent. Some looked too incredible to be real. Each drawing was made with charcoal and looked amazingly detailed.

"How is he a sciff? He's already a grown man?" Thorne asked as he flipped through the scrolls; the one he was holding now had a man with a tall neck and pointed ears, and an elf.

"A sciff was needed urgently after the departure of the harbor master's son, and he was available."

Thorne grunted. "What I saw was not a young impressionable boy – that was a man with a purpose. These, " he stabbed at the scrolls on the table and the bronze ring on his finger caught the light, "are not from the mind of an ordinary sciff! Where is he from?"

"Hunter's Grove," the watcher answered.

"What else is known about him?"

"He has no parents and his uncle is a carpenter."

"And you know that because you found out or because that was what he fed you?" Thorne asked, setting aside the scrolls and moving to the rest of the room. A black cloak hung on a nail in the wall along with a sack bag; a pair of sandals made of goat's hide sat on the ground below it. The bed was small, and unremarkable. Thorne moved to the only window in the room.

"That is what he said, My Lord," the watcher answered.

Thorne peered out the window, down three stories; it was the only way the sciff could have escaped. He ground his jaw. That wasn't just some sciff boy, he was definitely a man that knew what he was doing. "It was no mistake that he was here. He was in that room and he saw what was on that map. He also heard everything we said. I don't believe the odds that it was all a coincidence, and even if somehow it is, he heard what we said."

"There's no telling how much he heard. It might have been nothing, locked in the room."

"Maybe, but I have a feeling he heard it all. And if he did, there's no way he's can be allowed to be walking around. Besides, if he had nothing to hide, he wouldn't have run. He knows." Thorne stared down at the back of the building. Then he looked over the wall that circled Walrea to the small patches in the distance. Beyond them, an hour's journey down the stony road, was Hunter's Grove.

The Lord Watcher knew, regardless of who this sciff was, if he had escaped Walrea with the knowledge he had learned, there was a chance he would spread it. And, though it may sound crazy to those who didn't yet know that King Edmond was trailing the edge of death with his illness, there were those who would know the truth, should the news find its way out. It was going to create a problem that wouldn't go away easily.

The inner workings of Walrea were supposed to be secret. If Thorne's words made it to the palace, it would put a dent in the plan and make things incredibly uncomfortable.

"This has happened because of you, L, so you must deal with this. And you need to do so quickly," the Lord Watcher said. He turned to leave, but stopped at the table. Thorne picked up the drawings – the one of the elf – and stared at it. His brows pinched and his nose flared.

The Lord Watcher's face went from thoughtful, to upset, to sour. "Find this sciff and end this," he said.

***

Old Ron opened the door with a drink in his hand. "Wylie! Miss me already? You old bastard," he shouted, already drunk even though they had seen each other less than an hour before.

Wylie looked different than when they'd trudged through the forest together earlier. Old Ron noticed he was wearing his cold expression, one he had once said looked like the gaze of death.

Ron downed the rest of the ale and thudded the cup onto a small stool next to the door. He stepped outside and closed the door behind him. "What is it?" he asked Wylie.

"I need it," Wylie answered.

"I can see that. But why? What's happened?" Old Ron led Wylie away from the house towards the barn.

"I can't tell you. It's better that I don't."

"The hell it is, Wylie. I want to know, that's why I'm asking. You haven't talked about it in ten years and now you come for it, and you won't tell me what the hell is going on?"

Wylie stared at his oldest friend. His grey hair was now thinning. As much as he wanted to reveal what he'd learned, he knew there was a chance that anyone with the knowledge would be cursed with the burden of the secret until they were eventually found by the Order, and he wasn't going to put that burden on Ron. Not when he would have to get his own family out of the town. Not now.

"Trust me, old friend. You are better off not knowing."

Ron clearly wasn't satisfied, but he also knew better than to try arguing with Wylie. He turned around, and almost sulkily took the lead off a barrel. He looked back at Wylie. "It's in there," Ron said. "Your ring, spell."

***

Olin saw only darkness.

He blinked hard, turning around again and again but there was still nothing. He heard no sounds, not even his own heartbeat. Everything was still. He called out as loud as he could, but even his own voice didn't make a noise in the nothingness. Screaming did nothing.

All of a sudden, he felt water covering his feet. He looked down, unable to see the water. But soon he felt his legs go under. There was nothing to do to save himself, nowhere he could go, nothing to latch on to for help.

"Breathe."

He suddenly heard a voice. It came from within his own body, but it was strange, unfamiliar. His breath was already labored; he was on the brink of drowning; the water had reached his waist and was still climbing and he could feel his knees sinking into the mud below.

"Breathe."

He was breathing heavily, quickly, the air coming in and out like it was burning. He was breathing, but it wasn't stopping his body from slipping under. He would soon be able to float his hands in the water as it rose up chest. Half of his body was in the mud now. Anything he did only seemed to make it worse.

"Breathe!"

Enraged barely described how he felt about this voice telling him to do the same thing over and over again while he was drowning in water and mud. He had breathed more times in the last minute than he had in his entire life before. If breathing was going to help, if it was going to pull him out, lift him out of the mud by even an inch, then he would have been walking on water by now. He had been breathing, and flapping and screaming soundlessly, and now the water was taking his voice.

He raised his face to catch one more breath of air, cursing the crazy voice. Then the water covered his head; he felt it enter his nose, his mouth, and down his throat. It felt as though arms were gripping at him. He couldn't breathe if there was no air. Breathing wouldn't help him now, and the quiet was consuming him, while everything else swallowed him. But the annoying voice still insisted. The air did not matter, all he had to do was convince himself to keep breathing.

Eyes closed in the depth of the water, he let it all go. He stopped fighting. Just when the strange voice began to grow distant and true oblivion looked certain, his eyes flung open, and he looked down to see a ball of light form around his right hand. He looked at the other hand, and it was the same. He could suddenly see the water and the mud below. Uncertain, he clasped his hands into fists and felt his whole body shoot out of the water.

Olin's eyes opened and he gasped awake. A great force like a quake shook him back to consciousness. Only then did he hear it.

"He's not here!"

His uncle's voice was coming from the living chamber. Olin snuck to doorway, pressing against the wall, just as he had in the secret room at Walrea when it had all started, only this time he didn't have the benefit of remaining unseen. Olin held his breath; he could feel the sweat drip from his chin to his chest beneath his tunic.

"He's your nephew, isn't he? Where else would he be?" an eerily familiar voice responded to his uncle and Olin's heart thumped even harder. So much for hoping the watchers hadn't noticed him.

"Olin hasn't been here in weeks! The last I saw of him was when he left for Walrea, and I couldn't care less where he is. Now get out of my house before you regret it."

"You're only being given the chance to come clean and make your death quicker. Where is the boy?" the watcher said again.

"You definitely are deaf for a watcher," Wylie said.

His words didn't seem to please the watcher, who drew a knife from his side and let it fly. Wylie raised his hands, his right hand fixed so his thumb was pressed against his little finger and the rest of his fingers pointed up. A shield appeared, stopping the knife. Using his left hand, Wylie drew a series of rings to widen the shield.

From where he stood, Olin stared in shock at Wylie and the rings of shields revolving around his hands.

The watcher threw two more knives, but Wylie was quick enough with his shield. When it was obvious that Wylie was prepared, L stepped aside and another watcher with a red mask took his place.

Wylie eyed his nephew by the door, unable to say a word to him as the red watcher took up his stance. The new watcher put his right foot forward, preparing to split himself, then clapped his palms together. The effect was a strong pulse that shook the room and disoriented Wylie, who now struggled to hold his shield in place. Olin watched as his uncle stepped back. Then he saw the handle of a knife sticking out of Wylie's belly.

L had taken advantage of the red watcher's display to find a crack in the shield. Wylie groaned, face paling as he struggled to hold the shield together as he bled out.

Olin gasped. Unable to stay hidden, he grabbed the sword by the bed and rushed out of the chamber to stand in front of his uncle. "Wylie!"

"No, Olin, get back!" Wylie yelled.

"I thought you said he wasn't here?" L asked, drawing another blade and stepping forward. He looked to the red watcher, who took his stance again, preparing to release another pulse.

Wylie knew what was coming. "Olin! Olin step back! You have to go!" he said.

"I'm not going anywhere!" Olin held the sword with both hands, prepared for whatever came through his uncle's shield. He snapped his gaze between L, the red watcher, and Wylie, whose blood was now dripping from the knife in his gut, but he was still struggling to stay on his feet and keep the shield up.

"Listen to me, Olin. You have to go!" Wylie said again, his eyes locked on the red watcher, who clapped his hands and released another pulse of energy just as Wylie turned swiftly to throw what was left of his shield over his nephew.

A confused Olin suddenly found his uncle standing in front of him, the handle of the knife between them. Wylie groaned louder as L's second knife sunk into his back.

"No!" Olin screamed, reaching for his uncle.

Wylie looked down at the black ring on his hand; he had hoped he would never have to use it again, but there was nothing else left. He repositioned the ring on his blood-soaked hand, and at once he could feel it pull energy through what was left of the blood in his body.

Wylie shoved his nephew to the side and, drawing on the power from the ring feeding on his blood, he manifested a new shield, ten time bigger than the one he'd made before, and threw it at L, snapping the watcher in place. The red watcher was about to create a third pulse, but a red-eyed Wylie yanked the knife from his own back and threw it, hitting the red watcher right between the eyes just before his hands could meet.

A confused and terrified Olin watched as his uncle drew unfamiliar signs in the air, chanting ancient words. "Edrmeius, hakus ad-incurium!"

A red glow tore through the wall next to Olin and widened into a portal.

"Wylie," he called.

Wylie lunged forward, gripping his nephew by the shoulders harder than he ever had. The cost of the spells were already taking a toll on him, and blood began to drip from his nose and ears.

Olin looked terrified as his uncle stared into his eyes. "Go! Find ... Cyrus," Wylie said, his voice almost a whisper.

Before Olin could protest, his uncle shoved him through the portal and closed it.

Wylie fell to his knees after his nephew disappeared; he could feel the ring aiming for his heart, clawing its power around it as he faded. He fell again, this time to the side, unable and unwilling to use any more of the ring's power, but knowing there was no prying it off his finger. Wylie yanked the knife out of his gut and stabbed his own hand at the root of the ring finger. He groaned in pain, digging deeper until the finger, and the ring, fell away from his hand. Once he was no longer wearing it, he felt the ring's power slither off quickly as the spell broke.

Wylie was left completely drained, blood pooling from his missing finger, his side, and his belly. He coughed hard and even more blood spattered over the floor. Wylie could feel his insides churn and his breath stiffen in his throat.

Seeing the end, he thought of it all – the memories he'd blocked away and forgotten, the ones that ached the most. He thought of his family, his brother, Ilda. Wylie thought of Olin and the relief that he was safe away from the watchers battled with the agony of leaving him behind.

As Wylie's eyes slowly closed, he wanted his last thought to be of Olin getting as far from Ravinshore as possible. But the face of his nephew wouldn't be the last thing he saw. Between the slits of his bloodied eyes, on the brink of losing consciousness, he saw the masked face of a watcher leaning over him.

CHAPTER SEVEN

T horne couldn't remember the last time he had been to a house like this. He stared from atop his horse, angry that he'd had to bring himself here. The watcher in front of him climbed off his mount and held the bit as Thorne descended, his black cape flying. As his boots touched the ground, he looked left and right, but there was no light coming from either of the houses in the distance.

The Lord Watcher walked through the front door, stepping across the pool of blood, which had spread across the floor when the body had been dragged away. Thorne glanced to his right to see the watcher with the red mask bent over a chair grotesquely, the handle of a blade sticking out of his forehead. To his left, Thorne saw char marks and signs of energy against the wall. His gaze passed over L, who was standing firm. The Lord Watcher walked to the man on the ground.

The body wasn't moving. It looked as though all of his blood was on the floor of the room; Thorne noticed the severed finger and the knives nearby. He noted the ring but turned instead to the wall Wylie was facing. Just like by the door, there was a charred mark, a sign of the energy that had passed through it. Thorne exhaled.

"Where was the boy?" he asked.

L stepped over Wylie as he led the Lord Watcher to the room where Olin had been hiding. Thorne stepped in, scanning the entire room. It held a few clothes hanging on nails, a small chest pushed against the wall, and a bow resting against a table, the arrows sticking out of a satchel. L held the oil lamp in his hand, allowing Thorne to study the bed carved from dead wood. The rare furniture was of no interest to Thorne, but he took a step closer, staring at the sheet that had been thrown over top. He yanked the sheet from the bed and inspected it closely. A handprint seemed to have been burned into it. He ground his jaw.

That sciff wasn't just some boy, and Thorne knew it.

Nothing else in the room was remarkable enough for him to pay attention to, so he turned back to the body on the floor, stepping in the blood. "Turn him over," he ordered.

One of the watchers accompanying him pulled the limp body up, holding it in a sitting position so that Thorne could see his face properly. A sound resembling a gasp came from the body.

Thorne scoffed in disbelief when he saw who it was. "And who would have thought?" he said. "Old Wylie."

There was no response, but Thorne wasn't having it. He crouched, grabbed Wylie by the jaw and squeezed hard. Wylie grunted and partly opened one eye.

"You were always meant for the rot. I really thought you had already succumbed. Was this you? Were you trying to crawl yourself back to where you don't belong? Did you send your son – or your nephew, is it? – to do your dirty work because you're too impotent to do it?" Thorne asked.

Wylie grunted again, and his eye remained open as he stared; his bloodied face didn't betray whether he recognized Thorne or not.

Thorne scoffed. "How comfortable of you to not remember," he said. The Lord Watcher reached for his mask, and all three watchers instantly averted their gazes as Thorne pulled down the mask to reveal his face, jaw tight and lips pursed in a wry grimace. "Remember now?"

Wylie blinked, hard. He exhaled and his brows furrowed in realization. Thorne put his mask back on and the Lord Watcher rose. "I knew there was something more to that sciff. This explains much, but I am far from satisfied." He turned to L. "Where did he send him?"

"I couldn't tell," L said.

Thorne looked down at the man who had carved himself a life as a humble carpenter; he was completely different than the man he'd known before. "It's my fault now, though it was your mess, L, from the start. Underestimating that sciff was on me. If I'd had any idea who his uncle was, I wouldn't have wasted so much time. Oh, Wylie, I don't suppose you're going to make it easy for me, and tell me where you sent your little spy of a nephew now, are you?"

Wylie blinked and grunted, this time louder than before, giving the impression that he was trying to say something.

Thorne bent over, bringing his face level with his old acquaintance. "Did you say something?" he asked. He leaned in a little, hoping for the impossible to happen and for Wylie to give him a straight answer. But what he got was a flimsy swing of a knife that Wylie had somehow managed to get his hands on.

"Oh, so not dead yet?" Thorne asked, standing. "Good, that's good. 'Cos I'm going to dig out where you sent that bastard from your head, and it's always better when they're alive."

CHAPTER EIGHT

"**D**o you have it or not?"

"Of course I do, I'm just undecided as to whether I'm willing to sell to you. The pieces of the barrel you shattered are still in the corner of my stall. I see them every day."

"And do you really think the best thing to do is to refuse profit just because you still haven't forgotten a little incident that happened almost a fortnight ago?"

"A fortnight? It was four days ago! And you call having a barrel of Elm's milk strewn all over my stall after your spell an incident?"

Yondi shook his head. "Giodin, now, we both know that's not true. It was all a misunderstanding. I did the spell in self-defense – it came as a reflex. I thought you were going to come at me and so I acted, you must understand that?"

The potion merchant didn't look anywhere close to understanding what had happened the last time Yondi had visited his stall. Yondi had said he might be tempted to let everyone know that the merchant sometimes added ale to his "tooth medicine" to make it stronger before selling it, and Giodin had not taken kindly to the threat. In his irritation, the merchant had moved towards Yondi, and the mage's apprentice had panicked, unleashing a ball of energy to force him to back off. Yondi had blabbered a last-minute apology as the merchant had chased him away from the store. There had been no sale that day.

"And is that going to bring back the potions I lost?" Giodin asked.

"Look, I'm here now, okay? And accidents happen all the time, but I wouldn't want to take my money elsewhere. Though I hear Adam sells for a cheaper rate now." Yondi shifted his weight to the other leg and crossed his arms, turning casually and stretching his neck, pretending to check out the stall a few yards away where Giodin's mortal enemy and fiercest competition had set up shop. He forced a thoughtful look on his face, continuing to stare at the other stall, only glancing at Giodin out of the corner of his eye. Yondi watched as Giodin's nose flared and his brows pulled even tighter at the mention of his competition.

"Go ahead, go there! You know he sells fake potions and steals the slugs he has? The ones he doesn't steal are diseased. Half of the things he sells do nothing and that's if you're lucky and they don't explode in your face when you try to cast a spell." Giodin waved his hand, dismissive, with a forced look of apathy as he turned around and made his hands busy.

Yondi held back a smile. "At least he's willing to sell to me. Who knows? I might just find his better than yours, assuming it doesn't explode in my face," he said.

Giodin scoffed loudly, back still turned, but Yondi could hear him muttering angry words before he turned around, face no less disgusted at the idea of being compared to the other man.

"Everyone knows no one else in Queen's Hill sells better potions than I do. No one!"

Yondi turned his lips downward. "I know. But what can I do? You won't sell to me. And by the time I tell my master about it, and he tells his friends about how you turned his apprentice away, soon the word will spread, and people will start wondering if you'd turn them away too. And they won't bother stopping by anymore when they learn they can get whatever they want somewhere else." He shrugged, cocked his head, and raised his hand in the direction of the competition as he took a step forward. He still kept one eye on Giodin, too.

Giodin rubbed his chin, with a look of a man who was watching his money inching away. "You wouldn't do that!"

"Will you sell to me?"

The merchant stared at him and Yondi could see the contemplation in his eyes — it was easy to see him weighing the options of remaining angry about an almost empty barrel of Elm's milk over losing Yondi's master and his influence.

Yondi spread his hands as he stepped away from the stall; he could feel Giodin's eyes working to hold him back with each of his three steps.

"Wait!"

Yondi turned, brow raised; his face didn't betray the smile he was holding back. "What will it be, Giodin? I cannot stand here forever. My master will soon return, and I'm not going to tell him I didn't get what he wanted because of you."

Giodin stared at him and grunted, then the merchant turned and fetched an average-sized jar half-filled with oros – small blue slugs. "How many do you need?"

"Just three will do," Yondi answered, and he watched as the merchant placed the jar on the table, fetched a smaller jar, and used a pair of tongs to remove three slugs.

Giodin had to be quick while he transferred the oros because the creatures had the tendency to grow bigger when they felt stressed; they could grow to become as big as fifty times their actual size. Oros were usually harmless to humans, but were one of the creatures that mages and sorcerers used for their potions and spells, due to the slugs' magical potential. Because of that they were worth a lot to mages. But they were difficult to harvest or collect – depending on the form the creature took when discovered.

"See, not that hard after all," Yondi said as he collected the jar from Giodin and dropped a silver coin in its place.

Giodin didn't look like a man getting the better end of the deal as he took the money and watched the mage's insufferable apprentice put the jar in his satchel and break into a smile before hurrying away.

Yondi needed to fetch one more thing before he returned home. He had gotten everything his master required, except for the Elvin dandelion from the woods closest to the Black River. He had chosen to find the dandelions last, hoping they would have had enough time to blossom with the sunrise, making them easier for him to find.

The apprentice hastened away from the market, rushing through fields of tall grass towards the woods. With one hand, he held the satchel with its jar of oros in place. He wanted to get all of the items home before his master knew about it so he could have time to practice on his own. His sandals slapped against the dirt of the field and spores of the grass danced through the air as he passed, clinging to his trousers and his tunic.

Yondi reached the woods, cutting past the tall and skinny trees with only the sound of his own steps following him. As soon as he reached the Black River, Yondi's gaze was at once caught by something unusual on the bank. As he drew closer, his steps slowed as he realized what it was.

Someone was lying face-down in the dirt, and they weren't moving.

***

He was drowning. He needed to breathe, find a way out. All of the water felt like nothing as he pushed. His hands, he remembered. The pulse had sounded like an explosion and it rang in his ears. He opened his eyes and this time it was Wylie lying face down in a pool of his own blood with the watcher's blade sticking out of his back.

Olin stared at his uncle's body and dropped to his knees in the blood. He put his hands on Wylie and nudged him, calling his name and getting nothing. Olin pulled the knife out of his uncle's side, letting out a small trickle of fresh blood. He held the knife in one hand and blinked to see both of his hands soaked in blood, as if he'd been the one to burry the knife in his uncle's gut in the first place. Olin dropped the blade and turned his uncle over. Wylie's eyes were bleeding too.

"Go!" he heard, "Go! Find Cyrus!" Wylie's voice screamed again.

His uncle was on the floor, dead, but Olin could still hear his voice. Olin's face twisted as he felt himself being sucked away through a hole in the air; his screams only lasted as long as he could resist the displacement. The moment he entered the hole, Olin felt a dizziness he couldn't explain, and his attempts at a scream – just like in the water – was voiceless. He grew dizzier and fainter so swiftly that he lost his complete sense of consciousness in a heartbeat.

***

Yondi found himself standing a few yards away from the body. He looked around, eyes scanning fervently for anything or anyone that might answer why the ... fellow was lying face deep in the unforgiving mud of the Black River. He found nothing. The river here was more like a stream; the main current began a few miles downstream, north of the town and the kingdom.

Yondi clutched his satchel as he took a small step closer. He couldn't be sure he wasn't about to fall into a trap; what if the body sprung to their feet once he was close enough, and then his accomplices dashed out of the woods to strip him of what little he had? Yondi had never experienced bandits before, but he had heard of something similar happening to a traveling merchant once on the road to Duken. Queen's Hill was far from being a home to saints. He didn't have more than a quarter of a silver, so no one would profit from robbing him, unless they were willing to sell the oros and the rest of what he had in his bag that belonged to his master.

Still, if they robbed him and didn't harm him, that would be fair, Yondi thought as he drew closer to the mysterious body.

"Hello?" Yondi called softly as he approached. He bent over and picked up a small stick. "Hello," he said again. The apprentice looked one more time for signs of an ambush before he poked the fellow with the stick.

"Mister." He assumed it was a man, given the mudded trousers and the soaked tunic.

When the body didn't even twitch, Yondi dropped the stick and bent over to touch the man with one hand; the other hand he held ready for anything. Hoping he wasn't about to touch a dead body, Yondi turned the man over. The face was covered with matted hair. He was a stranger. Yondi froze as he saw something else – the young man had been hiding a sword underneath his body. Yondi hesitated rather than try to wake him again.

He had no wounds Yondi could see, yet his color was pale compared to the mud around him.

He was alive, but he had stains of thick dark crimson on his shirt. Yondi had seen enough blood to know when a stain was ominous.

Yondi was still frozen in place, staring, when the body suddenly sprung awake with a gasp. Yondi didn't move his hands – one still prepared for the worst and the other trying to decide between keeping the young man at bay and reaching out to help him. Yondi watched with his mouth agape as the stranger opened his eyes.

Olin opened blood-shot eyes to see an unfamiliar face crouched over him. He blinked hard and startled back, dragging his ass through the mud with his hands. He was within reach of his own sword, but he eyed it, realizing his possible error. He raised his muddy hand. "St – Stay away from me!" he yelled, panic filling his voice.

Yondi frowned – not exactly what he had been expecting. Then again, it was a stranger lying belly-down in the mud with no shoes. What had he really been expecting? Yondi kept his own hands higher, this time, in a stance to show he intended to keep the young man's wishes. After a moment of both of them waiting, hands in the air, each eyeing the sword in the mud, Yondi saw a hint of confusion in the stranger's face as his eyes moved quickly around.

"Are you okay?" Yondi asked.

"Who are you?" Olin shot back in response.

"I'm Yondi. Who are you?"

Olin looked from Yondi's face to his attire, to his satchel, before looking around again – but nothing looked familiar.

"Are you from around here?" Yondi asked.

Olin frowned. It depended. He wasn't sure. Where was here? Who was Yondi? Why had he been leaning over him? What was in the bag he was carrying? What would Yondi do if he tried to pick up his sword? Olin needed to have that upper hand before he said another word.

He didn't think twice as he leapt forward and snatched his blade from the ground, pointing it at Yondi, who still had his hands up, but had lowered them enough so he wouldn't be caught off guard should the stranger try something.

"Okay," Yondi said. "You have your sword. If you don't want to answer or be disturbed, I'll get up and gladly be on my way now."

Yondi got on his feet and Olin did the same. At least he tried to, but the dizziness returned, as if the earth was turning on its head and the ground was slipping from beneath his cold and muddy feet. He struggled to keep standing for a moment, trying to hold the sword still.

"Are you okay?" Yondi asked again.

Olin shook his head to stop the world spinning, which turned out to be a bad idea as he instantly felt like a mallet had been smashed against his brain. He dropped back down to his knees and threw up.

"Oh, all right. So, is that an answer?" Yondi asked.

Olin wiped his mouth with the back of his hand. Having learnt his lesson the first time, he rested his weight on his sword before he slowly rose. "Where is this? Where are we?" he asked.

Yondi's eyebrows rose. "That's the Black River behind you. We're in Faidon," Yondi answered.

"Faidon?" Olin asked, the surprise apparent on his face.

"Yes, Faidon, the old town. We're in Queen's Hill," Yondi said.

Olin's eyes widened at the words. Queen's Hill. Wylie had sent him all the way to another kingdom?

Wylie! The memory flooded in. How he'd gotten here. The end – the watchers, his uncle being stabbed, throwing himself in the path of the knife to save him; he remembered Wylie bleeding out, the terrifying look on his face as he'd cast spells to create the portal. Olin remembered Wylie falling just as he'd shoved him through the portal. Cyrus – he remembered that, too. Olin raised his hand to his head as he turned and saw the hills. He gripped the sword harder as the pain of what had happened to Wylie clung to his chest. What had he done?

"Are you lost?" Yondi asked, clearly seeing the distraught look on Olin's face.

"I ... I need to find someone," Olin said.

"Alright. Who?"

"Cyrus," he said without thinking.

"Huh ... there are quite a number of Cyrus's here in Faidon, not to mention all of Queen's Hill. Do you maybe have something else he goes by that could make it —"

"Who are you?" Olin raised the sword at Yondi again, returning to their earlier stance. The apprentice had a hand readied in his own defense.

"I believe I just told you," Yondi answered, wondering for a moment if memory loss was one of the things plaguing the young man. "My name is Yondi."

"Yondi. Wh – Who do you work for? How did you find me?"

Yondi scoffed. "I'm an apprentice to a mage here in Faidon. Actually, more like the Grand Mage. And I found you by chance. I came to the woods looking for Elvin dandelions." He nodded behind him to the woods. "I need to find them for my master before he gets back," he said, placing his left hand on his satchel.

Olin eyed the satchel, his mind weighing the odds that Yondi was telling the truth. What if he was still in Ravinshore, somewhere on the outskirts, and Yondi was just a watcher in disguise? But, considering what had happened the last time he'd encountered a watcher, he doubted he'd be standing there still talking if Yondi was one.

Olin lowered his sword. "Can you help me find him? Cyrus?"

"It depends. Will you stop pointing the sword at me?" Yondi said.

Olin looked down at the sword in his hand; it was his only possession and connection to home, to his uncle. The same sword he'd been useless with when it had mattered the most.

"Come on, this way." Yondi nodded.

Olin eyed him before he took a step, then another, a myriad of thoughts and questions in his head as he followed.

"Do you have a name?" Yondi asked.

"It's Olin."

CHAPTER NINE

A lden eyed the woman riding in silence; she had barely said more than three words since they'd set off from Ravinshore. He had seen many people from different continents and different parts of the world – foreigners came to Ravinshore all the time, voyagers and adventurers and merchants and royals and nobles. Alden had seen and met a fair number of them, and it had always been an experience, but this was different. This was only his second time meeting someone from Maedro, and the merchant he'd met before had offered a lot more words than this woman did. He was tempted to wonder if that was how Maedrian women behaved – incredible silence and reservation as their trade or trait – or if she was just uninteresting.

Isabelle, for her part, could feel the escort's eyes on her as they crossed the Dead Field, halfway to Duken. She would have perhaps engaged him more had she not been assigned to him unwillingly. Isabelle preferred to travel alone – it allowed her to focus her senses on her task. Company was only a distraction, a distraction that King Edmond could not afford.

"Are all Maedrian women this quiet?" Alden said, finally breaking the silence that had lasted the hours since they'd resumed their journey after breaking for the night.

Isabelle considered not responding. She wasn't obligated to say a word to him; she was on a mission for the throne of Ravinshore, and he was simply an escort.

"I didn't think all Ravinshore men snored in their sleep," she finally said.

Alden's face whitened and twitched, and he gripped harder at the reins as the horse trotted forward at a marching pace. The response was clearly not what he had expected. "I ... I don't snore,'" he blurted.

Isabelle remained quiet, hoping that the realization would keep him quiet for a few more hours.

"Even if I did, it's a sign of good health."

Quiet ensued for another moment, giving the sorceress the hope that she might get her wish.

"So, are all Maedrian women against small talk?" he asked again.

Isabelle sighed. "What is the usefulness of small talk? It will only distract from the journey. I don't like distractions," she said.

"Oh, but distractions can be good. Like in this case, they help the time pass quickly and make the journey less boring."

"This is not a luxury trip. It doesn't matter how boring it is, as long as we succeed in what we are supposed to do. I didn't think I would have to remind a King's Guard this," Isabelle said.

Alden shook his head. "Shame that you think talking would make me unable to do my job. I would think it wouldn't be a bother to you. But I guess doing two things at a time is not for everyone." He shrugged.

The escort looked ahead and Isabelle turned to glance at him; his words felt like a dig, one she couldn't let pass. She couldn't help but feel like he was questioning her intelligence. Normally, she wouldn't have bothered to dignify that with a response, but he looked so content and sure of his assumption. Of course she could do more than two things at once. He was only saying that because he had no idea who she was, what she had done, or what she could do. If only he knew she had the power to force his horse to throw him five yards away while she sat here talking to him. She wondered how he'd feel about doing two things at once then.

"You know I'm missing my daughter's birthday for this? I'm loyal to the throne, to King Edmond of Ravinshore, and I'm sworn to pursue this course and protect him with my life. And I will. I do not question my missions, ever. I do not question *this* even though I barely know anything about it. The throne tells me to go and that's it."

Isabelle felt a wave of remorse for the man. She heard the pain of leaving his daughter in his voice even though he tried to hide it. He was looking to the east, and the hills they were soon to climb.

"You think about your daughter on every mission you go on for the king?"

Alden looked ahead. "I think about her all the time. And it doesn't stop me from giving everything for my missions. If anything, it makes me better, ensures that I do whatever is needed of me to return to Ravinshore, return home, safe."

"How is it possible? Which do you put first? The king or your family?" Isabelle asked, studying him for the first time. He had short black stubble and square jaw.

"My daughter – she comes first in my heart, always, I live and die for her. The king, the throne – I am sworn in service to him. The king comes first with everything else. Me being here should give you your answer. The king's duty comes first."

The sorceress was tempted to ask an impossible question, but she knew he'd given the answer already and couldn't make him say it out loud. Which would he save, if he had to choose between his daughter and the king? Isabelle knew there was no response that wouldn't doom a man like him, but she had a good idea which way the soldier would choose, should that be his last duty.

"What's her name? Your daughter?"

Alden turned to face her; it was the first time in hours they'd met each other's gaze. "Mary," he said, a smile on his face. "Her name is Mary and she is eight today. All grown."

"Ah, Mary, a beautiful name," Isabelle said.

"Yes, and she's one beautiful and strong-willed daughter. Just like her father," Alden said.

Talking about his daughter seemed to change the man's face, brightening his features. Isabelle would never make him answer that question. "I'm sorry," she said.

"Huh? For what?"

"About your daughter, that you have to miss her birthday. I'm sorry."

Alden shrugged. "Believe it or not, she would have kicked me out of the house herself if I had told her that I wanted to stay when the throne needed me," he answered proudly.

**

Edmond was a troublesome man, but a just king. Queen Ariana knew her husband better than anyone alive, and she was sure that whoever was responsible for his fate hadn't targeted him because of a wrong he'd committed as king.

As a father and husband, Edmond could be trying. Life with him was full of subterfuges and pranks that had often made him insufferable when they'd been much younger. Even so, Edmond wasn't a troublemaker when it got dangerous; he was the type who would rather find an amicable solution, avoiding confrontation and only choosing to attack as an absolute last response to any situation.

Ariana knew he wasn't oblivious to the fact that there were those who thought him meek; meekness didn't belong in the ruler of Ravinshore. But Ariana also knew that her husband preferred to show that side to the people, he chose to be the opposite of the image of a terrifying tyrant. Because if he'd wanted to use fear to impose his rule, the Queen of Ravinshore knew that her husband could have dowsed the entire kingdom in it. She knew.

The people gossiped that Ravinshore had a Queen Ruler, rather than a king, because she had been the face of many of their hard decisions. The whispers hadn't escaped her. Hadn't escaped him, either. Edmond shared almost everything with her, including the affairs of the kingdom, and when a decision would make him be perceived as a stiff, it was Ariana's voice that carried the message. They were a pair.

Edmond never kept anything from her, even the things many kings would have chosen to keep from their queens. She knew about the time he had sent one of her handmaids packing because he'd noticed the girl looking her way too often. The queen knew when her husband wanted to murder someone for what they'd done with his own hands – like the time a drunk farmer had clubbed his own son to death for forgetting to feed the goats. Ariana had been there when Edmond had acted on the urge. She had been the one to arrange for the prisoner to be taken to the hidden dungeon beneath the palace, where she had watched as Edmond had unleashed his anger on the man; she had not let it pass that day.

Ariana knew everything about her husband, and yet she had missed the moment a traitor had wormed close enough to bring him down.

Ariana climbed into bed and laid beside him; she placed her head on his shoulder and her arm across his chest. She could hardly feel anything. It was as though his heart was no longer there and his breath was absent. But she could sense the faintest, feathery push of his chest against her arm. His heart was barely beating. As she listened, she wondered how long he could hold on with that slow thud. She missed the rhythm it had used to be, before. She missed him awake and alive. Ariana missed her husband and it hurt to think about how she could very well never have him back again. Ravinshore would crumble, would mourn in disarray, but no one would be more wrecked than her.

If Edmond didn't wake, if he wasn't healed of this poison, if the King of Ravinshore died from this, Ariana wasn't sure if she would be able to keep quiet. Roaches would scramble out of their hiding places to whisper and stir trouble and the Order of Walrea would squash them one at a time. But that might not be enough. The Order was there to stop wars before they were even planned, but the murder of the King of Ravinshore would anger so many people.

"There will be questions, Your Grace, many of them. It will be an uproar that the Order might not be able to quiet. Telling the people might do more harm than good," Ole said from his place standing behind Ariana, who was walking through the gardens as part of Ole's plan for the people to see that she – and by some extension, the king – were in good health. The queen kept her face carefully blank, to neither conceded or deny the fact that she was grieving.

"You've stated your case, and I have listened, same as yesterday. But the rage is building in my heart and I don't know if I will hold back should Edmond not ... open his eyes again," she ended the sentence with almost a whisper. "It grows by every day that passes that I'm unable to look the culprit in the eyes and ask them why they did this. My rage stirs with every moment I don't have my husband back and Ravinshore's king is left on the brink, his life force hanging by a thread."

Ariana fell quiet as they walked near a group of people. She exhaled and smiled at her youngest, who was waving vigorously at her from afar. The queen turned to face her Court's Counsel and Ole adjusted his stance. She stepped towards him, closing the distance between them so only he could hear her next words.

"This will not end well for Ravinshore, Ole, if my husband dies."

Ole swallowed hard, his eyes fixed on the queen's hair to avoid her gaze. He couldn't speak, not when she was this close.

"Speak," she ordered.

"Your Grace. I know there is much to ponder concerning the evil that has found its way to the palace, but if I may say: we cannot rule out one possibility."

"And what is that?" the queen asked.

"The very thing you are expressing right now – anger." He could look at her face now. "The person, or group of persons, that has done this must surely have a motive, and as far as His Majesty is concerned, he *is* Ravinshore. An attack on him is an attack on the kingdom to which a natural response would be outrage, chaos. War. Whoever it is could be looking for your reaction as the fuel to feed the flame they have sparked. A flame that would consume Ravinshore," Ole said. "It is absolutely unforgivable, what has been done, but more than anything you have accomplished in the past as the queen of this kingdom, what you do at this moment will ultimately determine the fate of all Ravinshore. And by extension, Duken and Queen's Hill, Your Grace."

Ariana stared at him, anger at the tips of her fingers. She balled them into fists. Then exhaled, doing the very opposite of what she really wanted to do, which was scream at the man in front of her, scream at the guard standing yards away from them, scream at everyone who was responsible for keeping her husband safe. Most of all scream at the person who had brought this upon her, scream so loud and long that their head would explode.

Instead, the queen unfurled her fists and looked to the window of the room where her husband lay.

"Which is why I need you to find me someone to direct this rage at instead, Ole. My husband will not die in silence. I will burn every house in Ravinshore down to find his killer if I have to," the queen said.

CHAPTER TEN

L evyna had just learned she was a dreamer.

Some mages could show signs of their powers much later than others; some would never find out, unless placed in circumstances that forced their powers to manifest. Levyna was an aquamot, and her magic allowed her to do almost anything she wanted with water.

For years she'd thought that was all there was to know of her power. Until a month ago, when she'd had her first dream.

She'd dreamed of blood dripping from the insignia of the Queen's Hill King's Guards, and two days later she learned that a former King's Guard had died, stabbed by bandits on his way to Duken. When she'd heard of the death, she'd shaken it off as a coincidence, until four days later, when she'd had another dream, of a white rose losing its last petal as the stalk decayed.

Exactly two days after, the queen's oldest seamstress died in her sleep. Levyna heard of it when she'd been in the garden with Veronica, the princess of Queen's Hill. Unsure, she had asked the princess what the late seamstress's name had been. Levyna had dropped the tulips she'd been holding when Veronica told her that the Queen Mother had given the old maid a popular name – White Rose.

Since then, she'd had a few more dreams that had seemed like nothing: a wolf drenched in blood and a crown thrown into a black pit that consumed it. It had been weeks and she'd heard nothing of a bloodied wolf or crown.

The crown had terrified her – it could only mean the throne or the king. But she hadn't seen any signs of the kingdom being thrown into a disarray. She saw King Ranald almost every day and he couldn't have been livelier; so was his wife, the queen, and the rest of the royal family. It had almost convinced Levyna yet again that maybe her dreams had no meaning and the previous ones of the guard and white rose had only been coincidences.

Then a week ago, while she'd been napping, she'd seen a pale horse die in her dreams. Barely a day later, the king's otherwise healthy stallion had died in the stable.

Now, Levyna sat on her bed with her blanket clutched to her chest; she hadn't moved since she'd woken from her slumber. She had dreamt again, and this one had been more terrifying than anything she had ever seen before in her unconscious state. She had dreamed of two objects – a ring and a single eye – buried in the dirt. She didn't need to wait to know what it could mean. Levyna had seen it before: the golden ring engraved with a black eye was worn by only one person in the entire kingdom of Queen's Hill – the Palatine of Queen's Hill.

A knock sounded on the door and Levyna jerked her head at her mother's voice.

"Levyna." Her mother opened the door, walking to her bedside. "Is everything all right?" she asked, concern pulling her face taut. "You look pale."

Levyna stared at her mother, struggling to find the words to explain what she had seen.

"Levyna?"

"Where is Father?"

"Preparing to go and meet the king," her mother answered.

"I – I need to see him," Levyna said, urgency in her voice.

"Okay ... Why? Is something the matter?"

"I ... I don't know, Mother. I think so," she said.

Her mother's face pinched as she sat herself next to Levyna on the bed. "What is it?"

Levyna told her mother about the dreams, all of them, and how they seemed to be coming true. Then she told her mother why she was terrified about the most recent dream.

Just then, Levyna's father walked in, and both of their eyes locked on his hand and the ring wore.

If her dream was true, then something would happen to her father, the Palatine of Queen's Hill.

"What has both of you staring at me like that?" her father asked.

Levyna looked to her mother, still unsure how she was supposed to tell him. Her mother gave a soft nod and Levyna recounted it all again.

"I've been having these dreams now for the past month. At first I thought it was nothing until ..." she paused to think about how to say it.

"Levyna, you will have to speak, young woman. I'm not a mind-reader," her father said.

"I dreamt about the King's Guard insignia covered in blood and then an old guard died. I saw a white rose flower lose its petals two nights before the queen's seamstress passed. You remember the king's horse that died, too? I dreamt about it the night before, as a paddle horse that drowned."

The palatine stared at his daughter, face serious, recognizing the pattern she was trying to make him see. "How long has this been happening?" he asked.

"Just about a month now," Levyna answered.

"And you're sure about these dreams?"

"I am," Levyna said.

"But that's not the reason why she looks so pale now," her mother revealed, staring at her father. Both of them looked at her, then, waiting but Levyna could only look at her father's hand again.

"Father, this time my dream was about a ring and an eye being buried in the dirt," she said.

Her father's brows pinched. "What?" He stared at her in confusion.

"A ring with an eye on it," her mother explained. "The symbol of the Queen's Hill Palatine."

His brows rose and he lifted his left hand to look at the ring on his middle finger. He stared at it for a moment, realizing what they were insinuating. He chuckled loudly. "Nonsense," he said, to Levyna's horror. "I was willing to think that maybe there could be something to your dreams but this –" he pointed the ringed hand at her "– this is not it. Your dreams don't mean what you think they mean, Levyna."

"But, Father, I saw it, just like I saw the rest before they happened."

"And you said it yourself – you saw other things that have failed to come to pass. So perhaps it's just a coincidence that you're putting too much belief in."

"She's scared, Fredrik. Listen to her, what are the chances that she's not wrong and her dream means something?" her mother said.

Levyna's father fell silent for just a moment before he looked between his wife to his daughter and back again. He turned around, preparing to walk away. "Perhaps you should stay in today and get some rest. You would be amazed how rest can help the mind."

"I'm not imagining things, Father!"

"Of course, I'm not saying you are, Levyna, but I still think you should get some rest. We can talk more about this when I get back." He reached the door, and Levyna and her mother shared a quick petrified glance before her mother hurried after him.

"Fredrik," she said, putting herself in front of him.

"She believes she's dreaming about all these things. She needs to rest. Don't tell anyone else about it or it might become a problem. We'll deal with this when I return," Fredrik said.

Levyna's mother scoffed. "She's not a problem the palatine has to fix, Fredrik, she's your daughter!"

"I am aware of that."

"What if she's not wrong? What if what she saw is true and her dreams are happening? What if it happens, Fredrik?" His wife looked down at his ring, mind racing as she took his hand. "What if ..."

"There hasn't been a dreamer in Queen's Hill in over a century. And the last one didn't find it kind when she realized the burden of what she was seeing. It's not something that can be assumed, no matter how worried you are. Levyna needs rest. That's what I believe. Nothing is going to happen to me or my ring." Fredrik removed his wife's hand from his and walked away.

***

Olin had never been to Queen's Hill before. He had always wondered what it was like, hoping he would someday find his way there, but he'd never really found the chance. The only other palace he'd been outside Ravinshore was Duken, and that had been years ago.

Olin stared at everything they passed, following Yondi to his master's house to at least find Olin a pair of sandals to wear before they figured out how to search for Cyrus. A barefoot man walking around Queen's Hill with a sword in his hand was definitely going to draw attention. Olin was a spectacle, covered in mud and dirt, not to mention the blood. Considering that Yondi's home was still a distance away, and they would have to pass through town, they would have to think of a disguise.

Yondi pulled Olin to the side of a road, and waited, then cast a spell to remove a robe that a passing rider had tossed behind his horse, pulling it into his own arms instead. Exhilaration flashed across his face; that had been only his third attempt at the spell.

Now, Olin walked through town wearubg the robe to hide his sword and blood-stained clothes; it covered his face as well. But it didn't stop him from seeing the rest of Queen's Hill. It looked a lot like Ravinshore, only with less dirt and more magic.

They didn't talk much, focused on trying to get off the streets quickly. While Olin was happy to experience the town and the kingdom from beneath his robe, he couldn't help but dart his eyes around for signs of watchers, even though he knew that there was no way the Order of Walrea could be in Queen's Hill.

They reached Yondi's master's house, and Yondi opened the door and let him in; Olin followed, tracking dirt into the house. He pulled the cloak off his head and turned to face the apprentice.

"When do we go and find Cyrus?" he asked.

Yondi shook his head. "I've told you. There are a couple of people by that name in Faidon and more in Queen's Hill, and you don't seem to have any idea what the one you need looks like or does for a living. Do you?"

Olin's face pinched; he'd had no time to ask while his uncle had been being killed by the watchers. There hadn't even been time for him to consider questions before Wylie had tossed him through the portal. His silence confirmed Yondi's assumption.

"But I need to find him, and I need to do so quickly."

"And I have agreed to help you." Yondi walked to a table in the room, removed the satchel, and took out the jar of oros. He placed it on the table, then removed the rest of the bag's contents.

"While we try and find this person, perhaps you want to make yourself look less noticeable. And put that away," Yondi said, nodding at the sword Olin was still holding.

Olin gripped the sword harder. He looked at the blade. Letting go of it didn't feel like something he should do. None of it felt right – getting clean, resting while everything went to hell. The boy in front of him had no idea about the events that had thrown him out of his own kingdom. He ran his hand through his hair.

"Look." Yondi stepped away from storing the dandelions on a shelf and turned to Olin. "I don't know what happened to you that led you to being buried in the dirt by the Black River, or why you need to find this man, but I have promised to help as much as I can. You can go ahead and leave if you want to. Maybe you can find him on your own, but maybe you stand a better chance with the help of a mage," Yondi said. "You could meet my master and maybe he could help. He knows more than I do, and if you talk to him, there might be something he can do to make the search easier."

Olin's face relaxed a little, but the urgency was still in his head. He looked to the side of the room and walked there to rest the sword. He removed the cloak and dropped it on the chair. Yondi pointed at the back chamber where he could clean himself up.

"Take your sword with you if it makes you safer, but there really is no need for it here. I'll get you a new shirt and you can clean the pants yourself."

Olin nodded, eyed the sword, then exhaled as he left it behind to rid himself of his uncle's blood.

***

Olin jerked awake and sat up, breath heaving and gaze daggering in every direction till he found Yondi, sitting by the table with his hands raised in front of him and a book open beside him. The apprentice seemed to be trying out a new spell and didn't notice him immediately.

Olin shot to his feet, rubbing his hands over his face and then ran them through his hair as he walked over to Yondi. "I need to find him."

Yondi sighed. "I thought we talked about this already and you understood? Do you remember something new that might help you find the man?"

Olin shook his head. "No, no. I'm not talking about Cyrus. I mean Wylie, my uncle. I need to – I need to find him. He might still be alive. I need to get back to Ravinshore and get him out."

"I don't think that's a very wise idea, Olin."

"I don't care!" Olin, now wearing the shirt that Yondi had loaned him and a pair of new trousers, leaned on the table for support as he shook his head. "You didn't see him, or what he went through. All of it was because of me and he still chose to get me out instead. I need to go back and find him. I must at least try!"

"And how do you plan to do that? From what you've told me, the entire Order of Walrea is probably looking for you. How do you intend to hide from them once you set foot back in Ravinshore? They will find you and your uncle's sacrifice will have been for nothing. Even if he's somehow still alive, which, from what youv'e told me, sounds very unlikely, he would have been captured by the watchers. And even if, for some reason, he was kept alive and you're somehow able to reach him, how do you think he would feel seeing you in Ravinshore after he nearly bled himself to death to get you out of it?"

Deep down, Olin knew all of these things were true, but he couldn't let himself simply abandon Wylie. His uncle's last act had most likely been shoving him through that portal, but it was easier for Olin to hang onto the hope that he was still alive somehow, a hope that came with the fear of Wylie being hunted or tortured by the watchers.

Yondi could see the panic strangling Olin. Yondi couldn't imagine how he would react in Olin's place. The myths of the watchers were common across all the three kingdoms, whispers of their true identities. He couldn't imagine living the rest of his life in fear of every shadow and new face, each a potential enemy just because he'd discovered that the watchers were responsible for the king's sickness. It sounded as unreal as it possibly could. Yondi was still struggling with whether or not he believed it. Stories like that didn't just ruin lives, they ended them. But he couldn't think of a reason Olin would lie, not when he knew it was a death sentence.

"I should have stayed. I should have fought like he taught me to, I should never have let him get me out without saving himself too," Olin said as he lowered his head, hair falling across his eyes.

"And you would have gotten yourself killed trying to take on the watchers. What would have happened after you escaped from your house? Ten more watchers would be hunting you. What you've learned is probably the greatest secret of the decade, if not the century, Olin. An entire kingdom's fate. There was a reason that your uncle created the portal that led you *here*, and not just somewhere else in Ravinshore. Maybe it's because he knows that, when you find this Cyrus person, you might stand a chance here. Or you could just decide to walk away from it."

Olin turned to Yondi, hearing the echo of his uncle's words. "You think I should run."

"I think what you've stumbled across is a reason to run, if you like being alive. Even if you find the Cyrus person, you don't know if it'll end there," Yondi said.

Olin stared at the apprentice, who looked away, returning to the book open beside him. Yondi read it again, then positioned his hands to create the spell outlined in the book. Olin watched as a thread of power sparked for a moment, and then fizzled out to the apprentice's evident frustration. Yondi had magic, but like everyone who did, he had to learn to use it.

For once, Olin wished he had powers of his own. Even if the only thing he could use it for was to learn if Wylie was alive, and save him. If only.

CHAPTER ELEVEN

O lin snapped his gaze to the door as it flew open.

He almost leapt for his sword, but only sprung to his feet as a middle-aged man toppled his way into the house.

The man tilted as he struggled to keep himself upright. His brown hair was messy and thinned, exposing his scalp in a small bald patch surrounded by a lighter shade of brown. He wore a robe that looked soiled with whatever he'd been drinking – most likely cheap ale – and his belly protruded above the rope belted around his waist. The man had a bottle in his hand, and Olin watched as he turned it over, then frowned at the fact that it was empty. The realization seemed to irritate him and he threw the bottle to the side.

The man belched loudly and placed his hand on his belly, then he glanced at Yondi, who was now standing a few yards to his left. Then he turned his gaze on Olin. The sciff watched as the man's eyes narrowed. For the moment of stillness, the man stared, eyes drooping and brow cocked. Olin hoped it wasn't who he thought it was.

"Yo – Yondi, did I leave a guest in the house before I left?" the man asked.

"No, Master," Yondi said quickly. "He's my guest."

"Hm."

Olin was struggling to hide his disbelief. This man was the master Yondi had spoken so well of, the same one who was considered one of the most powerful mages in all of Queen's Hill? The man who might be able to help him find Cyrus? Olin endured another long stare from the mage, who walked past him and headed straight for the chamber. Yondi hurried after his master, who had landed on a bed and didn't look to be getting out of it for the rest of the day.

Yondi stepped out of the room and closed the door behind him, coming face to face with an unimpressed Olin.

"What is that? Is that who we're waiting for?" he asked.

"I know how it looks, but trust me, it's not really what you think," Yondi answered.

Olin scoffed with is hands turned up. "How is it not?"

"Master Posdel can be very ... unusual, but it doesn't take away from the fact that he's a brilliant and powerful mage."

"Who is also smashed right now. And I'm guessing the fact that you're not surprised means this is normal. Is he always like that?"

Yondi glanced at the closed door and stepped away. "No. No, he's not always like that. But sometimes he does that to deal with things that can be difficult to explain."

"How is he going to help when he can't even tell who he left in his own house?" Olin asked, eying the closed door skeptically.

Yondi shook his head. "Look, he'll snap out of it in a couple of hours and we can tell him everything. I promise he's much more than he looks right now. You're here already. A few more hours can't hurt."

"Except you might be wrong and it very much could hurt. A few hours could mean the difference between whether or not I reach Cyrus in time to figure out why my uncle wanted me to find him, whether or not I'm able save King Edmond and the Kingdom of Ravinshore, or whether I can maybe even still save my uncle. A few hours could be everything."

Yondi sighed. "Of course, you're right, even a minute is too much, sometimes, but you have to understand what I mean. Part of the reason why you're still here is because I know he will likely know something to help you. And, consider what your problem is: a secret you cannot go and reveal to just anyone, not even here in Queen's Hill. So, if you still want my help, I say we wait for my master to wake so he can hear your story."

***

"Tell me again how you managed to escape the Watchers of the Order of Walrea, twice?" Master Posdel asked, disbelief in his voice as he stared intently at the young man standing in the room next to his apprentice.

Posdel looked a sharp contrast to the man who had stumbled into the house less than two hours before, and his voice was firm as he spoke. The seriousness in his eyes was just what Olin had been hoping for.

"I only managed to escape because of the portal my uncle created. He's the reason why I'm here, and why I need to find Cyrus," Olin said.

Posdel turned to Yondi. "Of all the things you could have bought home, you chose the biggest trouble in the whole of the three kingdoms?" he asked. Yondi had no response for his master, who looked like he wanted to strangle him.

"Adium Insefato!" The mage raised his right hand and turned in the air, casting a small gust of wind whirling around the room. "A bit more privacy," he said.

Posdel stepped away from the boys and walked to table that held the jar of oros. "I'm not a fan of the Order – Red Flame or Walrea or the Three – but I don't seek to be involved in their business either," he said. "I have survived this long knowing what not to get involved in, and in one afternoon, my bloody apprentice brings it right into my home." He set the jar down, harshly enough that Yondi feared it might break.

"I am sorry," Olin said before Yondi could speak. "He only wanted to help, he had no idea what had happened, but ... I don't have to be your problem. I'm only still here because Yondi thinks that you might know something to help me find the man my uncle asked me to. I don't have to be here any longer. I just need to find him so I can get back to Ravinshore as soon as I can."

Posdel stared at Olin. "As noble as that sounds, you are naïve to think that the Order will give up if you're no longer there. Red Flame wouldn't, and from what I know, neither would Walrea," he said. "The fact that you're in Queen's Hill might give you some time, but you cannot be sure that you're safe from them, not completely." He gave his apprentice another look that could have been translated into several forms of annoyance. "Who is this Cyrus your uncle has asked you to find?"

"That's the thing, Master —"

"Yondi, if I need you to talk, I'll ask you. Right now, just stand there and try very hard not to say anything," Posdel said.

Yondi quieted at once and Olin glanced at him before he answered, "I have no idea who he is or what he looks like. My uncle only told me his name as he was sending me through the portal. I'd never heard of him before then."

Posdel's face pulled into a thoughtful frown. "And you have nothing that could hint at who this Cyrus is? You don't even know if he goes by that name."

"I've told you, I don't."

"Yes, I've heard you," the mage said, walking back to the table. "But considering the fact that you have been under a terrible amount of stress trying to escape one of the deadliest forces in the three kingdoms, it would be forgivable that your brain has hidden vital information from you, disguised as something you would otherwise deem unimportant." To Yondi, he ordered, pointing, "Get me the bowl."

Olin watched as the apprentice fetched a clay bowl from the shelf and brought it to his master. "Wylie never told me anything about Queen's Hill. We planned on leaving for Black Castle at dawn, and he said I would stay there and he would find a way to handle it. That was as much as he had told me before ... before the watchers attacked," Olin said.

Posdel opened the jar, dipped his hand inside, and pulled out one of the slugs. The animal squealed as it was moved to the bowl next to the jar. "What about your parents?" Posdel asked.

Olin looked startled. "What about them?"

"Where are they?"

"They're both dead," Olin answered, pain palpable in his voice.

"Do you remember any of them ever mentioning Cyrus?"

Olin scoffed. "Don't you think I would have told you if I did?" he said, voice a little louder.

Yondi looked between the triggered Olin, his master, and the magical slug slowly increasing in size in the bowl.

"You cannot be too certain. Like I said, the mind can hide things from you sometimes."

"My mind is fine!" Olin yelled.

Yondi turned to him. "Olin."

"What?!"

"Encephus, ignatias ad-interus," Posdel said the beginning of the spell as placed his hands over the bowl and slowly pulled away. Threads of light, the same color as the oro, appeared out of the creature, linking them together. The mage was controlling them.

Yondi looked at his master; he had never heard that spell before and wasn't sure what he was trying to do. The oro writhed and squealed, an irritating sound. His master didn't stop and continued to weave his hands; the threads of light from the creature grew and it squealed even louder.

"Make it stop!" Olin shouted.

Yondi turned to find Olin with his hands covering his ears, face contorted in agony at the torturous sounds from the creature.

"Olin?" Confused, Yondi moved towards the boy, who stepped back quickly. Yondi looked back at his master, who hadn't even turned from what he was doing, continuing to drain the oro of its light. The slug's brightness had dwindled; it was no longer growing and started to shrink instead. Yondi watched in dismay as the creature gave one final shriek, then was silent.

"Step away," Posdel said.

"What?"

"Step away, Yondi!"

Yondi stepped back, out of his master's way, and Posdel turned, cupping a ball of light in his hands. Yondi's eyes widened as his master threw the ball at an unsuspecting Olin, who suddenly dropped his hands from his ears and fell to the ground like a sack of stones. Yondi's mouth gaped, looking from Olin on the floor to his master, who was dusting off his hands and frowning.

"Wh – what just happened?" Yondi demanded.

"I'm not sure yet, but we'll find out in a minute. Get his legs and help me move him to the chair."

Yondi stared, aghast.

"Yondi!"

The apprentice snapped out of it. Uncertain, but trusting his master, he moved to Olin's legs and lifted him.

***

Olin slowly opened his eyes. Yondi gasped. He didn't understand – Olin's eyes were glowing blue, just like the light that had struck him. It was only for a moment, then he blinked and it was gone. Yondi looked to his master, as if to confirm if he'd seen the same thing.

"Olin," Posdel called. "Can you hear me?"

Olin grunted as he blinked again, his head lolling to the side. He was sitting in the chair, with Posdel and Yondi in front of him.

"What did your uncle tell you before he sent you through the portal?" Posdel asked.

Yondi glanced at his master, wondering why he was asking the same question as before. It made no sense to him.

Olin grunted, then said something that wasn't coherent.

"Olin, I need you to remember what your uncle told you before you went through the portal. Who did he say you should find?"

Yondi didn't understand. "Master, we already know who his uncle asked him to find."

"Yondi, keep quiet and you might learn." Posdel, with his gaze still on the barely-conscious Olin, called the boy again, "Olin?"

"Find ... Cy ... rus," Olin muttered.

"I need you to remember everything, Olin. Go back there and remember everything,"

Yondi watched as his master gripped Olin's head and the sciff's brows furrowed even harder; his eyes were still closed.

"Go on ..."

"Find ... Cy ... rus. For-ger," Olin said slowly, following it with a heaving cough.

Yondi's face showed his astonishment at the words. He looked at his master, who looked satisfied, but not surprised. His gaze turned thoughtful as he let go of Olin's head and stood.

"How did – How did you know?" Yondi asked.

"The mind is a bottomless trap," his master answered vaguely.

Olin coughed a few more times and finally opened his eyes, keeping his head upright and looking like he'd come back to his senses. His face pinched as he looked between Yondi and Posdel. "What happened?"

"The Cyrus you're looking for is a forger. That was what your uncle told you. This makes the search much easier now," Posdel said, turning and walking returning to the table that held the bowl of shriveled oro.

"What?" Olin said in disbelief.

"You said it."

Olin looked at Yondi and then away. He put his hand on his head; it ached terribly, almost as bad as it had earlier when he'd first woken up on the riverbank. "I remember it now. Why am I just remembering it? Did you do this? Did you put it in my head?"

The mage scoffed as he took a small mortar and pestle and placed it on the table next to the bowl. "I did no such thing. I barely helped you remember what you'd 'forgotten' you'd heard," he said. "Like I told you, Olin the mind is a bottomless pit. You will only ever remember a fraction of the things you see and the things you hear and when your life is in danger or you are threatened, as you were when facing the watchers, your mind will pick what it needs for your survival in that moment. Before you ask, I didn't know whether or not there was something locked away, I merely gambled."

Olin sighed and Yondi silently agreed with his irritation. Yondi stepped away to join his master, who took the dried-out slug and placed it in the mortal and started to pound.

"So now what?" Olin asked, who had stayed seated. He'd learned his lesson at the river, and was less quick to try getting to his feet with the way his head felt.

"The headache will pass in a few minutes. As far as the man you're looking for, I know of only one man named Cyrus in all of Queen's Hill who used to be a smith. He was one hell of a forger when he was younger. Just like his father and his father's father." Posdel pounded the oro harder; it was quickly beginning to look like dust. "But he didn't bother to keep to the trade for long before he found his way out of the dirt and the molten ore to something else. He grew bigger than it, and never returned. What did you say your uncle did for living again?" he asked as he turned around.

"Wylie is ... was many things." Olin paused to recognize the change in the tenses he had used. "He was a carpenter towards the end. That was what most people knew him as. He was a hunter too, but before that, he was ..." He looked over at the sword resting against the wall at his side. "Not many people know this, but he used to be part of the Ravinshore King's Guard for King Edmond's father, King Landen," he said.

"Hm," Posdel said. "I guess it's possible that the two became acquainted sometime during your uncle's varied past."

Olin got to his feet. "Where do I find him? Cyrus, the forger."

"He doesn't go by that anymore. You will do yourself a favor in remembering that when you see him," Posdel answered, still pounding away at the ash of the oro.

CHAPTER TWELVE

W ylie knew when someone was being kept alive to be used. He was more than familiar with the practice. The hope of taking his last breath in his house in a pool of his own blood had vanished the moment he'd realized who was behind the mask of the Lord Watcher. Had Wylie not been too weak, it would have been a pleasure to spend his final moments knowing that he'd taken the bastard with him.

There were men whose hearts were changed by their experiences, turning them into soulless creatures. Thorne was not one of those men; the Lord Watcher of Walrea had never had a heart to begin with. Whatever sat in his chest was a lump of charred mass pumping vile through his veins endlessly. And Wylie had missed his chance to carve it out. Again.

Wylie lifted his head at the sound of the steps, feeling the ache of his injuries. He didn't feel like a man alive; he had lived past his time and he knew it. What he'd done with the ring, how it had consumed him and clung to his heart ... he wasn't himself anymore. Death was looking like the perfect escape from it all, since he had managed to send Olin to safety.

But Thorne had stopped the bleeding, burnt his wounds, and given him water just so he could continue breathing for a few more hours, here in this place. Wylie turned his head a little; he could recognize a dungeon when he saw one. If he'd one more guess, he would say that he was below the grounds of Walrea.

The gate to the cell opened. Wylie turned to see the watchers standing guard walk in; two of them stepped aside for a third watcher to step forward. Wylie recognized the eyes now.

More than twenty years ago, during Wylie's role as a Captain of the King's Guards, he'd caused a stir when he'd spoken against the watchers being given free reign to do as they pleased. It wasn't uncommon for people every once in a while to talk ill of Walrea and what it stood for, but having it come from someone who was as close to the throne as a King's Guard didn't sit well with many.

Wylie hadn't announced his disbelief of the Order for the world to hear, but those close to him then had known where he'd stood, and it had soon caused division among the ranks of the guards. Everything had turned on its head when one of the men, who was rumored to also be secretly against the Order, had ended up with his throat slit in his own bed. The man had also been one of Wylie's friends outside of the King's Guard.

Wylie had hid his outrage afterwards, but then the day after, the King's Guards escorting one of the king's guests to the palace were attacked by bandits, helped by another sorcerer. The clash had been brutal, and had seen five of the eight guards killed at the hands of the bandits, who also managed to steal many of the guests' possessions. The rumor that had followed was that the bandits had been rebels supposedly against the watchers, and that they had succeeded in the attack because they had a man inside – Wylie – who wanted to get revenge for what had been done to his friend. But since watchers' identities weren't known, and the rebels couldn't storm Walrea, they'd decided to take it out on the King's Guards to hurt the kingdom.

The guards that had survived the attack blamed Wylie, sure he could have done more to stop it had he wanted to. One of them had lost his brother to the bandits. The boy had been young, a little older than Wylie's own nephew was now, and he'd never gotten past his rage at Wylie, blaming him for everything that had happened.

After the disruption the rumors had caused, as the bandits and rebels were soon found dead one after the other all over the kingdom, Wylie had removed himself from the King's Guard and disappeared. He had gone into hiding for years in Black Castle before he returned. Only one man in town had known who he really was, besides his nephew, and Old Ron had always been on his side from the time they'd served as King's Guards. Wylie hadn't thought anyone else would remember him, but he'd apparently been wrong.

"You've had enough rest, old man. It's time to tell me where you sent your shit-stain of a nephew." Thorne's voice was cold.

Wylie's jaw tightened and he shook his shackled hands. He heaved a bloody phlegm and spat it at the feet of the Lord Watcher, nearly hitting what he aimed for. "I will bite and chew my own tongue out before I ever tell you anything. You will never get the satisfaction of finding him."

Thorne chuckled. "Bold of you to think that I have any true need of your bloody tongue and the words you want to twist with it – the lies. I only ask you again because I thought being a step further away from death might have given you some idea as to why telling me might be the better option. Save yourself the hell of having me dig it out of you. But since you've insisted." Throne reached to his side and brought out his dagger. "Hold him still," he ordered the other watchers.

They moved to either side of the prisoner – the first prisoner to be held in the dungeon of Walrea in over ten years – and forced him to his knees, Wylie could only do so much against the ache of his body. He hadn't recovered from the ring draining his life force. What little resistance could muster ended after one of the watchers elbowed him in the shoulder, followed by a knee ramming into the back of his leg. He grunted as his knees met the ground. The chains clanked, and his breath sounded close to collapse as the watcher held his head up so he was forced to watch what Thorne was about to do.

The Lord Watcher swiped the blade across the heel of his own left palm, then returned the dagger to his side. Thorne stepped forward, holding his hand in a fist over Wylie's head, allowing the blood to drip on his forehead as he began to mouth his spell.

"Raigielario," he smeared the blood over the prisoner's head, "agniticus filla et-mentorio!" Thorne grabbed Wylie's head on either side of his temple with both of his hands as the watchers stepped back. A red glow emerged from the blood and the light threaded into the Lord Watcher's hands like a fountain.

Wylie's mouth gaped; he gasped for only a moment before it all went dark for him.

"Filla et-mentatio!" Thorne repeated and threw back his own head; his eyes glowed a soft red and his hands began to shake around Wylie's head. The watchers saw the dark brown of the prisoner's bloodshot eyes slowly fade. Wylie's eyes turned white as he trembled in Thorne's hands.

It felt like his mind was being carved with a dagger; Wylie could feel Thorne's spell reach through his memories, from a few moments before as he was held down, back to the hours before they'd met. Wylie tried to resist, but it was futile and only made it a thousand times more torturous. Thorne's spell left no memory untouched, all the way back to when he'd collapsed in a pool of blood, then further back to when he'd shoved his nephew through the portal. The spell found the last words he'd said to Olin, and even the memory of his thoughts as he'd created the portal.

Blood seeped from Wylie's ears and nose and soon his eyes as Thorne tightened his grip, digging as much as he could from his mind. Each memory he sucked out of the prisoner's head brought Wylie closer to becoming empty. Already defeated by the struggle, and the drain on his own magic from the ring, Wylie was powerless; a tear slid down the side of his face before the thread of light finally dimmed, this time leaving the man with nothing but a void to his end.

Thorne took his hands away and the watchers stepped back. With his hands still chained behind his back, a dead Wylie dropped to his side. His head hit the stony ground, leaving his ghost-white eyes staring at the wall ahead of him.

***

Thorne stepped out of the cell with the watchers. L and the nameless watcher followed him a couple of yards away before the Lord Watcher stopped and turned to the second man. "Get rid of the body," he said.

"Yes, My Lord." The masked watcher bowed and hurried away, leaving Thorne and L alone in the dungeon.

"There has still been no word from the palace?" Thorne asked.

"None, and it has me concerned. Nothing has been said about his situation, it's as though the palace is not willing to let their subjects know," L answered.

Thorne exhaled. "Of course, they're not. They understand that revealing the king is ill will certainly come with consequences. They have assumed it's better to keep it quiet, see if they can find a way for him to recover like nothing ever happened." He scoffed. "I almost find their hope impressive."

"And what if ... they find a way?"

"A way to do what?"

"To help him."

Thorne ground his jaw. "Do you remember the last time you started on a conversation like this?" His features were hidden, but his eyes gave away his disdain. He glanced beyond L to the cell they had just left, where Wylie's body was still very warm. "It created a mess that I'm now having to deal with, in addition to everything else we have planned." Thorne ground his jaw again and looked away for a moment.

When he returned his gaze, he released a swift pulse of energy at L, throwing the watcher against the stone wall of the dungeon and pinning him to it, legs dangling a foot off the ground. L quickly began to struggle to breathe.

"I warned you, did I not? That if you ever gave me a reason to hear your doubts again, you wouldn't have it easy."

L grunted, his expression stuck between trying to get air in his lungs and trying to give the Lord Watcher a response that would pacify him.

Footsteps approached. Men to remove Wylie's body. Thorne raised his left arm to the direction of the dungeon stairs and made a supinating wave of his hand that slammed the door shut, loud enough that the wood could almost be heard cracking.

"Look at how much of a problem your stupid questions have caused! I have a dead carpenter in my dungeon and a bloody sciff all the way in another kingdom, because even when I gave you the chance to take care of the mess you created, you managed to make it worse. Is it old age?" Thorne cocked his head, uncaring about the watcher's struggle. "Are you growing so senile in your middle age that you're suddenly unable to understand the madness of questioning the plans of the Order? My plan? Or is it complacency that has turned you so soft and incapable of accomplishing the task the Order demands of you?"

L's struggles began to dwindle as he slowly succumbed.

"We are approaching the most critical point in the plan and I'm still being questioned by my right blade? I'm tempted to snap your neck in two right now and have your body fed to the hogs."

L gave no response; his breath was almost non-existent as the full weight of Thorne's spell pressed even harder on his body. A moment of quiet fell before he felt the sudden release of weight. He fell to the ground, landing on his knees and hands to avoid hitting his face. L coughed and clutched his chest.

"There will be no next time, L. You cannot continue to be a watcher and show even a semblance of a second thought through your actions. I will steal the air from your lungs for good if you ever give me a reason to doubt your ability or your trust in the Order. Do you hear me?"

L nodded vigorously on his knees before rising to his feet. His breath was still labored as he stood to face Thorne. "Never again, My Lord," he muttered.

Thorne's eyes held part resentment and part regret. Had it been any other watcher, he wouldn't have shown mercy. Anyone else wouldn't have even gotten the chance fix the mess they'd created by letting the sciff get away.

Throne knew he might be losing his edge by giving L a warning. A decade ago, he would have erased the watcher and every evidence of his failure before it had time to fester. It wouldn't have been allowed to spread all the way to Queen's Hill. He wouldn't have left the task of catching the spy to his right blade – he would have hunted the sciff down himself within an hour of realizing his identity. It all would have ended there.

So the thought of giving L yet another chance to redeem himself felt like he, the Lord Watcher, was losing his touch. Thorne looked at L and let out an angry exhale. There was much to be done, and L, his right blade, would be needed for it. As he himself had said, they were at a pivotal moment in a plan that had taken a decade to arrange. Crippling his right blade with his own hands could end up costing more than his rage was worth.

King Edmond was proving to be more of a stubborn bastard than expected by remaining alive with the poison in his system; other men had only lasted three days before growing cold and stiff. But Thorne didn't doubt that plan was moments away from fruition; nothing the palace did was going to have any effect on the king.

"Has there been any whisper from the needle inside?" he asked.

"None, My Lord. It has been quiet ever since the king's touch was established."

"Not that there should be a need, but that should tell you something – everything. The plan is taking its course and whatever scrambling the palace is doing will yield nothing but futile efforts," Thorne said. Still, he thought that he perhaps needed to make an appearance to test what games Ole and the queen were playing, keeping quiet about the king's welfare.

"Of course, My Lord." L seemed to have snapped out of his earlier skepticism; his doubts were now a distant memory of a lifetime before.

Thorne turned to the exit. "There is more to be done while we wait for Edmond to get out of the way, but for now I need to make sure that the rat Wylie sent to Queen's Hill is squashed for good this time."

L's face pinched as he seemed to realize what he needed to do. He bowed his head. "My Lord Watcher, I know I have failed before with this task, but I ask that you let me have one more chance to prove my worth to the Order and its cause by getting rid of the sciff myself," he said.

"You've had two chances to get to him, one more than is ever required. Now that he has found his way to Queen's Hill, I will not risk him running his mouth to the three kingdoms and causing any more headaches for us. I will take no more chances."

L dropped to one knee. "And with my life I am sworn to the Order of Walrea, that nothing but its cause shall be my crusade, that the last drop of my blood I shall spend to fulfill its acts."

Thorne tilted his head to look down at the man in front of him reciting the Watcher's Oath in a bid to earn his redemption. He was quiet.

"Grant me this chance, Lord Watcher. Let me redeem myself and the Order by erasing the mire I have caused. I will hunt the sciff in Queen Hill, I will search the entire kingdom front top to bottom until I find him, and I will make sure he never has the chance to say a word about

Walrea to anyone. And if he has, everyone single ear that has heard it will perish along with him," L said as he lifted his head. "I will make sure of that."

"It's Queen's Hill. You are not free to step into another kingdom acting as a watcher."

"Then I will capture him instead and drag him out of the kingdom. I will do whatever I have to," L answered, desperation apparent in his voice.

Thorne exhaled. A moment ago, he had been close to snapping the man's neck, yet here he was, now begging for another chance to correct his mistake, to act as his right blade, risking everything in another kingdom. If he was discovered, he would be executed at best, start a war at worst.

The Lord Watcher certainly felt compelled. "You may not need to do that after all," he said as he began to walk towards the steps leading out of the dungeon. "I know where exactly Wylie has sent him."

CHAPTER
THIRTEEN

O lin had learned that Cyrus had become part of the Queen's Hill Palace Officers, and the only way they could reach him was to find a way to the palace. He'd spent the night with Yondi and Posdel. Come morning, he'd woken to find the mage gone again, which left Yondi free to go with Olin in search of Cyrus.

"Are you sure your master won't mind the fact that you're coming with me?" Olin asked.

Yondi shrugged. "He all but told me I was free to do whatever I wanted, as long as it didn't result in him having to deal with the Red Flame."

"I still find it hard to believe that man is your master."

"Yes, I can see how it may look. But you got a glimpse of what he could do, did you not? I've been his apprentice for a while now and even I'd never seen him do that before. I'd never even heard of that spell. It wasn't in any of the spellbooks I've read. My master's character can sometimes make people miss his true form; it makes them underestimate him. It's true that he has challenges though. Many of them are because of his powers, though you might not believe it. He sees things and sometimes it takes a toll on his mind. He hardly ever sleeps through the night. But if you're able to look past that, you'll find out the truth yourself." Yondi looked ahead. "He's very gifted. He does magic like I've never seen anyone else do."

"How are you able to learn anything from him?" Olin asked as the pair inched towards the main market.

"I learn a lot simply by watching and listening, but he teaches me – he does – when he's not in one of his foul moods. He can be very different – determined. I've gotten used to him. I understand when he says things, even when they don't sound like a lesson. When I find it hard to create a spell, as long as he's not out of it, he shows me how. He says my magic will grow as I learn more, and soon he will have no need for me. I know that was his own way of telling me I would soon not need *him* anymore."

Olin glanced behind for the third time as they walked; he still saw nothing and looked ahead again. "Do you think you know enough to leave?" he asked.

"I could stay for another year and still not have learnt half of the things he knows. I'm eager to find my way soon, but I hope I can get him to teach me how to do some black magic, at least. I don't want to be a sorcerer or anything, I'd just like to know. It would be nice to have that kind of power, unlike spells of Red Light."

"Red Light?" Olin asked.

"Yes, those ones he says he would never teach me and I should never learn because they consume the soul of the mage," Yondi answered, catching Olin when he glanced back yet again. "Is there something you're looking for?"

Olin shook his head. "No, nothing. But it feels very odd walking in the open and not being in a hurry. I think we're being followed."

Yondi snapped his head back, not trying to be subtle. He found no signs of anyone paying them a suspicious amount of attention. "I don't think we are."

"How can you be sure? I have a feeling someone's watching."

"Maybe, but not here. No one cares who we are here, if you're not trying to buy something from them. Besides, you're wearing a cloak, it should help," Yondi said. "You're in Queen's Hill, remember that. The Watchers of Walrea cannot do anything to anyone in this kingdom."

Olin wished he was comforted by the idea, but after what he'd seen them do the last time they'd caught him – how he'd thought that they weren't following him until they were suddenly there – he wouldn't dismiss the possibility of anything now, even if a centuries-old decree between the three kingdoms said otherwise.

"What about your master? What if he makes a mistake and says what he should not when he is ... not himself and someone hears who shouldn't?"

Yondi scoffed. "No. That's one thing I know will never happen. I don't know how he does it, but there are some things I know he would never let out no matter how smashed he gets. And those are the same things he wouldn't even think about saying to someone else when he's himself. Also, he meant it when he said he doesn't like anything that brings the Order's attention. He never talks about them."

"You sound like you're in his head, like you're with him and can tell when he's about to say the wrong thing. A smashed man has no control over his tongue."

"And I would pick my master, pissed-face and unconscious, to save my life over anyone else in the Kingdom of Queen's Hill. I know him," Yondi said.

The two walked in silence as they drew closer to the streets leading to the palace. Olin gripped tighter at the sword beneath his cape, trying to prepare himself for whatever he might encounter. With each step he took, he fought the memory of what had happened to Wylie. Yondi had mentioned Red Light, and Olin's mind flashed back to what his uncle had done, what he had turned into after doing that magic to take out watchers and save him.

Yondi eyed Olin. Though he had fallen silent, he still looked very cautious of everything, even with the hood of the cloak covering his expression. Yondi thought about what had happened earlier when his master had cast the spell to make Olin remember – the way he had reacted to the squealing of the oro, and especially how his eyes seemed to have changed color for a moment. And then Posdel had asked about Olin's parents, specifically if either of them had been mages, and Olin had said no. His father had never had magic and neither had his mother, though his memories of her were far fainter than that of his old man. When Posdel had asked if Olin had ever done magic before, Olin had told them that the only person who was a mage in his family had been his uncle, Wylie. When Olin had asked what these questions had to do with helping him find Cyrus, Posdel had said he was only curious.

Yondi didn't buy that it was the only reason. They'd both seen how Olin had reacted to the oro – different, agitated – unlike nothing either of them had seen before. Still he had no magic, showed no signs, even though one of the most powerful spells had brought him to Queen's Hill through a portal. But he had never recited a word of a spell to as much as light a flame. It left Yondi wondering what, then, had made Olin's eyes glow the way they had.

"So what do you plan to say to Cyrus when you see him? Do you think he's someone you can trust with what you know?" Yondi asked.

"I don't know yet. I guess the fact that he was the only one Wylie thought I should find when it mattered the most meant that Wylie must have trusted him. Besides, I really do need to tell someone that can do something to help."

"Do you?" Yondi asked. Olin turned to him with a quizzical gaze. "I mean, you did say that your uncle didn't really want you trying to do anything about it in the first place and he planned on having you hide at Black Castle."

"Not hide," Olin corrected. "He just wanted to go there because it would be safer than staying at home, and he did plan on doing something about it."

"Alone. Was that not what you said?"

Olin stopped in his tracks. He turned his back to a wagon following a carriage passing by – the type of the carriage that showed they were getting closer to the affluent part of the kingdom.

Olin waited for the carriages to leave before he spoke. "You weren't there. Alright? Whatever Wylie might have thought best obviously changed when the watchers found us and killed him. There's no way I'm keeping quiet about it now. Regardless of who Cyrus might turn out to be, once I meet him and tell him about what has happened to Wylie, either he helps me get back to Ravinshore or I find a way myself. I know Walrea has eyes everywhere and they'll be waiting for my return, but I don't care anymore. Wylie is dead and there's a very good chance that King Edmond is too, all because of the very Order that was supposed to protect the kingdom. If Walrea succeeds in killing the king, and I don't speak up about what I know, I will never forgive myself. The throne and the people of Ravinshore will never forgive me. It doesn't matter if the adversary is invincible," Olin said.

Yondi exhaled and fell quiet. He had no idea what Olin was going through, but he could very well imagine the pain of being told to let it go and keep silent in the face of potential disaster. Especially after his uncle had been one of the first to suffer because of him. The anxiety in Olin's eyes had not dimmed the slightest since Yondi had found him at the bank of the Black River. Yondi knew there was nothing he could say to make Olin reconsider returning to Ravinshore, with or without this Cyrus's help.

***

The little girl she was traveling with wasn't her daughter. The fact that the sea had nearly claimed them didn't change what she was there to do. Ilda hadn't known it would storm, or that it would be mad enough to shake the ship like it had, but save for the fact that it had almost killed her and the child, it had turned out to be an even better cover for executing her task.

Ilda had also been grateful for the kind and mysterious man with the black scarf who'd sat with them in the cabin, taking the attention off everyone else. There was a chance that maybe one other person on the ship could tell who he was; she'd been able to make it out before they'd even boarded the ship. From the way he'd waltzed past everyone, right up to the boatswain, thinking no one else had noticed what he'd done, to his silent demeanor and his eerie look, she could not have asked for a more perfect decoy. Of course, the poor man had no idea he'd been a decoy, just like he'd had no idea that the little girl with the small leather sandals and the curious eyes had been her original decoy.

Ilda had noticed the medallion in the man's restless hands; she had signed to the girl to go and see if she could get it from him. Ilda had no material need for the object, except maybe so she could mark the memory of the journey. Ilda only needed the girl to make an approach and an impression, not converse with the Black Scarf. After all, the child could neither hear nor speak, not since she'd been born. Ilda just needed her decoy to be seen – so her *decoys* would have their stage. It would distract till she got off the ship.

The girl belonged to a farmer and his wife, her neighbors who'd died of illness days apart when the child had been just a year old. Ilda had taken the child to care for when no family came to claim her, and the poor baby knew no better than her.

As she'd held the child – who she'd called daughter as they'd boarded to avoid suspicion – Ilda had eyed the group of merchants carefully. The girl had slept like the world ending wasn't her business. Ilda, meanwhile, had joined the rest of the people in the cabin, panicking as a group stepped outside to help. Black Scarf had remained in the cabin, and Ilda had begged him to help watch her daughter while she spoke with the captain. He'd agreed, and Ilda had stepped out for the slightest moment.

The reason she had been on the Flea, sailing to Edenborough, standing alone in a poorly lit storage room among barrels, had been for this purpose. She had been deep in shadow, so deep that it had hid the color of her attire as she'd jabbed the needle into the merchant's neck, then disappeared into the shadows again. She had waited behind a beam while the merchant's partner arrived, carrying the extra lamp. Immediately, she'd doused the room with a daze spell that lasted the five seconds she'd needed to escape. Ilda had returned to the cabin to resume the part of a terrified passenger, and no one had ever been the wiser.

And when the Flea had arrived at Edenborough, the poor mother had got off the ship, leading her little girl by the hand, whispering an unregarded "thank you" to the Black Scarf who had set off down the street quicker than anyone else. Ilda had wondered how she had been lucky enough for fate to work in her favor so perfectly. Very different than the fate of the merchant, who had been about to be found black-veined, dead in a cabin on the ship.

Ilda had seen the medallion in the girl's hand; she'd caught the moment the Black Scarf had slid it to her. Ilda had thought it had been a gesture of kindness, some kind of wish or perhaps a dream of redemption in the form of the gift to the strange child. She had seen many like that man, old and young alike, dropping off bits of themselves in the form of material possessions in an unspoken hope of returning the piece of a soul they could no longer find because of the things they'd done. Black Scarf had been subtle – she thought that he might succeed as a watcher, but he belonged to the Three, judging by how unbothered he had been and the way his gauntlet had been strapped with three laces. Someone should teach him not to dress so conspicuous in public.

Now back in Ravinshore, after making an immediate return crossing on the next ship leaving Edenborough for Duken, despite the storm scare, Ilda stood behind the bar with a tray of jugs filled with ale and bread in her hand, eyeing her newest mark, who had just entered the pub in the company of two others. Unlike the merchant on the ship, this was someone Ravinshore would feel when she killed him.

CHAPTER
FOURTEEN

I t hadn't been a completely smooth affair, even after Isabelle had learned of Alden's daughter and his sacrifice. But she certainly engaged more than she would have if she hadn't known. More than half of his conversation was about his daughter, and the other half was questions about Maedro and what it felt like to do magic. She still thought he talked a bit too much for someone expected to be alert at all times. Did he speak this much when he was around the king? Still, she didn't find it too insufferable as it made the time pass quickly.

As they entered Duken, Alden grew silent and she glanced at him, noticing the frown on his face; she followed his gaze to the side of the road.

"Something's wrong," he said, slowing his horse.

Isabelle saw nothing but she slowed as well. "What is it?"

"I don't —"

They followed the road around a sharp bend to find a wagon blocking the road, tipping precariously on one wheel. A heavily pregnant woman sat nearby, holding her belly and groaning. The grimace on her face made her distress obvious. She was alone.

Isabelle's eyes widened; she snapped her gaze to Alden. "We have to help her."

"We don't have to do anything. We can be on our way so you can reach where you're needed on time."

"What? Why would you say that? Can you not see that she needs help? She's probably in labor!" Isabelle said, voice growing louder.

"I do see what's in front of me, Isabelle, and though you may be right, I feel strongly that something is wrong. Someone else will pass soon enough, and they can help her. Trust me," Alden said. The serious look on his face was completely different than the one Isabelle had grown familiar with for the better part of a day and a half.

Isabelle frowned. She had no reason to listen to him – he was no more than a perfunctory companion on this trip, as far as she was concerned. She pulled at her horse's reins and the beast stopped. She ignored Alden's dismay as she climbed off.

"Wait, Isabelle!" Alden called after her, but Isabelle was already at the woman's side. He cursed under his breath as he brought his own horse to a stop and leapt down.

Gathering his reins, he paused to grab Isabelle's horse as well, and looked around, eyes hunting for anything lurking in the woods.

"What happened?" Isabelle asked as she dropped on her knees by the woman's side. The woman groaned loudly before she opened her eyes.

"I ... I was heading back to town when the wheel suddenly broke. I tried getting down and then I slipped." She pointed at her right leg. "The pain is fine, but I think ... I think my baby is coming."

"You were traveling all by yourself, in this condition?" Isabelle touched the woman's leg.

The woman let out a scream at the touch. "Please ... the baby," she said. She screamed again and a small stream of fluid slid down her legs.

"Is this your first time?" Isabelle asked, pulling the woman's dress up to examine her.

"No," the woman answered. Her tone had changed, turning brisk and loosing the sobbing and groans that had laced her previous responses.

Isabelle looked up to meet an alarmingly straight face. At the same time, she heard Alden scream. She heard a swish through the air and turned to him to catch him as he dropped to the ground, an arrow embedded in his chest. Shocked, Isabelle snapped her gaze back to the pregnant woman, only to see the flash of a heavy fist, knocking her backwards.

Isabelle fell to the ground, hitting her head on a stone. The pain flashed through her body, and she blinked through a moment of dizziness, head throbbing, before the sound of Alden's groan jolted her up. She tasted blood and felt it slowly slide down the side of her head.

"What took you so long?" the pregnant woman said.

Isabelle looked up to see men springing down from the trees and appearing from the woods. They approached the woman, who was getting to her feet.

***

Olin and Yondi stopped by a building a few yards from the palace. The famous castle was the tallest in all of the three kingdoms, and looked magnificent even from this distance. It had taken almost an hour of walking to make it from Faidon to Castle Grove where the palace was located. Based on how the people looked and the opulence of the buildings, this was where the elite of Queen's Hill resided. They peeked at the entrance to the palace grounds, which was manned by two guards standing on either side of the wooden gate. It was open and they'd seen a couple of people approach.

"Is that it? Can we just walk in?" Olin asked.

"This gate only leads to the grounds; the palace's entrance is further. It's not really that easy to get in. It also has more guards, but we don't need to go to the palace, we just need to reach the grounds, and hope that we find who we're looking for there. But you need a reason to enter. Mostly it's by invitation or special circumstances."

"We can't really tell them the reason we need to find Cyrus."

"No, of course not. But we'll still find a way in."

"How?"

Yondi sighed. He spat on his palm and used it to tame his wayward hair. He straightened his posture. "Some good-old confidence," he answered.

"What? That's your plan?" Olin didn't sound reassured.

"Do you have a better idea?" Yondi turned, waiting and Olin's silence gave him the answer. "Alright, then. Just trust me and let me do the talking."

Olin didn't protest. He trailed a step behind as they approached the gate. He was busy trying to avoid lurking eyes, but he could have sworn that Yondi's steps suddenly turned to strides akin to someone walking confidently towards their own house.

They were stopped by the guards' outstretched arms, but Yondi only scoffed.

"Who are you and what business do you have at the palace?" one of the guards asked.

"We are here for Cyrus. He has demanded our presence and is expecting us at the moment," Yondi answered.

"Who?"

"Did you not hear me? I said Cyrus," Yondi said, voice firm.

"Look, boy, I don't know who you are or what you think you're up to, but if you know what's good for you, you'll make yourself scarce at once," the second guard said.

Olin glanced at Yondi; his face pulled into a frown as he cocked his head. "Really? You don't know who I am, yet you think you can speak to me like this just because you guard the gates of the palace grounds?" Yondi looked from one to the other. "Tell me something, which of you should I say gave the order to deny us entry after Cyrus has been waiting for us, for him –" he pointed at Olin "– for hours? Which one of you turned away his important message to the king?"

The guards' faces seemed to contort in unison at the mention of the king, but Yondi didn't back down.

"If you must, send word to Cyrus and tell him that the people he's expecting have arrived and are being held at the gate. Then watch the messenger come back without a tongue. But, if you insist that you'd rather find out for yourselves then we'll turn around. I just need to know whether I should turn you both in, or just one of you when Cyrus finds us.

Yondi's displeased gaze remained fixed on the guards. Olin watched the men look at each other, an unspoken debate passing between them, arguing who would give the final order to refuse the supposed messenger for Cyrus.

"You say that he's expecting you?" one of them finally asked.

"Like I said, you can go ahead and confirm if you need to, but make sure whoever you send isn't someone you care about." Yondi's voice was firm.

The guard exhaled and stepped aside; his partner hesitated a moment longer before he did the same.

"Wise choice." Yondi nodded as he walked ahead. Olin followed.

Olin made to turn around, but Yondi stopped him.

"Don't turn, keep walking."

"How did you – how did you do that? How did you know they would believe you?" Olin asked, voice quiet as they hurried away from the gate and across the grounds.

"To be honest, I didn't," Yondi answered. "I merely hoped that the fear of mentioning the king and the urgency of the matter would stop any questions." He sounded a little excited as they arrived at the building next to the main palace.

Olin was in awe of what Yondi had done. The apprentice looked like he hardly believed it himself as he glanced around.

"Now we really need to ask somehow how to find Cyrus. I don't think your confidence will get us past the real palace guards," Olin said, eyeing the ones waiting in front of the palace.

Yondi looked and sighed, knowing Olin was right. There were people walking across the palace grounds, some dressed in robes and a few in tunics. Yondi spotted a young black man that looked close to their age and hurried towards him.

"Please, we are looking for Cyrus, where do we find him?" Yondi asked.

The young man pointed to the balcony of a nearby building, where a man was standing. Olin and Yondi followed his gaze, but Olin yanked Yondi out of sight of the building a moment later when another man joined Cyrus on the balcony.

"What is it!?" Yondi asked, questioning the assault.

"I – I know that man," Olin said.

"Cyrus?"

"No. The other one."

CHAPTER FIFTEEN

"**W**e had to be sure there weren't more of them," Isabelle heard one of the bandits say.

Isabelle pulled her eyes away from Alden. The pregnant woman was on her feet now, and had walked to grab the blade offered by one of her accomplices. Isabelle couldn't understand how this woman – this heavily pregnant woman – could be a part of this operation given her condition. Isabelle had seen the water proving she'd been in labor. Where had it come from?

"Next time you make me wait that long, I'll cut off your balls and feed them to you," the woman said, pointing her newly-acquired dagger at the man. He didn't give her a response. "I had to bloody piss myself before you showed. It was disgusting and had better be worth it.

Now, what the hell have we got here?" She looked back down at Alden and then to Isabelle.

Isabelle flicked her eyes back to Alden. The arrow still protruded from his chest. He screamed again when one of the bandits stepped on him to stop him from reaching for the sword next to him.

"Shall we get this over with, before the road gets too busy? See what you can find," the woman ordered. One of the men gathered the horses while another began searching the bleeding Alden.

The woman focused on Isabelle. "If you want to live to be stupid again, take off all of your jewelry and give them over," she said.

Isabelle wore a silver ruby ring on a finger of her left hand and a black amulet on her right wrist; she wasn't eager to part with either of them, but she didn't say this out loud. She watched as Alden was searched for anything of value. Alden didn't look like one of the Ravinshore's King's Guards; instead of his armor, he wore a tunic with a cape over it, a pair of trousers, and leather boots. He was dressed for traveling, and looked like anyone from the three kingdoms.

"Hurry, take off his gauntlet," one of the men said to the one searching.

"I said hand me your bloody jewelry, broad, can you not hear me?" The woman stepped closer, waving the dagger in Isabelle's face.

Isabelle could still taste blood from the punch, but she said nothing, watching as the bandit pulled off Alden's gauntlets. The man froze, then looked up at the others. "Oh, shit."

"What?"

"Look," the man handed the gauntlet to another bandit, whose eyes widened. They both looked down at Alden, then towards the woman, who had turned away from Isabelle and risen to her feet.

"What?" she demanded.

"The gauntlet – it's Ravinshore leather," the bandit holding the gauntlet said.

"So what?"

"It's got the marking inside." The look of dread on his face was mirrored by the others.

Before the woman could demand to see for herself, one of the men screamed as Alden jabbed a dagger into his foot. Alden then pulled the blade free and sliced at the man's heel in a swift move.

The other bandit reached for a knife at his belt and aimed at Alden, but a wave of energy threw him across the path and into a tree, impaling him on a branch.

Shocked and horrified, the remaining bandits turned to see Isabelle, who was supporting herself with one hand, the other raised against the now-dead bandit. The woman lunged at Isabelle, dagger in her hand and pure madness in her eyes.

"Exunis!" the sorceress commanded, and the root of a tree shot out of the ground, tripping woman and landing her on her face. Isabelle then waved her hand and the woman was swept into another tree. They could hear the sound of her bones breaking on impact.

The bandit Alden had stabbed tried grab the sword nearby, but Alden, still lying on the ground, kicked the man's bleeding leg, tripping him backwards. Alden then growled as he turned himself over and drove the blade in his hand into the side of the man's neck. The man stopped moving as blood spurted around the knife.

Then Alden let out a groan of pain as another arrow pierced the back of his thigh.

The last bandit shot another arrow, but it fell short of Isabelle, who had both hands raised to deflect it into the wagon behind her. The bandit readied another shot, but didn't get the chance to aim as Isabelle pointed her arm at a tree and waved towards the archer.

She watched as his eyes bulged and the arrow fell short a yard in front of him. His bow dropped from his hand. The bandit gasped and coughed blood as he dropped to his knees. He was stopped halfway to the ground by the thick foot-long tree branch buried in his chest.

There was no more movement, save for the startled horses. Isabelle looked at Alden to find the him face down on a dead bandit. She got on her feet and hurried towards him, falling to her knees by his side and turning him over to see his face.

His eyes were closed and he was quiet. This was not the kind of silence she'd hoped for. The sorceress put her head to his chest to listen; she could hear his heart beating slowly, along with the wheezing of his shallow breath. He was drowning in his own blood. She laid him out on his back and pulled the arrow from his chest. Blood gushed from the wound and Isabelle quickly placed both her hands over it. Alden coughed, spitting out more blood. Isabelle shook her head vigorously as she pressed harder against his chest.

Isabelle exhaled deeply as she raised her head to focus her energy. She'd spent half of it dealing with the bandits, but she let the rest flow through her, every bit that her body could take, down her hand into Alden's chest. He coughed more blood but she didn't stop. She hung on, feeling her own body quiver. Isabelle looked and saw the magic threading out of her own veins into the Alden's body. Soon, she began to feel the heat in her hands, and took them off his body. The hole in his chest had closed.

Isabelle gasped, holding her breath as she looked from the healed wound to Alden's face. He opened his eyes in time to see her exhale before her own eyes closed and she dropped to the ground beside him.

***

Isabelle opened her eyes to see Alden's bloodied face; his mouth was moving but she couldn't hear what he was saying. She blinked as he reached down and tore a piece of his cape to dab the side of her head where it was still bleeding.

"Can you hear me?" he said again.

Isabelle nodded and relief spread across his face. "Okay, I need to get you up. We need to get out here. Can you get up?"

Isabelle blinked, and nodded again. Alden helped her sit up and pulled her to her feet. It soon became obvious that she was too weak to stay on her feet. Alden caught her before she fell, groaning when it irritated the pain of his injured leg. Before Isabelle had woken, Alden had yanked out the arrow and tied a piece of cloth stolen from a dead bandit around the wound to stop the bleeding.

After he'd been free of the arrow, Alden had rushed to Isabelle, realizing what she must have done to the bandits and finding no sign of the wound on his chest.

And now she was awake, and trying to say something.

"What did you say?" he asked, hoping she would repeat herself.

"R – river," Isabelle whispered.

"River?"

He could only think of one.

Alden did the only thing he could – he scooped Isabelle into his arms and carried her to the horse, managing to get her on it. She seemed like she was about to fall, so Alden held her up until she could steady herself. She wasn't completely unconscious, and so wasn't totally a dead weight and was able to help by barely clinging to the beast.

"Hold on!" he said as he hurried back to pick up his gauntlet and sword. He sheathed his sword and rushed back to the second horse, grabbing the reins so it wouldn't be left behind. Alden then climbed behind Isabelle, wrapping his arms around her waist to grip the reins as they set off, with the second horse following beside them. Isabelle leaned against him. Alden could feel the heat of her body; it felt as though she was burning. The pain in his thigh quickly became secondary as they hurried away from the scene.

Alden didn't know what had happened, but whatever Isabelle had done had saved him. He was the one that was supposed to keep her safe.

Ole had told him that this woman couldn't lose a strand of hair from her head. Ravinshore depended on her mission. Alden clutched her tighter as they rode through the woods, further into Duken and straight for the Black River.

***

An hour after Isabelle and Alden had fled the scene, two riders arrived, slowing their horses to halt as they saw what was ahead of them.

"Bloody hell. What the hell happened here?"

"Bandits," the other said. The horse moved ahead a few paces before the rider dismounted. He pulled his sword from beneath his cape and walked towards the closest body – the man was on his knees, wedged between a tree branch and the ground. He moved his gaze to the one lying in a pool of blood. As one, the guard and his partner looked in the direction of the man impaled on the tree.

"What the hell did this to them?"

"Something or someone who didn't like being ambushed," the guard with his sword drawn said. He looked away from the impaled bandit and back to the broken wagon. There was no horse attached. He saw traces of a trail of blood, leading away from the bodies. He looked from the wagon, back to the bandit with the knife sticking out of his neck and stepped towards the body. He stared for a moment before he crouched to observe the hilt. He pulled out the blade and a small pool of blood followed. He looked at the blade even closer.

"What is it?" his partner asked.

This blade. A single stab with no room for error. The bandit had been dead at once. He glanced at the body's leg, turning the limb to observe what had been done. A stab and then a slash, in quick succession to destabilize the enemy. It had all the signs.

"Do you see what I'm seeing?" He showed the blade to his partner and pointed. "The neck. He was dead in a moment, but look – the leg, the cut. What do you think?"

His partner frowned and darted his gaze back at him. "These are from someone who knows what they're doing, a man who knows how to kill."

"Someone trained, like a King's Guard." He sheathed his sword.

Both men hurried back to their horses, knowing fully well who they were following. They might not have been able to tell what power had manipulated the tree branches, but they knew how to recognize the killing marks of a trained Ravinshore King's Guard.

They had been ordered follow Alden and the Maedrian woman, keeping enough distance that they wouldn't be seen. They were responsible for making sure that nothing happened to them, especially the woman.

They remounted their horses and hurried into Duken. Whatever had happened, the fact that Alden had killed wasn't a good sign, especially if whoever had killed the bandits with the branches was still out there, still after them. Keeping a distance was no longer an option, not when Alden or the Maedrian woman could be hurt.

The guards began to pick up the pace, hoping to find the pair before it was too late. They were all too conscious of what Ole had said of the woman's importance. In no simple terms, her life was more important than theirs.

CHAPTER SIXTEEN

Yondi hurried after Olin as he stepped around the corner of a building to hide. Yondi wasn't sure why Olin was running away from the very man he had traveled through a portal from another kingdom to find. All Yondi knew was that Olin had recognized the other man. But that was it. Considering what they'd had to pull off to enter the palace, Yondi wanted to know what was going on.

"Wait, Olin, stop." He grabbed Olin's hand before they went any further. "What's going on, who is the man, and why are you running from him?"

Olin turned so Yondi could see his eyes. He had known Olin for just over day, but the look in those eyes was instantly familiar. It was the same look he'd worn when

Yondi had found him by the bank of the river – a look of terror. His face was pale and pulled into a permanent frown. If it had been colder, Yondi would have seen Olin's breath steam in the air.

Olin knew who that man had been. Olin would never forget those eyes. Even if he forgot the face – which he never would – all he would need was those ghostly grey eyes for him to know. The look in that man's eyes as he had thrown knives at Wylie, while Olin had just stood there, unable to help, wasn't something he would ever forget.

"He's one of them!" Olin said. "He's a watcher!" he whispered.

"Wh — what?" Yondi wasn't sure he'd heard right.

"I know that man. I can never forget those eyes."

"Watchers aren't supposed to be seen, Olin. You can't see their faces. No one knows who they are. How can —"

"I know what the hell I'm saying! I know that man because I saw those eyes, and he was there. He was there when we were attacked, he was the one who threw the knives that killed Wylie. That watcher killed my uncle!" Olin said again.

Yondi was speechless for a moment. Mouth agape, he glanced back, as if he could still see the men on the balcony even though they were out of sight.

"Hold on, Olin, how can you be so sure? It's a very long distance to recognize someone who'd been wearing a mask. Besides, you only saw the man with Cyrus for less than second, are you sure you —"

Olin snapped. "Look, Yondi, if you don't believe me, that's fine. I have many flaws, but my memory isn't one of them. Even in the worst moment of my life, I never forget a face, and I might not have seen him without his mask, but I've seen those eyes. I don't question how you're able to do magic. This isn't something I can explain either. I don't need you to believe me, but I know what I saw!" he said, struggling to keep his voice down.

"Okay, okay ..." Yondi answered. "It's not that I don't believe you, but you have to understand how very unusual it is. It's not common, but it is also not unlikely."

Yondi remembered what had happened the day before when his master had used the oro on Olin. The questions his master had asked must still loom over him. If magic wasn't too far from Olin, then what he said could very well be likely, Yondi thought.

"It's not unlikely, Olin, so I don't think you're mistaken," he said.

Yondi's words instantly had an effect. Olin didn't look happy, but he looked a little less distraught at the fact that Yondi believed him. His shoulders relaxed and his jaw unclenched and he finally looked away from Yondi's face, over his shoulder to a man and a woman who were passing by. Olin had about ten thoughts flooding his head at the same time, but the one that pierced the loudest was echoed by Yondi out loud:

"So if the man – the watcher – who killed your uncle is talking with the man your uncle told you to come find, what does that mean?" Yondi asked.

"It means I don't quite think Cyrus is the same man Wylie thought he would be sending me to," Olin answered. "We need to go. I need to get away from here." Olin turned away.

"Wait!" Yondi called, but was too late to stop Olin from crashing into a woman who had appeared out of nowhere.

Olin's wrecked nerves and panic made him shove her away, and the woman landed on her behind before he realized his mistake. Olin stood there for a moment, staring at the young woman. She looked up, eyes misty, too quickly to be from his assault. She'd seemed distracted, but was soon fixed on Olin's stare.

"Olin!" Yondi whispered to snap him out of the state he was in.

Olin quickly reached down. "I'm sorry, I'm sorry I wasn't looking," he said. She took his hand and Olin almost let her go at once. She rose to her feet and he apologized again. "I'm sorry," he said curtly, before turning to Yondi and signaling for them to leave.

"Sorry ..." Yondi whispered to the young lady as he followed Olin away from the scene. "Olin, wait!" he called. Olin barely slowed till Yondi caught up with him.

"What?" Olin asked.

"Are you really sure you want to leave? You don't want to find out what Cyrus has to say or at least know who he is? Do you think it's wise to abandon approaching him when you're this close?"

"Even after I told you about the man he's talking to? The watcher from Walrea who wanted me dead and most likely still does?"

"I'm not rejecting what you've said, Olin, but there are always two sides to a story and you have one. You don't know what Cyrus's side is or why he's talking to that man. He may not know who he truly is."

"So I should believe that it's just a coincidence that the same man that murdered Wylie is right here in Queen's Hill and is talking with the same man that Wyle used his last words to tell me to find?" Olin asked.

"I don't know, but don't you think there's even the slightest chance that it's possible? Or, in the worst case, that the man is here because he knows what your uncle told you? He was in the room, after all," Yondi said.

Olin shook his head. "No. He might have been in the room but he couldn't have heard what Wylie whispered. But even if he had, how do you expect me to approach the man now when the Order has already gotten to him?"

"He could still be on your side. You never can tell."

"Maybe. But I would like to think that I could tell, because of Wylie. If there was one thing he taught me, it's that loyalty cannot be bargained. Wylie must have thought Cyrus was still the man he knew. Clearly, he hadn't been up to date. If he were here now, there's no way he would tell me to walk up to the same man who was treating a Watcher of the Order of Walrea as an old friend, not when he'd tried to kill me."

Yondi huffed at the irony. Before he hadn't been able to stop Olin from trying to find Cyrus, and now there was nothing he could say to get him to rethink approaching the man. It seemed there was a twist waiting at every turn. Yondi watched as Olin hurried in the direction of the gate, then followed.

***

It was all she could think about. Levyna hadn't been able to get it out of her head – the dream where the ring with the symbol of the eye was buried in the dirt, the same ring that represented the Palatine of Ravinshore, Lord Fredrik – her father.

Her fears were made stronger by the fact that her father didn't take it seriously; he didn't think any of her dreams were anything more than coincidences, and it bothered her. Her mother, at least, took the dreams more seriously than her father did, but there was only so much she could do when the person involved refused to listen.

Levyna hoped she was wrong. She had never wished more to be wrong in all of her life. She hoped she wasn't a dreamer, or that what she'd seen wouldn't turn out how she imagined, like the others had. But there was no way to tell, not in this palace and not when the people of Queen's Hill were so skeptical of magic and those who wield it.

Her mother had set out to meet with a sorcerer in town to ask if there was a way to know the truth. She'd gone alone, not wanting to risk the wrong ears learning the news.

It had been over a day and nothing had happened. Her father was healthy and even more dismissive of the dream. He had refused to hear any more of it, sure that it was just her mind playing tricks. Levyna had hardly been able to sleep thinking about it, and when she had fallen asleep, she'd woken to nothing, no dreams or visions to clarify the truth, nothing new to tell how to stop whatever it was from happening.

Levyna, though not really in the mood, stepped out of her chambers and the palatine quarters of the palace to meet with the princess and her maidens. Levyna struggled not to be a buzzkill while they chatted away about preparing for the princess's birthday, but she eventually stopped pretending and zoned out in the middle of the garden, watching one of the servants bury a flower in the soil.

In her mind, she saw again the palatine's symbol being buried.

Levyna excused herself from the company of the maidens and hurried away, giving no real reason beyond that she was not feeling well. No one had noticed her eyes as she'd escaped. She was too concerned with returning to quarters without talking to anyone, and didn't look up until she slammed into the man.

He looked odd, and wore a strange expression on his face. Falling to the ground had knocked her mind out of it's spiraling thoughts about the dream, enough that she noticed that everything from the young man's stare to his hand was peculiar. She hadn't ever seen him before.

Levyna watched in confusion as the stranger in a cloak hurried away with his friend. She didn't know what it was, exactly, but she held the hand he had grabbed close to her chest, as if protective of it, unsure of what had just happened.

***

They made it out of the gate without drawing attention to themselves, and Yondi turned and nodded at the guards that had led them in earlier with a flash of a smile. They picked up the pace once they were away from the gate. Now it seemed like Yondi was the one being led and Olin was the one who had lived in Queen's Hill for the better part of his life as he navigated the crevices of the town with ease and Yondi followed.

"So, what are you going to do now?" Yondi asked.

Olin shook his head. The hood of his cape was pulled lower than before, now that he was aware that a watcher was in Queen's Hill. Most likely after him.

"I don't know, yet," he said. "I had really hoped that, for once, I would get the chance to fix all of this by doing the one thing Wylie asked me to do. I'd hoped Cyrus would be that chance."

"So did I. There was no way you could have predicted that a watcher from Ravinshore was going to be with him."

"There didn't need to be! All of this, everything, it never needed to happen. It's all my doing – all my fault!" Olin said, stomping his foot and kicking a wall, breaking his stride then continuing to walk. "None of this would have happened if I hadn't been so nosey. Wylie always told me to be careful, but I could never stop feeling invincible whenever I got curious. Now look at what it brought me! I got so curious that I found myself in the belly of the monster – the Order of Walrea. I got so nosy and saw things and heard things that I had no business being part of. I completely forgot where I was. And what did I do after I got the Order after me? I bring them home to the only family I have left. And just like he always has, Wylie used himself as shield, got himself murdered for my mistakes, and the one man he'd hoped could help turns out to be dining with that same monster. So, yes, Yondi, I should have known that something like this would happen before I stepped foolishly into that room!" Olin finished his rant.

Yondi remained quiet for a while as he watched and listened to Olin berate himself for what had happened. Olin still hadn't mentioned what *could* have happened, and what very well could still happen, if Olin had never uncovered that secret. The fate of an entire kingdom rested on that knowledge. Olin couldn't see it now, and Yondi knew this wasn't the best moment to tell him, not when he had lost his only family and one of the most powerful forces in the three kingdoms was after him. He didn't need to hear right now that what he'd done had been any kind of good.

CHAPTER
SEVENTEEN

I lda carried the tray to the back of the bar and tapped the barrel for three fresh cups of ale. She took them to the table for the new customers, making sure to give a long sultry glance to the first one she served. The three men might be sharing a table, but they weren't equal, she knew that. The sultry glance would lay the groundwork for what she needed to accomplish.

Ilda served at the pothouse most evenings and most nights, and though she didn't own the establishment, it was often assumed she did given how well she ran the place. It was the perfect job for her to catch whatever flies she needed. Like the man she'd just served, with his blond hair and large arms.

"You look good today, Ilda," one of the men said with a toothy smile, revealing his missing pair of front teeth.

Ilda nodded like she knew exactly what he meant. "I always look good," she reminded him.

"Bring us your best meat, some cabbage, and bread," the blond said.

"Of course," she answered.

"And another round of drinks," a third man with a thick beard and a red face added.

Ilda was a tall and fair woman with long black hair plaited into a braid ending at the small of her back and following her like a tail. For her to run one of the most frequented pothouses in town, she had to look soft when she served, but be able to put a wayward drunk in his place if she needed to. The dimple on her cheek appeared when she smiled and as she turned, she knew the men's eyes followed her. But looks and comments were all they would ever get. She served no man in Ravinshore more than jugs of ale, wine, bread, chicken, and whatever else the pothouse provided for their appetite. It didn't stop them from trying, however, even when they knew their drunken shenanigans would get them nowhere with her.

Ilda went to the kitchen and returned with the food for the table, making sure to throw extra winks at each one of them as she served. They smiled sheepishly; they always smiled like simple beings when she did that. Ilda served the plates and left, then returned with a fresh tray of wine, collecting the old cups and returning them to the bar. She made each man feel like she'd given him extra attention, tugging on the hopelessness that he might someday be lucky and get more. Ilda didn't usually do this to most customers, not unless they were special or she needed more of the coin that weighed down their pockets. Or unless she wanted something from them, like today.

While they ate and talked, Ilda continued her chores, having her help take care of the rest of the customers, and only stepping out to serve those she felt like taking on her own. There could never be sign of anything different than normal. Ilda had done this so many times that she didn't need to bother glancing in the direction of the man to check that all was well with him. He ate with his men, and they laughed carelessly. When she saw that the plates held only chicken bones, she returned and collected them herself, still offering glances like before.

"Another round of drinks!" the thick-beard man said, holding his cup up.

"No, that's enough for me. And I suggest it should be for you two as well," the blond-haired man said.

"Oh, come on ..." the toothy one cried.

"It's way too early in the day to get shit-faced," the blond reminded them as he reached into his pocket and slapped two silver coins on the table. "Anything else you want you pay for yourself. I suggest you don't forget yourself and do something I won't want to hear about." He stood up, and Ilda watched as he adjusted his belt. "I have somewhere I have to be," he added, then pushed the stool aside and walked away from the table, leaving Ilda and his men trailing him with their gazes.

"Well, I think it's never too early to have a good time. By the gods, I don't know how many more I'll get before my time comes," the thick-bearded one said as he gulped down more ale. He thudded the cup in front of Ilda's fingers as she took the money from the table. "One more of this, Ilda, will you?" he said, almost belching as he spoke.

"Sure," she said, taking the empty cup to be refilled.

Ilda eyed the blond-haired man as he left the pothouse. Her face remained indifferent as she filled the jugs and put them on another tray. She was sure she knew where the man needed to be and it didn't worry her. Just like the storm at sea on the Flea, Ilda knew it would be the perfect cover. There was no need for her to leave; she had no intention of stepping out of her pub regardless of what happened. They were here – his men – and they smiled sheepishly as she served yet another round of drinks and offered that flash of a dimple to turn their thoughts to mush and hide her true intentions. They were where she needed them to be – away from him and his destination a few streets over.

Human beings were nothing if not slaves to their own habits. This would be the perfect storm to hide her handiwork, and not even the rain beginning to pour outside would keep him away. Ilda knew once he stepped out of the bar, he would throw the hood of his cape over his head until he reached his destination. For the rain, yes, but mostly to keep his face hidden as he walked to the back of a building, stopped in front of a small black door, and knocked twice to be let in.

He would be greeted by a middle-aged woman with her bosom pushed up oh-so-desperately and alluringly to draw beseeching eyes. The woman would have a crooked smile and she would flash it at him, saying nothing as she directed him to the room upstairs with a nod. He was going to walk, still hidden, to wait in that special room for a moment before the door would open, and a zaftig young woman who was far too young for her looks would come in and close the door behind her. Once it was closed, the whore would lock the door and smile only briefly before commanding him to get on his knees. He would remain on his seat on the bed, staring at her in defiance and she would step towards him and slap him across the face. He still would not do as he was told until he was slapped again, this time harder, and the woman would again order him to his knees.

The whore would watch him keep his eyes on her as he stood. He would tower over her just slightly but she would not fret as his stare would soon lower, and he would sink to his knees in a genuflecting posture, leaving her looking down on him. She was going to take his face in her hand and pull hard at his short beard, and then she would take her foot and plant it between his legs and throw him backwards against the bed. He would groan as she pressed harder. The whore would then tell him to be quiet and take off his clothes, keeping his eyes on her so she could see his pain. With every piece of clothing he removed, she would inflict more pressure with her foot and yank his beard harder.

When he was naked and on his knees, she would ask him to crawl around the room on all fours like a budding child, a lesser creature. When he took too long to react, she would strike him across the face again until he dropped to his knees and began crawling while she grabbed a hold of his belt to begin lashing him across his back, and then on his ass, letting soft groans escape.

When she had had enough, she would ask him to place himself on the bed, where she would tie his hands over his head then climb on top of him and plant herself on his mast. As she undulated over him, she would cuss him for disobeying her orders as she twisted the flesh of his arms. The pain he felt was going to warm with the pleasure he sought, and he was not going to be able to tell the difference them as she rode him harder and twisted the skin of his arms and the hair on his chest tighter.

The climax wouldn't be as he had expected. As she slapped him across the face one more time, his eyes would go dizzy and he is grunt and groans would go quiet. The whore would cuss at him to look at her, slapping him harder and harder before she would move his head. The whore would stop and call his name and get nothing. She would pluck herself off him and place her ear to his chest just as he would begin to shake terribly and then stop.

She was going to scream, very loudly, needing to bellow at the top of her lungs, unusual of the volume of the setting, for the mistress of the establishment to come running to see what was wrong. While the whore fell to a corner of the room and held her hands over her naked chest and tried to cover her mouth, the mistress would walk over to the bed and call to him, nudge him and place her own head to his chest to listen to the deathly abundance of silence.

Her own breath would then cease as she would reach for his face and part his eyelids to find them flushed red with blood. The mistress would then turn to the half-naked man and the woman standing by the door playing audience, and move her gaze to the zaftig young woman who had serviced him, asking what the hell the whore had done to stop the heart of the commander of Ravinshore's army.

***

They arrived at Black River and Alden halted the horses and climbed down, holding on to Isabelle as he lowered her to the ground. She had held on as he'd ridden like a man with two horses, but she hadn't stopped burning and it had driven him to ride even faster. She'd hardly responded to his calls as he tried to keep her conscious. Now Alden knelt on the bank, Isabelle cradled in his arms.

"Isabelle?" he called. "We're here, Isabelle. What do you want me to do?"

She exhaled very weakly and Alden worried she couldn't form the words, but Isabelle managed to whisper again, "Take ... water."

"Take water? T – take you to the water?" Alden asked. He looked at the river. No other meaning came to mind. She was almost a hot coal in his hands.

Alden quickly stripped her of her cape and carried her to the water. He stepped in, boots still on, hardly caring about the depth of the water, and gently lowered her down. He had to submerge himself as well to make sure he could hold onto her while she was under.

"Come on ..." he said as he watched her face.

Nothing was happening. She wasn't opening her eyes. Isabelle was in the water, with Alden carefully holding her head above, but she still wouldn't wake. Alden cupped his hand, and poured in over her face to wash it. He thought he heard her gasp as he did so, so Alden went ahead and lowered Isabelle a little more, submerging her enough so her head went under for a moment. Alden then lifted her up and wiped the water off her face. Isabelle coughed and slowly opened her eyes.

"Ah!" he exhaled in relief, but her eyes soon closed again, and Alden, unsure what to do, held her in the water a little longer, waiting hopefully.

She had stopped burning, he could tell, but Alden still wasn't sure if he was supposed to take her out of the water yet.

He tapped her gently on the face again, calling her name, "Isabelle ... Isabelle can you hear me?"

The sorceress didn't respond at once, but she soon opened her eyes and Alden gasped. "Can you hear me?" he asked, and she nodded.

Alden stood, helping her up as well. He didn't bother asking if she could walk because she was already moving her feet, and all he did was help her to the bank and to the horses.

Isabelle sat on the ground, soaked to the bones as Alden ran back to get her cape, glad he had wisely left it behind. He threw it around her and she clutched it close, silent as she stared at Duken's side of the Black River.

Here it was little better than a stream, but they could see the water growing wider further away. Duken was different from Ravinshore. The landscape often looked colored by the mud from the river and the air was almost always damp, but it still took nothing away from the beauty of the kingdom, one Isabelle hadn't seen in over three years. But she wasn't here to hunt the landscape or the nostalgia of her memory.

Alden took off his wet shirt and squeezed it free of the water. "Are you okay?" he asked.

She turned to him and nodded. "I am." She watched as he waved his tunic in the air to dry it. "Thank you," she said.

Alden stopped and looked at her, his gaze wondering if she knew what she was thanking him for. "I have no idea what you did back there. I was halfway dead. I really thought I would die, till I opened my eyes. You took on those bandits all alone, and by 'taking on' I mean you destroyed them. I've never seen anyone do anything like that ever before, and I've seen a lot of warriors and a lot of sorcerers. No one has ever done that," Alden said.

"I didn't do it alone. And it was the least I could do, considering I was the one who fell for the trap in the first place."

Alden frowned. "You couldn't have possibly left a pregnant woman in labor alone by the side of the road. It would have taken something drastic for me to *actually* leave her there, despite what I said. When you've traveled that path enough times, you're bound to notice the feeling when things are unusual."

"You warned me," she said.

"I may have, but I could just as easily have been shot as we rode away and the bastards could have very well attacked even if we'd kept moving."

Alden threw his shirt back on and Isabelle spotted the hole in the cloth. She hadn't been able to mend it. She realized just how close she had come to leaving a child fatherless because she had been distracted. Isabelle could guess the thoughts that had played through his mind as he ebbed towards the end, and they wouldn't have been about the king of Ravinshore. It wasn't simply about her own responsibility anymore. She had almost taken this man away from his daughter, yet he was still thanking her.

Isabelle looked away and let out a breath. She got to her feet and pulled her cloak tighter across her chest. "I have to go," she said.

"Really? You've barely —"

"I must go, Alden." It was the first time she'd used his name out loud.

Alden stared at her for a moment and then nodded. "Alright. Let's —"

Alden fell quiet as he felt the sorceress's hand on his arm. He looked down at the touch and back to her face.

"Adoit et-ralsa," Isabelle whispered, and moved her hand to catch his head as he dropped to the ground, unconscious.

"I'm sorry, I must go alone," she said as she turned to her horse, separated it from the other, and grabbed her satchel. Then she climbed on the beast and rode away.

CHAPTER
EIGHTEEN

O f all the Watchers of Walrea, only the Lord Watcher was allowed at the palace. There, only three people knew his true identity – the Court's Counsel and the Queen and King of Ravinshore themselves.

Thorne stood in the corner of the throne room, cloaked completely in a black cape that covered his head as he stared at the seat of power itself – the throne of Ravinshore. Forged from gold and the swords of the kings of the past, those who had fought wars centuries before the Great War of Black River. The throne had seen many kings before King Edmond, all of whom had ruled by right as the true heirs of Ravinshore. The reign over the kingdom and its people was passed down from generation to generation by blood.

Thorne exhaled as he stared. Because of who and what he was – a watcher – he was hardly ever in the throne room long enough to admire the magnificence of the seat, but in its current state – devoid of warmth from the ruler – he had more time than he'd ever had to consider it.

The Lord Watcher remained still as he heard steps approaching. He kept his gaze on the throne until the other person in the room announced themself. Of course, he already knew who it was. The spring in Ole's step, which was almost imperceptible to those who didn't know him well, always gave him away to Thorne, who remembered how he had gotten the gait in the first place when he had been just a child.

"It's a thing of beauty, isn't it?" Ole said as he stopped beside Thorne.

The Lord Watcher exhaled. "Four hundred years and it still carries the power of Ravinshore. It is a thing of beauty."

"You know, when I was younger, my older cousin told us about the story of the War of Garedon, centuries before the Great War of Black River, and how it had been so bloody that the people of Ravinshore dug holes in the ground to hide from soldiers, digging so deep that they found gold. The gold they found was then used to pay mercenaries weilding magic to fight the wars for them. I used to wonder if the throne had been made of some of that gold clawed out of the earth by the bleeding hands of Ravinshore's royal subjects," Ole said.

"Whether it be the fable of the diggers or that of slayed emperors, the throne of Ravinshore belongs to the kingdom."

"I think you mean it belongs to the king – the ruler of the kingdom," the Court's Counsel corrected.

Thorne ground his jaw before he turned to face Ole. "Of course, the throne belongs to His Majesty," he said.

"What brings you here, Lord Watcher?" Ole asked, moving to place himself in front of Thorne's view of the throne.

"I've come to pay a visit to His Majesty," Thorne said.

Ole's brow rose. "Is Walrea of in need of so little of your attention that you have come all this way for a courtesy visit?"

"Coming to see His Majesty is not a courtesy visit. It would be mortifying if you claim you do not know that. To keep the king apprised of the affairs of the kingdom is more than just a visit of leisure or a sign of stale responsibility. Not where the Order is concerned."

"So you say."

"So it is. Now, I don't know about you and your sense of judgment, but I cannot help but notice that the palace is looking a little … light."

"Is that so?" Ole tilted his head back and forth, as if he could scan the entirety of the palace with that small glance. "I think it looks just right to me," he said.

Throne scoffed. "I am tempted, not for the first time, to wonder how the court has survived under your watch. Because surely you cannot say you recognize it. There is always an air to a palace with the king's presence. It's heavy, and palpable at the same. I struggled to find the feeling when I rode through the gates and entered these doors."

"Well, perhaps it's you who needs to check your senses again, Lord Watcher, because the presence of the king, His Majesty, King Edmond the Fourth, is very much overwhelming every single soul in this palace."

Throne nodded. "Then I would like to see him."

Ole sighed. "Unfortunately you will have to come at another time. Right now, His Majesty is unable to take visitors."

"He might, if you tell him it is a matter of urgency from Walrea," Thorne said.

"If it is urgent, then I suggest you tell me what it is so I can pass the message along to him."

"You are not His Majesty, Counsel, do not forget your place. As important as you may think you are, there are still things that do not belong to your ears, and I must convey them to the king in person."

"Then I am afraid you will have to wait."

"Till when?"

"Till His Majesty is able to attend your presence."

"Nonsense, Ole. Tell me now, where is the king?" Thorne took a step towards the Court's Counsel.

Ole said nothing to the Lord Watcher's demands.

"I believe he has told you exactly what you need to know," the voice came from behind, causing Thorne to step back and turn around. Queen Ariana stood there, seeming to have appeared out of nowhere.

"Your Grace." Thorne bowed. "I did not know you were there."

"The man has given you our response. I see no reason why you should still be trying to throw yourself in his face."

"Your Grace, as you know, my role to the king and the kingdom requires that I personally communicate with His Majesty. My demand of his whereabouts and his audience is in utmost fulfillment of my duties as the Lord Watcher of this kingdom, Your Grace."

Ariana stepped towards the throne to take Ole's place. Ole stepped to the side and bowed as the queen looked at the throne. "Your position as the Lord Watcher of Walrea is to serve Ravinshore, Thorne. You *are* very much still a subject to the crown of this kingdom –" she turned around "– so, when you are told that the king is not able to see you, you shouldn't have to be told twice."

Thorne's face didn't betray his true emotions. "Apologies, Your Grace. I know I need not remind you that the Order of Walrea exists for the kingdom's most severe ... challenges. We deal with them, and that requires that that the Lord Watcher of the Order is able to have access His Majesty, the king, not for matters of my own leisure of convenience, but to address said challenges and ensure that the kingdom continues to thrive as it always has, under the guidance of the watchers."

Ariana stepped forward. "The kingdom does not thrive under the hands of a bunch of faceless slayers, Lord Watcher, it thrives under the rule of the King of the

Ravinshore, His Majesty King Edmond the Fourth of his name, my husband!"

Ole bowed again from where he stood and Thorne, silent and unable to risk defiance so soon, followed suit by lowering his head.

"I apologize for my choice of words, Your Grace. Surely, I will not for any reason aim disrespect at the king or at the throne," he said. "It is just that when the king is concerned, it is my duty to confirm these matters with him, in person. I am obliged to not just convey what information I need, but to see that the king is protected."

"My husband is fine, Lord Watcher. If you have something of such dire importance that you are unable to tell the Court's Counsel because you think it is not *fit* for his ears, then you may tell the queen and Mother of the Kingdom." If her voice wasn't enough, and the watcher was struck with the challenge of comprehension, then crown on her head would remind him of whose presence he was in.

Thorne looked from the queen to Ole, realizing that he wouldn't be allowed to see the king. "I am sure that His Majesty is well. I will come another time to see him," he said. "But I would like to say, Your Grace, that the king's presence in the palace and the kingdom is always felt. And so is his absence." The Lord Watcher bowed to the queen once more before he turned and walked out of the throne room.

Ariana remained tense until the man was out of sight. It had taken much to remain composed and resist reacting to the bait Thorne had spewed.

"I'm sorry, Your Grace, I had no idea he was coming," Ole said, stepping forward to stand at the queen's side.

"That was his plan – the Lord Watcher has no regard for timing. It's meant to be a part of his duties, but this one takes a particular kind of pleasure in being insufferable."

"Oh, of that I am aware. Regardless, I think you made his place clear."

"Don't tell me you were fooled, Ole. You heard the man, he's going to come back soon, very soon."

"And he will come to find the same response, if that's what it takes," Ole answered.

"I have a feeling. I think he knows, or at least he suspects," the queen said.

"He cannot know. Only a handful of servants are aware, and all of them are sworn on their lives and that of their families to not let out even a breath of it, I am sure of that."

Ariana exhaled as she turned to face the throne that had become lonely since her husband's indisposition. "The Order was birthed in silence and obscurity, and Thorne doesn't enjoy being treated with disrespect. We might have kept him away for now, but Walrea is allowed to come and demand the king's presence no matter what. If Thorne does indeed suspect something, and I know he does, then he will be back. The man is a hound born in mischief."

"And he will return empty-handed again."

"You know what I would prefer, Ole? That when Walrea comes again to find the king, he is seated on his throne instead of lying limp and lifeless on his bed. My husband needs to wake up, and your sorceress needs to return.

Because every moment that passes marks the beginning of a different fate for Ravinshore."

***

Lord Fredrik had barely thought about his daughter's dreams passed the hour Levyna had revealed them to him. And the coincidences had been the only thing that had made him give them even that much thought. But he'd tried to put it out of his mind. The odds that his own daughter was dreamer didn't bear thinking about. It wasn't something he could entertain. He was the Palatine of the Kingdom, the king and the kingdom's right arm, and there was no way his own child was cursed with the burden of seeing the future. None of his ancestors, or his wife's ancestors, had been dreamers, and thus his daughter could not be.

Dreamers usually showed at an earlier age, too. And they never had magic. And they never had a life that could be envied, or one that lasted.

Levyna simply could not be one.

Fredrik ignored the silliness of the thought, ruminating instead on his mission to visit Ravinshore to pay King Edmond a visit and hear his thoughts on the storm the seers had predicted would destroy much of the three kingdoms' harvest. Fredrik had not protested his king's command, his mind set for Ravinshore, to leave at dawn with his convoy. He had told his wife and Levyna, and had wanted them to come with him. Fredrik was sure that the trip, and a few days away from the palace and Queen's Hill, was bound to change his daughter's gloomy spirit and her ridiculous notion about dreams of deaths.

Fredrik heard the door creak from where he sat with his eyes closed, relaxing in the tub and letting the evening pass. The water was still around him; his hands were resting over the edge of the bath.

"Is that you, Fiona?" he asked, hoping it was his wife. He'd told her about his bath and had hinted she should join after she was done with talking to Levyna. It had been the better part twenty minutes since then.

He opened his eyes, and was immediately disappointed. His wife wasn't in the room. No one was.

"Is someone there?" he called, hearing the door creak again, but no one answered, even though a servant was supposed to be close by. He exhaled and rested his head against the tub. His breath seemed to reach the lamp on the wall a yard away as the flame danced with an unseen wind.

Fredrik closed his eyes in the silence, but was opened them again as the door creaked even louder.

"Jakob?" he called for the servant.

There was no response. Then Fredrik was shoved down, beneath the water. He was being buried in it and couldn't push himself up. Fredrik fought a hand he couldn't see as it held him underneath the water, his arms flaying and his legs flinging out of the bath. He swung his arms around as his head was held below. He saw nothing but the silhouette of a figure as he struggled to see though the water, fighting furiously and hopping to latch on to something, anything, that would allow him air. But his efforts quickly grew futile as the water rushed down his nostrils and throat. Soon, Fredrik's struggles ended as the water took over and his eyes slowly shut.

Outside of his tub, bubbles of air escaped with his final breath. The palatine's right hand was pulled out of the water and placed on the edge of the tub to display the ring with the symbol of the eye.

The flame in the lamp fought against the breeze as it blew through the open window of the room. The silhouette made its way outside the window and up the walls, clinging to the bricks until it reached the roof of the building. It hurried to the room all the way on the other side of the roof, where it climbed down slowly, thudding with feathery steps as it pulled a mask off and shoved it inside its armor. The shadow stepped into the light of the torches and took the form of a man.

"Hell, Vernon, was it a child you had to push out?" the man's partner said, thinking he'd just returned from taking a shit.

Vernon, a palace guard with a scar across his face, placed a hand over his stomach, exhaled, and shook his head. "Sure felt like it," he said.

CHAPTER
NINETEEN

J akob opened the door and noticed the silence as he
walked in.

"Master?" he called as he approached, seeing only the
palatine's ringed finger resting on the edge of the tub.
His knees seemed to be unusually raised. The servant
didn't receive a response as he inched closer to the bath.
Then his breath ceased as he realized that his master's
head was below the bath water.

"M – master," Jakob called one last time before touching
Fredrik's hand and finding it limp. The servant dropped
to his knees and pulled up the palatine's body to confirm
the horror.

"No, no!" Jakob dropped the body and stepped away from the tub. Then he turned and sprinted out the door.

***

Levyna's mother returned from her visit to the sorcerer with the news that the truth of whether or not Levyna was a dreamer could only be confirmed by a spell, performed by a sorcerer who had known a dreamer before. The only alternative was if a seer followed Levyna into sleep, where they could tell if there indeed was magic in her unconsciousness.

"I think I want to, Mother. I need to. I haven't been able to think about anything else since I've had that dream about the palatine's ring, and I thought I would feel better, but it only terrifies me more." Levyna was sitting on a pillow on the floor in her room, her back turned to her mother who had her hair in her hands and was gently parting it as she made the braids.

"Your father is safe, Levyna," her mother said. "I know you're eager to learn the truth, believe me, so am I. Now that we know what it will take to confirm if indeed ... I see no reason why you need to rush things."

Levyna pulled her head away from her mother's hands and turned. "So you would rather I waited till someone died? And what makes you certain that father is safe? He is still the Palatine of Queen's Hill, is he not?" She looked up to her mother's face. "I thought you believed me?"

"Of course, I do believe you, and I don't wish for anyone else to die in your dreams. But you have to understand, your father is fine, despite the days that have passed since your dream. Maybe the ring doesn't mean him. You said it yourself, the dreams that came true before did so almost the morning after. None of them took this long. It's been almost more than two days now. I know I might sound selfish, but I cannot help but be hopeful that, even if my daughter does turn out to be a dreamer, then this one will not come to pass. As for the spell, the sorcerer will not do it alone. There will be other mages there, and should it reveal what we suspect, it will no longer be a secret, Levyna. It will only be a matter of time before the entire kingdom knows," her mother said, the worry in her eyes and in her voice.

"But I don't care, I don't!"

"Do not talk like that, Levyna." Her mother reached for her shoulder but Levyna shrugged her hands away.

"If finding the truth is the price I have to pay, then don't you think it's worth it?"

Fiona sighed. "You don't know what it was like for dreamers in Queen's Hill."

"Father said the same thing. So now you agree with him?"

"I cannot say that I do, but I cannot deny that dreamers have not been heard of in Queen's Hill for decades now, and not many people are kind to those who see death and announce it. That is one of countless challenges that awaits a dreamer. If you are declared a dreamer, Levyna, your life will be turned upside down. You will become an outcast amongst your friends and the other maidens, and they will never look at you the same way. So, you must understand why I am not so eager to have my only child declared a misfit in Queen's Hill."

"Am I not one already?" Levyna answered, shaking her head. "I can barely sit still for five minutes without thinking about the dreams. I ran out of the gardens and abandoned the princess and the rest of the maidens today because I couldn't afford to let them see how terrified I was. If the mage's spells don't confirm I am a dreamer, does that mean that the dreams will stop? And if it's not my father that I dreamt of, then who is it?" Levyna had tears brimming in her eyes.

Her mother knelt to pull her daughter close, unwilling to let go even if Levyna tried to shrug out of the embrace. She couldn't claim to know what her daughter was going through, but it was clear how terrified she was. Being stuck with a fate such as this wasn't a burden many could carry. And one that even fewer survived.

"I know you are scared, my love, but you don't have to be. I will do whatever I need to make sure that your life is not taken away because of this, but you have to trust me, and trust your father too."

"You would really have me not know?" Levyna asked, her head buried in her mother's embrace.

"Not in a way that will doom everything you have. I will tell your father what I have learnt from my trip this morning."

"He will not like the fact that you visited a sorcerer when you told him it was just your cousin."

"I can handle Fredrik, don't worry about him. I just want him to know that regardless of what I have learned, there is no way we are letting you become like the rest of the dreamers before. And if it turns out that you are not one, we'll deal with whatever is responsible for the visions, quietly, so you can live your life as my daughter, the most beautiful maiden in all of Queen's Hill."

Levyna exhaled deeply as her mother kissed the top of her head and rubbed her arms gently. "Aren't you just saying that just because you're my mother?"

"Oh, nonsense, baby. I say that because it's true, and everyone who has eyes in this palace and in Queen's Hill knows it. You're smart and you're gorgeous and all of this that worries you now will pass. We will make sure of that."

"But Father —"

"Your father will be fine, Levyna. We're in the palace, the safest place in all of Queen's Hill, and he's not going anywhere anytime soon. He is healthy and strong. Whatever that dream was, it is not for him. And I know it bothers you that it might mean something for someone else, but please, just trust me when I say that it is not your burden to bear," her mother said.

Levyna was about to question her mother further when a harsh knock sounded on the door. A maid's voice called through the wood. Levyna pulled away and glanced at her mother, seeing the same confusion in her face. Levyna trailed a step behind as her mother called for the maid to open the door. When she did, the servant's face at that moment told Levyna that her mother had been wrong.

***

"Perhaps there's another way we can learn if he's on your side?" Yondi asked.

Olin scoffed. "I would think you'd be glad that he's not who I thought he was, since you seem so concerned about me returning to Ravinshore. I've told you, I'm not willing to get close to that man, not after what I've seen," Olin answered. He was sitting on chair by the fire Yondi had started, resting while he ruminated on what he should do next.

"I also know that you don't plan to be quiet and do nothing."

"I don't. I'll find a way back to Ravinshore. Get to the palace and tell them what I know."

Yondi's mouth gaped. "Surely I don't need to tell you how crazy that sounds? The watchers are after you, and they will most likely know the very moment you set foot in Ravinshore."

"What choice do I have now, Yondi?" Olin looked up. "To stay quiet and protect myself while King Edmond dies from something the watchers have done? I no longer see reason in this conversation. The question ended for me the moment Wylie died trying to protect me. He died trying to save me and the knowledge I have of the Order's plans. I cannot and will not do nothing, and, as the man my uncle thought could help isn't one I can trust, I have to find my own way to Ravinshore, regardless of how dangerous it is. Of all the times I could have hidden away and kept quiet, now is the time I cannot afford to do that, not when the kingdom of Ravinshore might be in trouble."

"All I am saying is that there must have been a reason why Cyrus the Forger was the one your uncle thought about in the last moments, and I know that things don't look how you expected them to now, but hear me out. If you would wait just one more day —"

"King Edmond might not have one more day, Yondi," Olin interrupted. "He could already be dead for all I know! Whatever the Order has done, me finding out might have forced them to hasten their plans before I'm able to get the truth to the palace. One more day of waiting could let them succeed."

"For one, I don't think that the King of Ravinshore is dead. If he were, word would have reached Queen's Hill by now. The death of someone like King Edmond isn't something that can be hidden for as much as an hour. The news will spread like fire through the three kingdoms. But I understand what you mean." Yondi scooped the soup into the bowl and handed it to Olin, who just stared at it like he couldn't understand what it was. "Take it."

"I'm not hungry."

"Well, you might try to be stubborn with it, but you cannot prevail with whatever plan you hatch, let alone go against the Order of Walrea, if you collapse from an empty stomach."

"I said I have no interest in food, Yondi."

"And I heard you. Your mind might not want it, but your body does need it. You've had nothing all day, and barely ate anything yesterday either. My cooking isn't the greatest, but it keeps me and my master alive. It'll help you too, so take it." Yondi nudged the bowl against his arm.

Olin eyed it still, but eventually took it when he realized the apprentice wasn't going to back off. "Thank you," he said.

Yondi shrugged and took his seat with his own bowl of soup. "As I was saying, there's a way you can be sure if Cyrus isn't who he appeared to be today. Maybe he's on your side, and before you tell me how you're sure of it and you won't go near him, how about I do it?"

Olin's face pinched. "What?"

"I could go back to the palace and find a way to reach Cyrus myself."

"And do what? Ask him if he's evil now?"

"Well, maybe not in those exact words, but something close. I could tell him that my master heard word about a Ravinshore boy looking for him at the bar, and his reaction would tell me what I need to know. Well, not his reaction alone, more like his eyes."

"How?"

"There's a spell for everything." Yondi shrugged.

"Can you really do that? Have you done it before?"

Yondi sipped the soup. "No, I haven't, but I know someone who has – my master, and I could get him to teach me in time."

"That's even crazier than me going back to Ravinshore. How do you think you can manage that? If Cyrus is working with the Order, he might sense that you're lying, and even if he doesn't, there's no way he would let you get away from the palace without having you followed. You'll make yourself a target and lead the Order here."

"That will confirm whatever we suspect. Besides, I won't lead them home if they follow me. There are lots of places to get lost in Queen's Hill," Yondi said. "And don't forget that Ravinshore's Order cannot do anything in Queen's Hill. So, the best they can do is follow me."

"They could find you!"

"They won't."

"And what if they do?" Olin spoke like someone who had made the mistake of underestimating the watchers before and paid the ultimate price.

"Olin, I wouldn't have mentioned this if I didn't know what my fate would be in the hands of foreign watchers. But I've done nothing against the Red Flame of Queen's Hill, and in my own kingdom, Walrea cannot do anything but make empty noises. They wouldn't want to risk the wrath of the Red Flame either."

Olin scoffed and shook his head. "How can you be so sure? You sound like someone who hasn't seen what these people are capable of. I don't for a second doubt that they would kill anyone anywhere to keep their secret. Even if it means risking a war."

Yondi looked at Olin and exhaled. "There's a lesser chance that it happens than it doesn't. So ..."

Olin couldn't get the look of incredulity off his face. Yondi sounded like he'd lost his mind. "How do you even plan to get back into the palace and find Cyrus again?"

"That'll be easy. I've done it once before, remember?"

Olin stared at him. He was acting like this would be as easy as waving away a fly. But Yondi knew it hadn't been luck that had gotten them get past the guards earlier, and though Olin himself was almost convinced that there had been more to it, seeing as he himself had almost believed Yondi's act when he'd told the palace guards of the urgency of their meeting with Cyrus, there was no way they could be sure that it would work again. But Yondi seemed confident.

"Let me go back to the palace and try to find out the truth before you head back to Ravinshore, that's all I ask," Yondi said.

Olin stirred the soup in his hand quietly. The momentary silence was punctuated by kindling breaking apart in the fire, and the panic Olin was still feeling was held at bay behind the apparent calm of the shared meal.

"Why are you helping me?" he asked.

Yondi looked from the fire to Olin, and chuckled. "How is it not obvious? You pointed a sword at me and demanded that I take you to Cyrus and now you're in my house and my master is waiting for you to leave so he can tell me how much trouble I'm in. I want you gone as soon as I can so I can have my peace again," he said.

Olin glanced at the room. "You really call this peace?"

"Compared to your situation, I would say it is." Yondi chuckled. "I know a bit about fate and destiny, and I was told once that no matter how far you walk or run, your destiny is always going to be there. Fate too – you can't con it. If you ask me, there's a reason you walked into this secret, and that same reason is responsible for why I found you when I did. I've always wanted to be a great sorcerer, maybe not like a master, but better. To be remembered as someone who did something great, you know. So, if helping a stranger from a different kingdom is how I become that, then you can be sure that I'm doing this for myself, nothing more," Yondi answered.

Olin remained quiet. That sounded believable. The odds that he would have been found by someone like the mage's apprentice when he'd landed in Queen's Hill weren't so great, after all. Could it have been fate?

Olin only wished that their meeting wasn't accompanied by so much terror when he thought about it. Olin stirred the bowl and ate.

***

Isabelle rode into the town ignoring the gazes following her. They couldn't tell who she was, but though they didn't know she was a mage, her long dark cloak and the way she looked drew enough attention, which wasn't what she had been hoping for when she'd set out on the trip. Isabelle made her way through the streets, mindless of the stares as she hurried towards a house on the far end of town, almost bordering the next one in Duken. Riding through a final field, she arrived at the house just as dusk was setting.

Isabelle could see light through the window. She climbed down from her horse and led the beast to a small log to tie it up, then she walked to the door and knocked. A moment later, the door opened to reveal a man with a blond-white afro and a grey beard. His expression pinched as he stared at the sorceress.

"Isabelle?"

Isabelle sighed. "Hello, William."

William held the door open even wider, giving her a once-over from head to toe. "What are you doing here?" he asked.

"I need your help."

He chuckled in disbelief. "You do?"

"Yes, I do."

"The hell you do, Isabelle. Oh, you must have such confidence in yourself and your charm to have thought this was a good idea. Either that or you've lost your memories, woman."

"My memories are fine. I came looking for you because it's important," Isabelle answered.

"If your mind isn't lost in the tangles of some spell, then surely you must remember the last time we saw each other – you more than made sure to tell me you never wanted anything to do with me again. Whatever it is that has brought you here, you must have nowhere else to go."

"This isn't about me, William."

"Oh, please. And what makes you think I would care about whatever it is?" William said. "I came to you and asked for your help and you not only turned me down, but made sure no one else would help me. For all of the kindness you pretend to have, your true form showed then, and I haven't forgotten it. So, whatever it is that has brought you here, you can give up now, as much as I would love to hear how desperate you are and waste your time before I dash your hopes by telling you I'm not going to help you just to enjoy the look on your face afterwards. I'll give you the kindness you didn't show me then, and tell you right now that I don't care what it is. I don't want to know, and I will never help you. So, get the hell away from my house and off my land," he said, trying to close the door.

"I had no choice," Isabelle said. "I know what I did was terrible, but I had no choice. I couldn't let you do that to yourself, not when I knew what it would cost you."

William scoffed. "Really? Is that what you tell yourself to feel better? That you 'saved' me? You really cannot admit, for once, that you were just bitter and selfish and didn't want me to become as powerful as you were. You couldn't afford to let anyone else be. You delude everyone with your claim of righteousness while deep down, that's who you really are. But you can't admit it, even when you're standing at my door and asking for help."

"I've never claimed to be perfect, William, but whatever I did then, I did because I really didn't want you to destroy yourself."

"But that was my choice to make! Mine! That's what you couldn't get, wasn't it? That it was my decision to try and harness the power of the orb. I was going to pay the consequences of however it turned out, no one else."

"That's not true. You couldn't see it, but others would be hurt eventually, that's how it works."

"You didn't know that!" William yelled, stepping forward and pointing at her face. "You — you just assumed, and decided, and that was it. I got no help and lost my shot at the orb and you disappeared afterwards, just like you always do."

"William ..."

"Admit it. Admit you knew what you were doing, that you stopped me from harnessing the magic of the Twelfth Orb because you feared I would become more powerful than you ever will be, that I would take all of the attention away from you and you couldn't live with that," William said, staring Isabelle in the eyes. The flame from the lantern behind him cast a shadow across her face.

Isabelle couldn't admit it, though, because she didn't think it was true. She had betrayed the trust of someone she'd cared about before she'd left Duken and the three kingdoms for good. William had shared her affection, until she'd discovered his plan to use the Twelfth Orb's magic to make himself more powerful. She had not only refused to help him, but had told the Grand Sorcerer of Duken what he'd planned on doing. Everyone had seen William's plan as dangerous, everyone but him, and he hadn't been able to move past it. He'd it as a betrayal from the woman he'd loved. Isabelle had chosen the very night that William had planned on taking the orb to turn him in, and after seeing the look on his face afterwards, she had left. She hadn't returned, until now.

"I should have told you that I didn't agree with what you wanted to do, but you were going to go ahead with it either way. You didn't care what anyone had to say. So, I am sorry, William. I am sorry that I betrayed your trust to save you and I cannot make up for that. I will admit that I should have done better, but I will never say that I was even for one moment thinking about who would have the most power, because it's simply not true," Isabelle said. Her voice betrayed the ache she felt at defending the accusation.

William stood in silence for a moment, as if considering her words. Then he shook his head. "Well, it's not good enough," he said. "I don't care for your lies anymore."

He shut the door in her face, but before he could step away, it creaked and opened on its own to reveal Isabelle's steady gaze.

"I know you want nothing to do with me, William, but this isn't about me. It's King Edmond of Ravinshore."

William's protest died at the name. His frown turned bleak. "What about him?"

"He's dying," Isabelle said.

CHAPTER TWENTY

"**O**lin! Stay back, stay away! Don't enter the room, Olin. Do you hear me?! Don't enter that room, it will fall apart!"

Olin continued to hear the voice even as he gripped the handle of the door. He hesitated for a moment, as if to heed what the voice was telling him. Then Olin walked away from the door of the house to stand alone in the middle of nowhere. He turned to see tall hills that looked familiar, but soon the clouds gathered like a storm and he turned back to the door and opened it, ignoring the voice. The moment he did, he came face to face with the voice, and Wylie's bloodied eyes stared at Olin as he was forced to watch in horror as a faceless attacker threw a knife into his back.

"No!" Olin screamed, reaching to catch his uncle, who'd fallen to the ground. But Wylie's body turned to ashes in his hands and he stared at it in horror. Rage coursed through him, and Olin felt his hands burn as if they were on fire. He looked up at the attacker and tried to lunge at him, but Olin felt a sudden force yank him away, out of the room and out of the dream.

"Olin? Olin!"

Olin sprung up on the bed, eyes wide, covered in sweat. With bated breath and a heart barreling in his chest, he turned to the voice that had been calling. It was Yondi.

"Are you okay?" Yondi asked.

Olin didn't immediately respond. He exhaled before he nodded.

"You were yelling really loudly," Yondi said, looking at the bed he'd been sleeping in, just as his master stepped beside him.

The first thing Posdel noticed as he stared at the boys was the bed. The cloth was burned with the imprint of Olin's hands. Olin followed their gazes to his own hands; they felt fine, just like hands. But the bed proved otherwise.

"What did you say you are again?" Posdel asked.

***

"I'm a sciff from Ravinshore. What do you mean?" Olin answered.

"What happened?" Yondi asked.

"I – I had a dream and ... I don't know." Olin shook his head.

"Has this ever happened before?" Posdel asked.

"No," Olin said, sure this was the first time he'd nearly caught the be on fire. "What is this?" he asked. The boys turned to Posdel, who was much more sober than last time.

"My best guess is there's something about yourself that you either do not know or you have not shared with us, sciff."

"And what could that be? What do you mean?"

"I think your magic is forcing its way out of you."

Yondi's brows rose. "What?"

"Wh – what the hell are you talking about? Magic? What magic? I don't have magic, I never have, I'm not a mage," Olin answered.

"I thought so too, but the signs are clearly saying something different," Posdel answered.

"What signs?" Olin asked.

"Your reaction to the oro, the slugs. That wasn't normal, before or after I hit you with its essence." Posdel stepped out of the room. Olin stood and followed with Yondi.

"Not many people physically react to oros like that. It's a magical creature, so those that do react are usually ones with magic themselves."

"I don't have magic! If I did, do you think I would be here or *still* be here? If I had any powers at all, don't you think I would have tried to use it to help my uncle, to save him when the watchers came instead of standing by and watching them take him apart? Whatever you think this is, it's not magic. I've never done a spell in my life, not even as a joke, because I can't."

"You might not know that you can."

Olin scoffed and shook his head. "Your master is clearly drunk again!" he said to Yondi.

Yondi looked from Olin to his master, but couldn't give a response before Posdel spoke again.

"Tell us about your dreams," he said.

"What?" answered Olin.

"The ones you've been having. Tell me about them." Posdel reached for a bottle on the shelf and popped the cork only to find it empty.

"My dreams are no business of yours, and they have nothing to do with whatever you think happened."

The mage reached for another bottle, higher up on the shelf and uncorked it. He put the bottle to his nose and sniffed, blinking hard at the scent. Yondi and Olin watched as the man tipped the bottle to get a mouthful and wiped his lips before turning to Olin again.

"The situation you've found yourself in is making it hard for you to either see or accept it. Everything is connected, that's a rule of life. But if you say your dream has nothing to do with what happened, how then do you explain the fact that you burnt the sheets?" Posdel asked. He turned to Yondi and said, "You just couldn't find someone less prone to chaos by the river bank, could you?"

Olin had no response to the mage's question. He didn't know what had caused his hands to leave a mark on the bed, but he was certain it wasn't magic. It wasn't *his* magic, because he simply had none. The idea that Olin'd had any kind of power that could have given his uncle a fighting chance against the watchers and he had done nothing wasn't something he was willing to even consider.

"Oh, and word is the Palatine of Queen's Hill is dead," Posdel said casually.

"What?" Yondi said, mouth agape.

"Yes, the news spread quicker than anything. No doubt because of how he died. They say he drowned in his own bathing tub." Posdel shook his head. "But I don't know of even a child old enough to hold his hand over his head and reach for his other ear who would fail to keep himself up in a bowl of water."

"Does that mean ..."

"Yes, Yondi. Something definitely stinks from the palace."

"How can the palatine die so easily? Was he ill?" Olin asked.

Posdel downed another gulp and glanced at Olin. "He's the king's right hand. He takes charge of the kingdom in the absence of the king and the queen. The Palatine of Queen's Hill is not the kind of man that should die in a bloody bowl of bath water, ill or not."

"But that's hardly the news you need to hear," Posdel said. "The palatine died overnight, but apparently the man who will take his place has already been chosen."

"Who is it?" Yondi asked.

"If I had known that his ambition would get him this far, perhaps I would have begged to go with him to the palace when he left," the mage said. "Because whatever it is Cyrus the Forger is doing, it has gotten him as far an any ordinary man could ever go in Queen's Hill. Bath-drowned masters be damned."

***

That was too much of a coincidence and Olin knew it. Something seemed terribly off about Cyrus being prepared to become the palatine so suddenly after they had seen him with a watcher from Ravinshore. And then his lord dies mysteriously. Olin didn't know what had happened, but the thought raised more questions than he liked, and Olin was someone who lived for curiosity, even when it ended up causing him trouble.

"How is it possible that he is to become palatine?" Yondi asked.

"He must have impressed himself on the king well enough that not even a thought was given to someone else. It doesn't mean he was the only one considered, but all signs point to him being the next chosen. The kingdom cannot afford to be without a palatine for too long. But it's the king's choice."

"Do you still think you'll be able to walk up to him and ask about his business with the Ravinshore Watcher now?" Olin asked Yondi.

Posdel nearly spat out his drink. "A Ravinshore Watcher? In Queen's Hill?"

Yondi looked between his master and Olin, realizing the man had been gone all day and knew nothing about their adventure to the palace. "Yes. Olin claims ... Olin saw one of the watchers that attacked him and his uncle back in Ravinshore."

The mage was wide-eyed as he looked from his apprentice to the sciff. "You do know there's a reason watchers aren't known by the common men, don't you? Whoever sees a watcher in his true form has to die, even if it's the watcher's own family. What sorcery did you perform to see the face of the assassin?"

"None. I've told you already that I don't have magic. I was merely able to remember the man's eyes."

"You remembered his eyes? How is that possible?"

"I don't know. I've always been able to. I never forget a face, or eyes. I have a very good memory," Olin said.

"Is that so?" The mage's tone implied that he strongly believed this was connected to Olin's so-called magic. "So this watcher – he didn't see you at the palace?"

"We left before he got the chance to," Yondi said.

"And you're sure you didn't lead him back here instead? To the house?"

"Yes, we're sure. It was yesterday afternoon. Besides, we're sure we weren't followed," Yondi said.

Posdel let out a breath, then belched and finally dropped the empty bottle on the table. "You say your watcher was talking with Cyrus? The new palatine? Was that before or after you spoke with him?"

"We never spoke with Cyrus, and we're definitely not going to now. It appears Wylie got it all wrong, and it's hard to understand because Wiley is – was hardly ever wrong. He was the best judge of character that I knew," Olin said.

Yondi thought about it, but found it incredibly difficult to argue the need to find Cyrus now, even if a part of him still wanted to know. His plan of brazenly waltzing into the palace like he'd done earlier wouldn't really work when he needed to see the Palatine of the Kingdom. "There has to be something you can do," he said, turning to Olin.

"Yes, there is. Follow the plan that Wylie and I had before the watchers came – find my way to Black Castle and hope they can help me get word to the palace before it's too late," Olin said.

"There's really nothing else besides you going back to Ravinshore?" Yondi asked.

"Oh, come on, don't try and stop the young man from fulfilling his fate, Yondi. If he was meant to return to his kingdom, then that's what he must do. Now, will you stop the barrage of questions, my head hurts. If you aren't happy with his decision, you might as well go instead of him!" Posdel said as he walked into his room and finally dropped himself onto the bed.

Olin and Yondi watched as the mage rendered himself useless again. Apparently, he had only needed the extra bottle of wine to push himself over the edge and into his spent state. Olin was even less convinced that there was any way that man was anything close to being the powerful mage Yondi claimed.

Yondi had perked up at his master's words. "And what if I do?" he asked, turning to Olin.

"What if you do what?"

"What if I were to go to Ravinshore to Black Castle instead of you? That way I can deliver the message before the watchers know anything and I might just be able to reach the palace. Think about it."

Olin shook his head. "I think you might be out of your mind."

"Oh, come on." Yondi lowered himself on a small stool next to Olin. "Think about it for a moment, this could really work. The Order has no idea who I am, or that I know you. I would simply stroll around Ravinshore and be the perfect spy – or messenger, in this case. We could save the king, like you want, without risking your life."

"So you would risk yours instead? You really sound like someone who has no idea what the Watchers of the Order of Walrea are capable of. You might think they don't know you and won't discover you, but the Order has been around for six centuries, Yondi. I used to think they were meant to protect the kingdom from enemies or threats, not people who merely seemed to stand in the way of an agenda. Six hundred years of existence, Yondi, they *will* find you once they know why you're in Ravinshore. And even if they don't, you won't be able to convince Black Castle of who you really are, or what your intentions are. You will be a foreigner claiming treason by the Oder. You'll be lucky if you're not killed on the spot."

Yondi shook his head and sighed. "But you know, despite all of those things, I still stand a better chance of getting into Ravinshore and telling someone than you do even getting close to the border."

"Maybe, but there's no way I'm letting yet another person risk their life or die for my stupid mistakes. Not if I can help it, not anymore. I need to get to Ravinshore and it has to be today."

CHAPTER
TWENTY-ONE

I sabelle had convinced William to listen. She'd told him everything about King Edmond's poisoning and how his life force was being attacked, killing him in the most silent and slowest way possible.

William had listened genuinely, unlike his rash promise to spite her. The fact that it was a king – the King of Ravinshore – who needed aid calmed him. Isabelle had told him that she'd come looking despite what had happened between them because he was the only sorcerer she knew who was bold enough and powerful enough to attempt to cure the king.

William had let her finish before telling her he couldn't help. Again, he hadn't been seeking to get back at

Isabelle for her betrayal, but genuinely wasn't the one she needed, based on what she'd told him of the king's symptoms.

"Why?" she asked. "Do you still think this is about me? Shall I find someone else to come and beg you?" Isabelle couldn't quite believe that her former friend was sincere.

"I wish it were so, truly. I wish my ego was so big that I would refuse to help the king because he was unfortunate enough to have you as a healer. But that's not the case. You said it yourself, the magic of Egro can't be handled by just anyone, and as much as I would love for the king and the kingdom of Ravinshore to become indebted to me, I am neither a Grand Sorcerer, nor the one you seek," William said. "And that is the truth."

Isabelle fought herself as she stared at the man's eyes, trying yet to pick apart his words for any hint of insincerity, a habit that she hadn't let go of since the last time they'd met almost a decade before. Now it was magnified by his previous apathy towards her and her plight. But William gave no signs that he was lying.

Isabelle was at least in the house and away from the cold. William had let her in to hear what she'd had to say about the king after she'd insisted. She was sitting on a stool in the living room while William rested against the wall near the door, arms crossed and listening with a barely patient expression. The silence stretched before she spoke again.

"Who is it then?" she asked.

William glanced at her, jaw clenched as if weighing the choice of sending her away empty-handed now that he'd given his answer.

"Will you tell me at least, please?" she asked again.

"Her name is Gytha. She is the only Grand Sorceress in Duken, perhaps even the truest in the three kingdoms. I have never seen anyone quite as powerful as she is, not even you would be a match for her. She's the only one I know who can find a way around an Egro spell," he said.

"Where do I find her?" Isabelle continued to push her luck.

William stared at her. He'd seen how matted her hair looked and how the dress beneath her cape was splattered with mud from the road. She was trying to hide whatever it was she had been through to reach him. "She's a few hours ride from here, just after the Ope fields."

Isabelle tried to force a smile but caught herself. She didn't want to cause any more trouble. She just nodded curtly instead and said, "Thank you," as she rose.

Isabelle stood silent in front of him for another moment. She didn't know what else to say. He had helped her despite his feelings.

"I ... I cannot take back what I've done, William. And the truth is ... should I get the chance again, the only thing I would change is telling you where I really stood, and then maybe actually staying to face you after instead of running away. I know you think I betrayed you, and that I was selfish, and maybe I was – selfish. Because I couldn't let go of the thought of what would happen to you if things went wrong with the orb. I betrayed you to save you, maybe for myself. But afterwards, not being able to stand the look on your face ... it wrecked me.

"I cannot make you forgive me for what I did. If I knew how, I would try, but I genuinely wish you to know that I am sorry. And maybe someday you will see that I really thought I was trying to save you with what I did," Isabelle said, then she headed for the door.

She had just opened the door when William spoke. "Did you really come riding all the way here by yourself?" he asked, his gaze straight ahead, not wanting to give her a hint that he actually cared.

"Not really," she answered. "I was given an escort who rode with me until I arrived in Duken. We had a few ... challenges and I had to ditch him."

"I wonder why that sounds familiar," William said.

"He has a kid, a daughter. I couldn't let him die in the name of serving the kingdom, even if it was his duty."

"Of course, you always have your reasons, and you always know best. Don't you? Still, seem like a pattern to you?" William finally turned to face her.

Isabelle went quiet, then exhaled. "Thank you for the help, William," she said, opening the door wider and taking a step.

"Ope isn't really the most ideal journey to make at this time," William said quickly. "And I doubt Gytha will be pleased to have a visitor so late."

"I have no choice. I need to reach her as soon as I can. King Edmond doesn't have much time left. I don't know if he will live to see the next two days. And I gave my word to the queen, I must try," Isabelle said.

William sighed like he couldn't quite believe what he was about to say. "You have a choice. You could stay the night here, and before dawn we'll set out after Gytha. Surely the king will survive a few more hours."

Isabelle turned to him with disbelief in her eyes. "I don't want to be of any inconvenience, William. You have done more than enough," she said.

"That's my choice, and I don't know when I'll stop being angry at you, but throwing you out to Ope won't make me feel any better. So, stay, if you'd like."

Isabelle couldn't hold back the smile on her face as she glanced at her horse, turned around and closed the door.

***

At dawn William mounted his own horse, a hairy black beast, and set out with Isabelle to Ope. They arrived in town a little after sunrise and made their way to a house standing alone on the edge of the fields, just as he'd described. It didn't look much different than his own, save for the lack of a fence.

William paused to ask Isabelle to let him do the talking, then knocked on the door. It took only a moment for it to open. Isabelle blinked in shock.

"Can I help you?" the aged woman with a bent back answered.

"Huh, yes. We are asking after Gytha," William said.

"And who are you?"

"I am William, she knows me. And this is ..." He glanced at Isabelle. "This is Isabelle. She has come from quite a distance. We would like to see Gytha. Is she home?"

"Do you not know how early it is? And what business do you have with Gytha?" the old woman said.

"It's very serious business. Is she here? Would you please tell her William would like to see her?"

"Not until I know what the business has brought you pummeling at our door so early," the old woman insisted.

"It's —"

"It's about this." Isabelle opened her hand and showed a ring. William's eyes widened. He hadn't known she was carrying it. The old woman picked it up. The ring held the seal of Ravinshore crown.

"It belongs to Queen Ariana of Ravinshore. She needs the help of Gytha. Would you please let us see her?"

The old woman stared at the ring and slowly turned into the house with it still in her hand. William and Isabelle shared a glance before they followed.

"What does the queen want?" Her voice was changed. There was less trembling and more firmness. William turned to close the door, and when he looked back it was to see that the old woman they had been speaking to a moment ago had become Gytha, a much younger woman. The grey hair was now a dark shade of brown that fell to her shoulders, and her rich brows and Nubian nose painted a complete contrast to the old woman who had greeted them earlier.

"You couldn't spare the theatrics even though you knew it was me?"

"I had to be sure," Gytha answered. She turned to Isabelle. "Now, again, what does the Queen of Ravinshore need from me?"

"She needs you to help heal her husband," Isabelle answered. "King Edmond has been poisoned by Egro magic that is feeding on his life force through his blood. I last saw him three days ago and he looked very much like he was hanging on by a thread. He does not have long."

"How did it happen?" Gytha asked, surprise evident in her voice. Poisoning a king was no easy feat and wasn't something she heard every day. Not for three centuries at least.

"I don't know yet. I didn't wait to find out before I set off for Duken after I saw him. I realized quickly that there was little I could do to help him, and he would need someone who could handle that type of magic: a Grand Sorcerer. I came to find William and he said that you are the most powerful sorceress he knows. I hope this is true, because I really need your help. I gave my word to the queen that I would find the most powerful there is to wake the king. Please, will you help us?"

Gytha looked from Isabelle to William, then to the ring in her hand. She handed it back to Isabelle. "How can I be sure that this isn't some trap, and I'll be asked to answer for something I know nothing about? Only a handful of people could have wielded this magic. What if the king dies while I'm trying to save him? Will I not become a prisoner of the heartbroken queen and kingdom?"

"You have my word, Gytha. Nothing of such will happen," Isabelle said.

"I'm sorry but I don't know who you are or what value, if any, your word holds. That ring may be real but I have seen men, and women, do more with less."

"Then you have my word instead," William answered. "You don't know her, but I do. And though I haven't seen her in a while, she's the kind of person I would trust with my own life, even when I don't like how she does things. Which is why I know that for her to come and find me, King Edmond must be hearing the voices of his ancestors already. Please, Gytha help her, help us, and save the king."

Gytha exhaled and shook her head. "Can you not find a way to bring him into Duken?" she asked.

"No. He cannot be moved as I fear he's too frail. Besides, other than the queen and a handful of people in the palace, no one knows about his condition. You, William, and myself are the only people outside of Ravinshore's palace who know."

"And you came alone?" she asked.

Isabelle glanced at William before she answered. "Yes."

"You just lied," Gytha said.

CHAPTER
TWENTY-TWO

L evyna's mother had been wrong. Her mother had been wrong and her father had been wrong and now he was dead.

Levyna sat on the bed in her chamber. The water in her eyes was making it hard to see as she peered blankly at the room. She had felt it, she had sensed it, and she had dreamt it. Levyna had dreamt it but had still allowed her parents to tell her it was nothing. It could be nothing. The cruelty of remembering crouching in front of her mother, thinking about what would happen if the dream turned out to be about someone else and not about her father, like every essence of her body told her it was, pulled the ground from underneath her and made it feel like the world was spinning.

There was a guard at her door and a maid was on standby. Her mother came in and out of the room every hour. A message of condolence had come from the king; the queen had called on them in person. The princess had called on Levyna. Everyone else outside the palace was being kept away. Levyna had barely existed through it. She had shed tears uncontrollably through the night, and not even her mother had been able to keep her calm. So she had been left alone, perhaps with the hope that she would be able to cry herself to sleep. But she had been in this one spot since last night, blinking to keep her eyes from falling out of her head.

Levyna wasn't willing to close her eyes to sleep anytime soon. The idea of another dream kept her awake. The ache of the thought that she might have had something to do with her father's fate haunted her. And even if she hadn't caused it, she had dreamt about it, knew about it, and yet it had still happened because she allowed herself to foolishly believe that her dream had been wrong.

Her mother had journeyed all the way to the sorcerer for nothing. There was no greater confirmation that she was a dreamer than what had befallen them.

Perhaps this had happened as some kind of punishment for her doubt. Maybe this was the unspoken rite of passage that dreamers had to endure before their life of misery began and they ultimately became outcasts in the world. Levyna's thoughts were running circles through her head, echoing with the words of the servant who had announced the news along with the image, that image, of him in the bathing tub. The image of the ring resting on his finger. She couldn't get it out of her head, and it played endlessly in a loop as time seemed to breeze past her.

Levyna had settled on her bed, alternating between sitting up and pulling her legs against her chest so her chin could rest on her knees as the darkness of the dusk passed, the fogginess of dawn came, and the daylight pierced through the window of the bedchamber.

Since she had stopped believing that her dream could be about her father, after that day in the garden where she had abandoned the princess and her maidens, Levyna had not allowed herself to imagine any scenario of it actually happening. But she definitely couldn't have imagined it happening the way it had. Drowning in a bathtub in a bath chamber. It was unheard of.

It begged the question: if the palatine had been a victim of a subterfuge, had someone caused it?

Someone could have killed her father. And if that was true, then the possibility existed that perhaps something could have been done to stop it, if her father's death had been orchestrated.

It should have scared her, should have angered her, terrified her and left her out of her manners. But it was only a secondary thought. Levyna jammed that question in with rest of the unanswered questions that tortured her.

"Levyna, can you hear me?"

Levyna blinked and looked up at her mother, who was now sitting by her feet on the bed. Fiona's eyes looked just like they had when her grandmother had died, only Levyna knew this probably hurt a thousand times worse, considering the circumstances. And the fact that she had more or less known that it was going to happen and belittled it.

They had belittled death.

"You need to get some sleep."

Levyna blinked again, exhaled, and looked towards the window. She wanted the daylight to bore at her eyes so she wouldn't feel the slightest urge to close them.

"I know you're sad, but your body can only take being restless for so long. I'm worried about you."

Behind the ache in her mother's trembling voice, Levyna heard a mixture of the fear of losing her too and the regret she knew her mother shared.

"Sleep is the last thing I should think of allowing now, Mother. Would you not agree?"

Fiona knew what Levyna meant. This was more than just grief for her father. Fiona was quiet for a moment before she answered, "You cannot let it take hold of you that way." She shook her head.

"Has it not already? Is it not a little too late for that?" Levyna answered.

Her mother raised a hand to her face. "I am so sorry about your father. I should have listened to you. I should not have assumed. I should not have allowed him to ignore you. It was ungodly to have played down your fears and tried to make them seem so ..."

Levyna caught sight of the tear as it glistened its way down her mother's cheek. Fiona was torturing herself, and as much as Levyna hated the idea of her mother's pain, she was cursed with the same fate, if not worse.

"I will get to the bottom of this. I promise, I will find out what happened, I will," Fiona said.

If only it would make Levyna feel any less responsible. If only it would mean that she would never dream again. Then perhaps there would be some relief.

"What happens now? Do we tell everyone what I am?" Levyna asked. "Or are we still not sure?" She knew that had been harsh the moment it came off her tongue.

Her mother's eyes seemed to carry the ache anew at the statement, but she didn't hesitate with a response. "We tell no one," Fiona said. She dabbed her eyes with a handkerchief and beckoned for her daughter to look at her. Fiona inched closer and gently lifted Levyna's face by the chin. "Look at me, Levyna. I know I have failed you once and there is nothing I can do to bring your father back, but I promise you if someone did this to us, I will find out. The palace garrison is already investigating and they will not stop, not even by the king's orders. I will not allow them too.

"If I have to fight the entire kingdom to stop anyone from touching you, then I will. You will tell no one about what you are. You don't owe anyone anything, and if you ever choose to talk, it will be your choice. But as long as I live, you will not have your life ruined by this, I promise you."

Levyna stared at her mother behind a film of tears and wondered just how long it would take before they realized she couldn't keep that promise.

TWENTY-THREE

"**W**hat? No, I'm not lying, we came here alone," Isabelle said.

"You are still lying."

"No, she's not. We did, Gytha," William answered. "I swear we came here alone." He shared a perplexed glance with Isabelle.

The frown grew on Gytha's face. "If you say you came alone, then who the hell is that?" she asked, nodding in the direction of the window.

They looked through to see three riders approaching quickly, leaving a small cloud of dust in their wake. William stepped closer to the window and Isabelle followed him. He guessed by the subtle curse beneath her breath that she knew who they were. He glanced at her face and she blinked before she turned to Gytha.

"It's not what you think, Gytha."

"Oh, is it not? You've lied to me already and we haven't even set across the three kingdoms yet. How am I supposed to take any word from your mouth as worthy?"

Isabelle shook her head. "I swear, I didn't lie to you." She pointed out the widow. The riders were close enough for them to see their faces. "We did come here alone, but one of those men was the escort that the Queen of Ravinshore demanded acompany me. I had to leave him behind because he was holding me back. I didn't intend to lead him here. I actually hoped to achieve the opposite. You must believe me," she said.

The frown had not left Gytha's face. Her nostrils flared as considered whether or not to believe Isabelle. "If you came to Duken with one escort, why are there three men?" she demanded.

William was the one to answer. "If I had to guess, I would say that the other two are the guards that followed her escort. The ones she didn't know about. The Queen of Ravinshore must surely be desperate enough to want to be certain that nothing happens to Isabelle and that her mission is successful. By the way they're riding, I can tell they're trained. I would say they're not just part of the palace garrison but personal guards of the crown – Ravinshore King's Guards, which is probably why they were able to find her so quickly."

"Yes. Alden, the escort that came with me, is a King's Guard. I swear they're on our side."

"It hardly makes me feel better," Gytha said. "I do not like crowds, especially ones I am not familiar with."

"And they won't be in your way, I promise," Isabelle said.

Just as she finished speaking, they heard the sound of the horses coming to a stop and the thud of boots hitting the ground as the riders dismounted. No doubt the presence of Isabelle's horse was enough evidence to indicate she was inside.

Isabelle made for the door before Alden or any of his fellow guardsmen could make an unpleasant scene and put the already distrustful Gytha in an even worse mood. She opened the door to find Alden already waiting, and his expression grew from relief to annoyance. She'd expect no less from someone she'd abandoned after spending two days riding together.

"Isabelle," he acknowledged, a hint of animosity in his voice. He was standing steady, meaning the injury to his thigh had healed well. He looked much better now that he was no longer near death's door.

"You don't need to be here."

"And where am I supposed to be if not here, fulfilling my mission as instructed by the Crown of Ravinshore?" Alden asked.

"You really don't have to. I can find my way back. I'm trying to get what we came here for."

"And it is my sworn duty to remain at your side until you return to Ravinshore. Isabelle, that trick you pulled —"

"It wasn't a trick. But I apologize for it. Still, you do need to leave," Isabelle said, glancing back to make sure Gyntha wasn't too angry.

"You don't seem to understand what he's saying, lady – it's his mission to be wherever you are and ensure *your* quest is successful and that you return to Ravinshore unharmed and undeterred," the tallest of the three men standing behind Alden spoke. "Alden cannot be anywhere other than here, and seeing what you managed to do to him before, I would say that neither can we. You have to let us in."

"She doesn't have to do anything." Gytha's voice came from behind Isabelle. She turned to face their host.

"And who are you to say that?"

"The owner of this property and someone you certainly don't want to speak to in that manner," William said from where he stood next to Isabelle. He didn't need to act imposing for his voice to carry weight.

"We're here on command of Ravinshore, that trumps everything else but the crown of the kingdom of Duken, and you —"

Alden turned to see the guard's eyes widen. Then his expression twisted. Alden blinked in shocked horror – the guard's mouth had disappeared, replaced with skin, making it seem as though he'd never had a mouth in his life. As if he were some creature with just a pair of eyes and fat nose for a face. The other guards stared in shock as he fell to the ground.

Everyone darted their gazes towards the door, where Isabelle had stepped back, looking equally clueless. As one, everyone looked at the Grand Sorceress. Gytha hadn't even raised a finger.

"What did you —" the second guard began.

"Please," Alden begged.

"Stop this at once!" the guard, apparently oblivious to Alden's caution, reached to his side to draw his sword, but suddenly found himself hit with a concussive pulse. He landed with a thud several yards away from the cottage.

Alden could do nothing but watch in awe as the man was tossed like he weighed nothing. "P – please ..." he said, one hand gripping the shoulder of his deformed and horrified comrade.

Isabelle looked frantically at Gytha, who still hadn't reacted to what was happening. Her expression was carefully unimpressed.

"Gytha ..." William said carefully. "They are a little too committed, that is all."

"That does not excuse the rudeness," the Grand Sorceress answered.

"No, it definitely does not," William said. "And I'm sure they've gotten the message."

Gytha glanced at him, then at Isabelle, who looked to be searching for the correct words to say. "They stay out. He can come in." She nodded at Alden.

Alden looked down in time to see the moment the guard gasped for air like he'd never breathed before. He helped the man up, looking across the yard to see the other guardsman slowly getting back on his feet. Alden abandoned them both, entered the house, and closed the door behind him.

"If what you have told me is true, time is not on your side at all." Gytha picked up the conversation like nothing had happened.

"Which is why this is a matter of urgency, Gytha. We would have arrived sooner had we not me with some challenges on the road." Isabelle didn't bother to glance at Alden, who knew what she was talking about.

"And what happens if we reach Ravinshore and it's already too late?" Gytha asked.

"Then, regrettably, all of this would have been for nothing and I would have failed my promise to the queen."

Gytha exhaled. "Perhaps next time you will be careful throwing promises around." She turned and disappeared into another room for a few minutes. By the time she came back, she had a grey-hooded cape covering her tunic dress. Isabelle felt a wave of relief.

"Does the horse outside belong to you?" Alden asked.

"No, and I will not be needing one." Gytha looked at Isabelle. "You say time is of the essence, do you intend to spend another day and a half riding back to Ravinshore?"

"I would rather not," Isabelle said.

"Then take my hand," Gytha said.

Isabelle obeyed without hesitation.

Alden's face twisted when he realized what was about to happen. "I – I have to come too," he said.

"Do you have magic?" Gytha asked.

"No."

"Have you ever traveled through a portal or jumped through reality before?"

"N – No," Alden answered.

"Then it may not work. I do not have the time argue and cannot be responsible for whatever happens to you."

"I understand."

"Do you?"

"Look, my mission is to make sure Isabelle arrives in Ravinshore with what she set out for. And I know she doesn't like it, but I cannot help that I was put in charge of her. I cannot return to Ravinshore unless she is by my side. Anything less and I will have failed and the crown may have my head. So, please, unless you intend to take my head off yourself, I go wherever she goes," Alden said.

Gytha stared at the guard. He seemed very determined, even though they could have disappeared by the time he'd finished his little speech.

"Very well," Gytha said.

"William?" Isabelle said.

William nodded. "You know where to find me." A smile she had not seen in ages appeared at the corner of his lips.

Isabelle flinched at the realization that he wasn't coming with her. After everything, he'd only made sure that she found the help she needed. She was surprised at how much she wanted him to say that he would be right behind her. But instead she mouthed a "thank you," because that was as much as she could demand of him.

William watched as Alden took her hand, and Gytha, raising her free hand, muttered a string of words and swirled her fingers as the air above them sizzled like lightning. At once all three of them disappeared.

William exhaled, glanced around at the room, and walked to the window, closing it even though it was unnecessary. No robbers would dare steal anything from Gytha without her knowledge. A death sentence would be better.

Finished, he walked to the door and opened it to find the waiting guards, who flinched at the sudden noise, undoubtedly still shaken by what they had experienced. He nodded at them both – the one who now had a mouth and the one whose ass was probably still broken – as he headed for his horse, the darkest of the five outside the cottage.

"Will you be needing these beasts?" he asked.

"Huh ..." The first guard couldn't figure out why he would ask.

"Because they won't," William said, nodding back towards the house.

"And why is that?"

"Because they're most likely already in Ravinshore."

TWENTY-FOUR

O lin had no horse, no carriage, and no means of travel except his legs, yet his mind was set on returning to Ravinshore.

Sitting on the chair in the small hall, he stared mindlessly at the sword on his lap. It had only just occurred to him that his presence in Queen's Hill was the result of being transported through a magic portal that had made the trip to the mountainous kingdom simple. Getting back wouldn't be so easy. It would take a day with a horse or carriage, and much more walking. In his desperate hunger to return, he hadn't truly considered what it would entail to make the return journey. He'd only been thinking about the consequences of being in Ravinshore, in the open and within reach of the Order.

Olin looked back at the room where Posdel still slept, wondering about the chances that he would know something about traveling without conventional means. But then Olin remembered the last time the man had spoken of magic, when he'd accused Olin himself of having it. Olin laughed at the idea again. He'd been a lot of things in his young life, but never magic. He'd never had the power to build or destroy, heal or break, or change reality like many did. He was not a mage. He had never felt any connection to magic.

But the oro ...

Olin didn't believe Posdel had full control of his faculties, no matter his skills and no matter what Yondi said. Whatever they'd seen happen with the oro was probably coincidence at best. A coincidence exaggerated by a man whose every other word made him insufferable.

But what did he really stand to gain with such a claim?

Olin turned his palms up and looked at them. His hands. The bed. *That* had been real. How did he explain that? He had no idea. It could have been anything. Or it could have been nothing. But he couldn't let anyone use it to keep him in Queen's Hill longer than he needed to be.

Olin found himself thinking that this was the type of moment that Wylie would have an answer he could really trust. Wylie would tell him what he should do, and even though they would disagree for a moment, Olin would end up doing what his uncle had wanted anyway and find out he'd been right.

But Wylie had asked him to find Cyrus, and Cyrus had turned out to be consorting with a Watcher of Walrea, and was now to be the Palatine of Queen's Hill after the old palatine had —

Olin was pulled out of his pensive mood by the front door opening suddenly and he jerked reflexively, leaning forward and gripping the sword. His body still seemed trapped in the trauma of the past few days. Before Olin could get to his feet, a figure stepped through the door.

"Moreen?" Yondi said.

"That sound had better be because you missed me."

Olin looked back at Yondi, who dropped the mortar and pestle on the table, expression brightening as he looked at his guest. "Of course I missed you!" Yondi said as he stepped towards her.

Moreen dropped her bag on the floor and the pair embraced. She was just a few inches taller than Yondi, and looked like she might be a few years older too. She took the apprentice's face in her hands and pulled it. "Bloody hell you've gotten uglier. I didn't think that was ever possible."

"Haha, very funny," Yondi said, slapping her hands away. "When did you get back in town?"

"Just arriving now. Had the wagon drop me off at the market and I trudged my way here," she answered. She ended with a glance at Olin who was still standing, seemingly lost, sword in his hand. "And who's the swordsman?"

"Oh, this is Olin," Yondi said, stepping aside to face both of them. "He's a friend of mine from ... around." He turned to Olin. "This is Moreen, my cousin, the great wanderer of the three kingdoms."

"That was a one-time thing, years ago. I have better things to do now," she said, with a look hinting she wanted to smack Yondi across the back of the head for teasing her in front of a stranger.

Olin studied her closer. She wore a tunic with a belt like a warrior and a pair of trousers and boots. Her dirty blonde hair was braided halfway down her back and the end dangled over her shoulder to her chest. She had large eyes, making her face unique with thin lips and a chin with the hint of an inch-long scar on her jaw.

"Does he speak?" Moreen asked, watching Olin gawk at her.

"I do," Olin answered.

"Oh, great. Good to meet you. Where are you from?"

Olin suddenly blinked hard at the question and then turned to Yondi.

"He is ... from Ravinshore," Yondi answered, disregarding the frown on Olin's face. "And as it happens, now that you're here, perhaps you can help us."

"Help you? With what?" Moreen asked.

Before Yondi could say anymore, Olin grabbed him by the arm and pulled him into a smaller room, leaving Moreen alone and confused.

"What are you doing?" Olin asked.

"Trying to get us help."

"By telling someone else that I don't know about this thing I'm not supposed to be talking about?"

"Allay your worries, Olin. I know Moreen. She's family. Someone I trust, and besides, she really could help."

"And how could she do that? Does she have magic that can send me back to Ravinshore?" Olin said, realizing too late that the example was too specific. It had been on his mind all along.

Yondi's face pulled into a frown. "No, Moreen has no magic. But what she does have is her skills as a traveler and her connections. She's just returning from Duken, where she's training to join the garrison and become a King's Guard."

"What?"

"Yes, a King's Guard. She's that good. And Moreen knows many of people all over the three kingdoms, trust me. Before you decide to leave, maybe you should see if there's anything she can do."

Olin still looked very uncertain. It wasn't just about revealing his secret to someone else, it was also the fact that he was diverging so far away from his original plan. But then his plan hadn't really been holding up. Still, it was a risk. "Do you remember what we're talking about here? It's watchers, Yondi!" Olin whispered.

"I know. And I know Moreen can handle just about anything, trust me."

She would have to. Olin had never met a woman who wanted to join a garrison before, let alone become a King's Guard. Yondi took his silence as agreement and led the way back to where Moreen had already made herself comfortable on Olin's chair eating an apple.

"So, what am I hearing about watchers?" she asked.

Olin's brows rose and he turned to Yondi.

"Ha! I should tell you she also has very scary ears," Yondi said, and then began to tell his cousin about Olin's ordeal, from how he'd learned the secret to how he'd watched his uncle die, and how it had now turned out that the one person who had been supposed to help wasn't who he'd thought, leaving him with the only one option: return to Ravinshore and reach Black Castle to inform someone and hopefully keep his head. And maybe save the king and the kingdom.

"I agree, it would be an impossible coincidence that your Cyrus just happened to meet with the man from Ravinshore."

"It wasn't just some man, it was the watcher that attacked me and my uncle."

"And how could you possibly know that?"

"He knows," Yondi answered his cousin, who glared at them both, clearly unsatisfied with the answer.

"I saw his eyes. I never forget someone's eyes. Never," Olin said.

Moreen looked at him for a moment before she spoke again, "Like I was saying then, I don't think it was a coincidence that they met so casually, and I definitely don't like the fact that the palatine has suddenly died, leaving a path for Cyrus to take charge. That being said, I don't think you'll be able to reach Cyrus so easily. Even if you did, it wouldn't be safe. But your plan to return to Ravinshore relying on nothing but your grit isn't safe either. You talk of the watchers. Of Walrea."

"I know all this. I've thought about it more times than I can count. I've played it over and over again in my head and I know what lies ahead. I've seen it first hand. I'm not unaware of the danger. But if this secret is true, then it's not just my own life at risk. I've already lost my uncle to this, I don't intend for anyone else to die, as long as I can help it. So, will you help me?" Olin asked.

Moreen looked from Olin to her cousin, who was standing by the table with an eager gaze. "What does he think?" she asked, nodding towards the mage's room.

"He thinks I should do whatever I want. He can't be bothered," Olin said.

And he thinks Olin has magic, Yondi thought.

Moreen looked thoughtful for a moment before she stood and stepped towards the door.

"Where are you going?" Olin asked. His tone made the question more of a demand.

"To do what I know best – find an answer."

Olin stirred. "Are you going to tell more people? If you are, then I might as well be on my way because the Order will beat you back here."

"Rest your worries, young man. The only way you'll get the help you need is if you tell someone what you need. But right now, I don't plan on divulging the details of your story, I only need to make an inquiry. If all this is true, there's only one group that can help – the King's Guards."

"You're going to Duken?" Yondi asked.

"Of course not. I know a commander in the King's Guards right here in Queen's Hill who might just be able to help. He's not a fan of the watchers or the any of the kingdoms' Orders. I'll have to see if he's available to hear you out. Hopefully he can either get your message to King Ranald or at least make sure it gets to Ravinshore, with you, of course."

"And how do you know you can trust this guard?" Olin asked.

"I told you, there is no love between him and the Order."

"And what happens if you can't find him or don't make it back quickly enough?"

"I don't plan on sleeping outside his door if that's what you're asking. Now, will you let me go or do you have more to say?"

"Yes," Olin answered. "I'm coming with you."

TWENTY-FIVE

T here were guards, manservants, maidens, cooks and groundsmen. To be thorough, they would have to interrogate every single one of them. Ole knew they wouldn't be able to hide it, if he went fishing, casting his net that wide. He would tip the true culprit into realizing something was wrong. But starting too small, interrogating only those who had been closest to the king, could also make the culprit suspect they were being hunted.

Whatever ruse he used could end up giving them away. So, having given his word to the queen that he would find the culprit, and conscious of Ariana's patience waning with each day that passed and King Edmond grew weaker, Ole decided to begin with the obvious –

those who were in the palace on the day the king had been poisoned.

"What is your place in the palace?" he asked his first suspect.

"I work with the kitchen, sir," the man in front of him answered. A completely white mustache hung beneath his nose. It looked like his beard had been cut not too long ago. The patches of hair on the sides of his head were also thin and white. The man was old, perhaps the same age as Ole himself, if not older, and it made Ole wonder how the man still managed to do his job without fail.

"And what precisely do you do in the kitchen?" Ole asked.

"I'm in charge of the slaughterhouse – I'm a butcher, My Lord. Been one for a good three decades, know nothing better. And I know it better than anyone else in all of the kingdom. You know this, sir," the man said, nodding at the Ole.

The butcher wasn't wrong. Ole of course, knew who he was. It had been Ole's wife who'd recommended the man for the position at the palace. His questions may have seemed unusual, but Ole wasn't in the business of caring about what people thought of him when he needed to be unpredictable.

That was something he and the queen had agreed on – whoever had attacked the king wasn't some simpleton roaming the palace corridors. They would be slippery, lurking, and doing everything to avoid suspicion.

"Of course, it must have escaped my mind. But remind me again how you came to work in the palace?"

The butcher glanced at the chamberlain standing next to him; they were the only other person in the room. He focused back at Ole. "My Lord, 'twas the then queen's chief maid, your wife, who hired me for the palace. I started at once and took over everything that involved meat in the kitchen. It has been ten years since and I have served Ravinshore without any discord," he answered.

"I see. And is that all you do in the palace? Deal with the meat?"

"Yes sir, My Lord, nothin' else."

"You don't wander outside the slaughterhouse in the kitchen?"

"No sir, My Lord, I don't got no reason to."

"Where do you stay?"

"I have a modest bed in the servant quarters, My Lord. But I also have a small house not too far from the open market. I live there with my wife and two daughters. I stay in the quarters when I am needed for a long period," he explained.

Ole paused for a moment, then continued, "So you have worked in the palace for ten years and you have never seen beyond the kitchen and the butchery?"

"I – I have."

"I thought you said you don't go anywhere else?"

"I don't, sir, don't wander," he corrected. "But once in a while when there's a feast, we move around – the servants. But never past the place of gathering – the large dining hall. We watch from windows and doorposts and corners to enjoy the feast after serving, and then we return to our post."

"And how often do you do this?"

"Only when there is feast sir, My Lord. A celebration. Never anytime else. And only for a moment or two, to catch a feeling of the merriment. I swear, nothing else," the butcher said.

"And when was the last time you saw a feast?"

The butcher's eyes dropped to the side as he tried to recall. "I – It was a fortnight ago, called by His Majesty's request. The feast to celebrate a month to the crown prince's day," the butcher said.

That was too far in the past, but the man had still been in the vicinity less than a week ago when the king had been poisoned. "Have you ever met the king in person?"

The butcher shook his head at once. "No sir, My Lord. Never been honored to."

"Do you consider yourself loyal to the king?" Ole asked.

"Of course, sir. I am loyal to His Majesty. I've been for the past ten years that I've worked in the palace. I've been loyal to the crown and the kingdom and will continue to be till the day I die."

Ole nodded. "I've had to ask you these questions because something has gone missing from His Majesty's possession. One of the twelve adamantine buttons of the king's black robe is nowhere to be found."

The butcher gasped and leaned forward. "I swear to you, sir, My Lord. I swear to His Majesty and the crown that I know nothing of the whereabouts of the missing piece. I have never been graced with touching even the helm of His Majesty's garment before. I swear by my life and that of my daughters' that I have not taken anything that belongs to His Majesty," the man said, almost dropping to his knees. He looked apprehensively from Ole to the chamberlain, who had still not said a word since entering the room.

"I hear you, you don't need to swear. I believe you. The truth is that I don't really think that you could have done such a thing. Not when you have so much to lose. Besides, you seem to be a good man who has devoted his life to serving the kingdom," Ole said and the butcher nodded to confirm the comments. "I've really called you here to ask something of you on behalf of His Majesty."

The butcher nodded his head, ready. "Anything, My Lord, anything."

"If, by some chance you come across someone, anyone, in the palace slaughterhouse, the kitchen, or anywhere else who you suspect could have the button in their possession, will you come quietly and find me directly?"

"Yes, sir, My Lord, I will. I'll go and search the servant quarters if that is what it takes."

"No. That will not be necessary. Don't do anything to bring a hint suspicion to the thief. Simply come and find me if you suspect someone," Ole said. "And, you shouldn't speak a word of this to anyone at all. Not even your wife."

The butcher nodded and thanked Ole as he was asked to leave. The door closed and Ole turned to the chamberlain, who was looking at the door.

"You don't think he's the one, sir?" the chamberlain asked.

"The palace corridors are a long way from the slaughterhouse. He simply couldn't get himself close enough."

The door opened and another man entered, this one much younger than the butcher. He was a little shorter than the old man, and had a head full of thick black hair. He wore a clean brown tunic cinched with rope like a true servant of the palace. He bowed to the chamberlain and Ole.

Ole looked studied him. He was young enough that he probably hadn't been born when the butcher had made his first cut. If he was older than two decades, it would only be by a few years, but shadows of a mustache were already forming on his face. Servants like him did the domestic work in the chambers of the palace. He still had ardor. Ole saw him quite often, usually at dawn when most of the servants began their chores.

"You work in the chambers, don't you?" Ole asked.

"Yes, My Lord. And anywhere I'm needed. But my post is in the chambers."

"Which ones?"

"The prince's, My Lord. I clean and serve the chamber of Prince George."

"And how long has that been your responsibility?"

"A little over a year."

"And how has it been so far?" Ole asked.

"A pleasure, My Lord. A great pleasure."

"Do you ever have to clean any other chamber besides the prince's?"

The servant nodded. "Yes. Sometimes I serve the younger prince, and sometimes I have to join some of the other servants in cleaning the halls and large rooms."

"And do you ever clean the king's chambers?"

He shook his head. "No, My Lord. Never have. Only the chamberlain and the king's hands are allowed there."

"Hmm." Ole stared the young man. "I would assume that you have come across His Majesty."

The servant nodded, face serious. "Many times, during my duties, I've encountered His Majesty," he said.

"And you're vast in the affairs of the palace?"

"Not more than would be expected of a chamber servant, My Lord."

"What do you know of the missing button?"

The young man shook his head. "A button? Nothing."

"The king's favorite attire is missing a rare button. It has been for the past week."

The servant's gaze stayed steady. "I haven't seen any adamantine button missing from the king's attire, My

Lord. Surely if I did, I would never even dream of keeping it. I would return it to the chamberlain at once."

The chamberlain and Ole exchanged glances. The Court's Counsel turned his gaze back at the servant. "Adamantine you say? I never mentioned what the button was made of."

The servant raised his face. "No, of course you didn't. I must have assumed because I've seen many of the king's attires laced with adamantine stones. But I have no knowledge of one that has gone missing."

Ole regarded the young man a moment longer before he spoke. "Well then, will you be willing to do something for His Majesty?"

"Of course, My Lord."

"If you happen to know of anyone who has helped themselves to the king's possession, if you see it or if there is someone you suspect at all, will you come find me at once?"

"Of course, My Lord," he said.

Ole nodded and sat back. "Where did you say you're from?"

"I never said, My Lord. But I'm from Ravinshore, born and bred in the cold of Hutton's Grove."

"And who will your father be?"

"Gordon, son of Heldera the carver, My Lord."

"And your mother?"

"Ramina, from Duken."

"Of course, the fair-haired dancer," Ole acknowledged. "You're Ramina's son?"

"Yes, My Lord," he answered, a smile on his face at Ole's recognition.

"How is she?"

"Healthy, My Lord," he said.

"Good. And how are your sisters, both of them?"

"Married, fat and happy, sir."

Ole nodded, and glanced at the chamberlain, who was lost in the familiarity. "He comes from a good family," he said. Ole turned to the servant. "You can leave."

The young man bowed and turned, but was stopped by Ole's voice.

"I know Ramina, quite well. She was close to the court once. Hell of a dancer, never to be forgotten. I know that she only ever gave birth to two children – a daughter and her youngest, a son near the same time Prince George was born. And, if I am not mistaken, the prince is preparing for his sixteenth birthday. If you are who you say you are, then you should be no more than a decade and a half old."

The young man was rooted on the spot, half-turned to leave.

The chamberlain's eyes widened and he looked from the Ole to the man and back, peeling himself away slowly from the wall.

"Who are you?" Ole asked.

The young man slowly turned around. His eyes were now thinned and empty of emotion, and his face looked as though the blood had deserted it. His lips tightened as he stared at Ole, who was rising from his chair.

"Who are you?" Ole demanded.

The man's nostrils flared, disgusted by the question. He exhaled as he blinked a glance at the chamberlain, who was sweating. He looked back at Ole. "You waste your time. There is nothing you can do. Edmond is nothing but a corpse waiting to rot."

The chamberlain cursed under his breath. Ole's mouth opened, and time seemed to stand still as they both watched a tiny blade shimmer as it appeared in the servant's hand. Before either of them could move, the assassin jammed the blade deep in the side of his own neck and drew it across, slitting his throat from end to end.

Ole trembled as blood spurted across his face, and he watched in horror as the chamberlain screamed for the guards and the king's poisoner dropped to the ground among a crimson pool of drying blood.

TWENTY-SIX

T he guard jerked as a gust of wind blew a small cloud of dust away from the front of the gatehouse. He glanced at his partner and got a nod to check it out. The guard moved cautiously to the east side of the fence then froze at the sight of Alden bending over and heaving violently.

"Is – is all well, sir?" he asked.

"He should feel better in a few hours, if his head doesn't explode before then from throwing his guts up," Gytha answered.

She turned to take in the view of the territory from the side of the palace. The vastness of Ravinshore was always a sight. The easternmost of the three kingdoms still left her paralyzed with memories. The air that had kept her awake so many of the nights she had spent in this kingdom still felt the same. A wave of anxiousness masked in silence washed over her as she was reminded of it all. Her kingdom.

"We need to get inside at once," Isabelle said.

"And who are you?"

"Here on the order of Queen Ariana," Isabelle answered, turning to the guard so he could catch a glimpse of her face from beneath her hood.

The guard's eyes widened. He recognized her from when she'd set out with Alden. Only they'd had horses then.

Alden pulled himself up, though it still felt as if the earth was shifting under him, and wiped his mouth. He cleared his throat and met the guard's eyes. "Let us in right away. The queen awaits," he managed to say.

The guard nodded and turned on his heels. Isabelle and Gytha followed him side by side while Alden trailed behind. The gate was opened for them enter, an uninterrupted path straight to the palace, where every waiting guard fell quiet and stepped aside at the sight of Alden and the cloaked women.

Isabelle held her worries at bay, hoping it wasn't too late and they weren't going to march into a hollow chamber where King Edmond had already passed beyond help. Despite everything, she hoped the promise she had given the queen didn't become meaningless. She didn't want to end up regretting it, like Gytha had warned. Isabelle didn't want to be proven a liar, and didn't want to prove Ole an old fool for bringing her to Ravinshore from Madero in the first place.

Isabelle hoped, and she had a fairly good reason to. She glanced to her left as the colossal doors of the main palace parted. The woman walking by her side exuded an aura of magic like she'd never felt before. Isabelle had been in awe of Gytha before she'd even set eyes on her, just from the way William had spoken about her. And then they'd met, and Isabelle hadn't even suspected the old woman would transform herself to reveal her true form. Isabelle had never obsessed over a mage's power, despite William's quarrel with her, but she did wonder what it felt like for Gytha to have that level of magic flowing freely through her. And if that little display at the cottage had been anything to judge by, the Grand Sorceress's powers were more than just phenomenal, they were something sane people sought to avoid. Isabelle just hoped that they would be enough to wake the King of Ravinshore from his mortal slumber.

Gytha had always known that this day was going to come eventually. It was inevitable – not that she would be walking through the corridors of the palace towards the dying king, but that she would be back in Ravinshore, after everything. She hadn't known how long it would take, but she'd always suspected something would have to force her to come back. This was force, but it didn't mean she had returned for good. Despite her feelings towards Ravinshore, she was not hard-hearted enough to do nothing when she'd been called to help save the king. Besides, even though she might not admit it, she wanted to know how Egro magic had found its way to the palace. Who had set it loose on the king?

Their convoy came to an abrupt halt as Ole appeared from a corridor to the left. Something was wrong. Though Alden was still struggling with keeping his own head on his neck, even he noticed the Court's Counsel dazed expression. Then he saw the blood.

"Lord Counsel?" Alden called before Isabelle or anyone else could.

Ole blinked. "You have arrived, good. There's no time to waste. We head to the chamber at once," he said.

"Are – are you okay?" Isabelle asked.

"I will be." He realized they were curious about the blood. "This isn't mine, and I have to worry about something else at this moment." He glanced at the guard standing next to him. "Where is the queen?"

"With the princes, My Lord," the guard said.

"Inform Her Majesty at once that the quest to Duken has arrived with company," Ole said and the guard bowed, turned, and hurried away just as the chamberlain stepped out of a room, wearing a similarly shaken expression. Ole turned to him. "Lead them to the chamber and wait with them in the hall. I will join you in a moment."

The chamberlain nodded and gestured for Isabelle and Gytha to follow him.

Alden didn't bother to move and only watched as the sorceresses continued without him. This was as far as his own role went. He would remain oblivious to the true purpose of the journey he had almost lost his life to. It was the curse of serving.

Isabelle stopped, then turned and looked at Alden, who seemed like he desperately needed to find a seat. "Thank you," she said with a nod.

Alden gave a vague, painful smile in return, and Isabelle turned back and joined Gytha and the chamberlain. A few paces down the hall, Isabelle asked the man, "Whose blood was that?"

"The king's poisoner."

* * *

"There is word from Queen's Hill, My Lord."

Ole exhaled as he shouldered himself out of the bloodied robe. The servant picked it up from the floor. "What is it?"

"It says Palatine Fredrick has passed."

Ole froze, staring at the servant with a pinched expression. "Frederic is dead?"

"That was the message, My Lord. He passed yesterday evening," the servant answered, dropping his face as he moved to the corner of the room to dispose of the blood-stained robe.

"How did he die?"

"He – he was said to have been found in his bathing tub."

Ole could hardly believe it. Surely, a man like the Palatine of Queen's Hill didn't just expire in a bathing tub. The possibilities swarmed his head. What he had witnessed in the interrogation made him that realize something more must have happened, but they could never know now. Even with the existence of the Order.

He dipped his hands in the bowl of water and washed his face and his neck to rid himself of the assassin's blood. Ole wiped as hard he could, struggling to push the image of the young man slitting his throat out of his head. Like he had told Isabelle – he had other concerns now.

He had ordered Alden to lock the castle down. No one was to be allowed to leave unless he was aware of it. The arrival of the sorceress meant that the king's health took priority, but the servant's betrayal wouldn't go unattended for long.

Ole took the towel his servant handed to him and dried his face. Then he got dressed in a new robe and headed out of his chamber.

It was time to decide Ravinshore's fate.

* * *

Queen Ariana stood silently by the door as her sons were engrossed in their studies. Watching them was one of the few things that comforted her, keeping her sane through the day despite the fact she was on the verge of losing her husband. More than on the verge. He was the palest she had ever seen any human, dead or alive. She could still hear the almost imperceptible thud of his heart in his chest – or she thought did, but the alternative wasn't something she allowed herself to think about, let alone prepare for.

If Edmond died, her world would change. If Edmond died, her children's world would change, and the weight of the kingdom would shift to their shoulders, hardly giving them time to grieve, without regard for the fact that they were still children. George was sixteen, he was already a man and she had no doubt that her son would grow into what was required of him. A revered leader.

But a mother could never stop the fear in the back of her mind of how quickly life could consume her child.

It would come fast, disorientating him. It would change him. It would change his brother, too. Ariana wished it wouldn't, but it would.

George had continued to ask about his father. Ariana had managed to tell him only that his father was ill and would get better soon. He had no idea that Edmond had been poisoned and was slowly dying. But he probably suspected it. He probably knew. George was a smart young man, just like his father, and not just in looks. She watched as he studied the scrolls the mage was showing him.

There was a world of difference between what life could become if his father died, and if the king was murdered. Queen Ariana exhaled and her hand slowly clenched into a fist. She was going to protect her children, no matter what. If Edmond died from the poison before help arrived, Ravinshore would burn, and it would rise from the ashes for her son to reign. She would make sure of it. Every single person that played a part in this would perish in front of her eyes before her son took his father's crown and was forced into holding the fate of the kingdom on his shoulders.

Just then, George turned in his desk and noticed her observing him. Ariana gave him a small crooked smile, even though she feared he would see through it. He smiled back at her, but the smile waned just as quick as his eyes darted behind her to where a guard had appeared.

"Your Grace."

Queen Ariana turned to the guard and raised a finger to keep him from speaking as she led him out of the room. A few paces from the study, she demanded, "What is it?"

"Lord Counsel has asked that I inform Her Majesty that the quest to Duken has arrived, with company," the guard said with his head bowed.

Ariana's eyes widened, and she felt a jolt course through her body, her heart drumming with a thud in her chest at the news. Isabelle was back, with company. Ariana wasted no more time. She pulled her floor-sweeping dress off the ground and hastened her steps in the direction of the king's chamber as the messenger guard and her personal company hurried after her.

Perhaps there was still a chance.

The queen flung open the chamber door and heads turned to watch her enter. From their stance, it appeared as though they had just arrived as well. Isabelle curtsied and Gytha followed, both women pulling down their hoods one after the other.

"Isabelle." Ariana sounded like a mother seeing her long-absent child. A mixture of relief and anticipation flushed over the queen's expression. "You're here. Did you find who you set out for?" she asked, looking at the Maedrian sorceress, then moving her gaze to the unfamiliar woman in the grey cape.

"Yes, Your Grace. This is the Grand Sorceress Gytha," Isabelle answered.

Gytha curtsied again. "It is an honor to make your acquaintance, Your Majesty, despite the circumstance."

Queen Ariana didn't know what she'd been expecting a Grand Sorceress to look like — an old mage with a head full of grey hair and eyes that carried the weight of years, maybe. But it hardly mattered, she couldn't have cared less that Gytha was hardly older than herself. "Thank you, Grand Sorceress. Now tell me, please, can you truly save my husband?"

Gytha glanced over at the royal bed, where the king rested in solitude, completely still. "If I'm not too late," she answered. Gytha glanced at Isabelle, then moved towards King Edmond.

Ole, quiet during the introduction, received the weary glance from the queen. "They are here now," he assured. "Your Majesty, there is something you should know."

"Can it not wait, Ole?"

"It can, Your Grace, but I think you would want to know at once."

She turned to him.

"The king's poisoner is dead."

TWENTY-SEVEN

"Levyna?"

She hadn't been asleep. She was sure of it.

"Levyna!"

At the sound of the voice she jerked back to consciousness, gasping as she opened her eyes to her bedchamber. Her mother was crouching over her, looking relieved. The same expression was mirrored by the maid standing behind her.

"Levyna, can you hear me?"

Levyna nodded. Fiona tightened her hand on her daughter's shoulder. "Are you okay? You've had me in a panic. The maid called and you never answered and she came to fetch me. I've called your name several times and you haven't responded. You only laid with your eyes open, staring at nothing but the top of your bedchamber," Fiona said, the worry in her voice. "My dear ..."

"Mother ..." Levyna glanced at the maid standing by and Fiona followed her gaze.

"Wait outside," Fiona ordered the servant and the maid curtsied before taking her leave. Once the door closed, Fiona turned back to her daughter. "Tell me."

"I must have fallen asleep," Levyna said.

"Asleep with your eyes wide open?" Fiona asked, brows furrowed.

"I've been terrified of closing my eyes since last night. I've willed my body not to accept sleep, or so I had thought. I laid here staring at the ceiling and, though I could see it and my eyes were open, my mind had gone on a journey of its own, Mother."

"I don't think I understand what you're saying, Levyna."

"I mean I was awake, but somehow I was also asleep," Levyna answered. "Even though I hadn't willed it, I slept. And I dreamt again, Mother."

Fiona stiffened at the words. "You – you dreamt while your eyes were open? You had a vision?"

"I don't know what a vision feels like, but I know that it came just like the dreams I had when sleeping." Levyna had dreaded it happening again, and had tried to avoid sleep for as long as she could, even if she didn't remain sane after the battle. But her revolt had been futile as the dreams had found her regardless.

"What did you dream of?" Fiona asked, the trembling was still present in her voice; it was almost a whisper. Her eyes were filled with a mix of apprehension and the grief that still lingered.

"A hand falling," Levyna answered. "I dreamt of two hands and one of them dropped, as if felled."

Fiona peered at her daughter, confused. "A hand you say? Whose? Was this hand familiar? Was there something on it like your —"

Fiona stopped herself from finishing the sentence, but Levyna already knew what her mother was trying to ask. That barrage of questions was no doubt partly an attempt to show that she was no longer taking her daughter's dream lightly. Still, Levyna felt the heaviness in the air. She hated that she had been made to stir this grief when her own father's body was hardly cold. And though the grief was far from abandoning her and the ache still pressed deeply into her chest, as though a stud rested on her bosom, the unwanted dream she'd just had was gripping her just as heavily.

It wasn't only because Levyna feared the dreams, but because she dreaded the fact that she already knew who the hand belonged to.

She had seen it once, and though it had been brief, Levyna remembered the encounter vividly. She remembered it now, the feeling of a pulse running through her body as she took that hand. It'd felt as though she had known that hand, known that person, for longer than the utterly transient moment they had shared in the palace hall. How ironic it was that in that moment she had been upset about a dream that had only ended up coming true anyway.

"I recognize the hand and who it belongs to, Mother," Levyna answered.

"Who is it?"

Levyna's face twisted as she thought about how to describe it. She had nothing beyond the fact that she had encountered the person by chance, the unusual sensation she had felt when they had touched, and the fact that she could somehow feel that they were close by.

"I do not know his name, or where he comes from." She looked towards the window as if to call to more of the memory as she gently touched the hand he had grabbed when he'd helped her from the ground. A complete stranger who didn't feel like one. One whose touch had spawned a web of a singular memory.

Levyna closed her eyes and exhaled, thinking perhaps it would help, then opened them to her mother's waiting eyes. "I don't know what to call him, but I have a strong feeling he is somewhere here in Queen's Hill."

* * *

"Your Grace, perhaps you might not want to be in the room for this," Gytha said.

"No, whatever it is you want to do, don't shy away on my account. He is my husband, I want to see everything," Queen Ariana answered.

Ariana hadn't waited on this precipice with him, breathed with his docile chest and hung herself around

266

his still body to be sent away as he was healed. If her husband was going to open his eyes again, she refused to be anywhere else.

Her heart was still recovering from the news Ole had brought. The shock of it still lingered at the tips of her fingers and toes. She hadn't expected it. She had needed the poisoner found so she could look into their eyes as she inflicted the cruelest of horrors upon them, releasing all of her pain and her frustration. She had been waiting for it, demanding it. She had wanted to know why. Why had they done it? She'd hoped to carve out the truth of who, if anyone, had been the mastermind.

Queen Ariana was not troubled that the man was dead. If anything, she harbored a fury that she had been deprived of the chance to be the one to wield the blade and see the life escape the traitor. It made sense that the poisoner would choose to go as quickly as possible, given the perdition that awaited him, which would have ended with his head on a pike. What had shaken her was how he had done it. A knife to his own throat was the actions of a man who feared nothing, who had a stone for a heart and river of sand for blood in his veins. A man like that could have done anything; he could have done more. He had worked in her son's chamber for a year. The thought burned through her as she moved her right hand to her belly.

Gytha stared at the queen, who had fallen silent, then nodded. She turned to the chamberlain. "We need a live animal. A small fowl or a bird should do," she said.

The chamberlain nodded and hurried away at once.

Gytha looked to Ole. "When he returns with the bird you are to lock the doors to the room, and no one is to be allowed to wander the corridor outside. If there are children around, keep them far away from the doors of the chamber."

Ole nodded and turned to leave.

"Don't let anyone near this chamber, Ole. No one," Queen Ariana added, meeting the Court's Counsel's eyes.

Ole knew at once what she meant. He wasn't needed to witness the result of the king's treatment. It was his duty to protect the kingdom in the queen's absence, even from those who thought they owned it. Ole bowed sharply and stepped out, opening the doors to the chamber to demand the guards relocate to the ends of the corridor. Just then, the chamberlain hurried past with a white pigeon clutched in his hands. Ole closed the doors behind him, and and turned his back. Now to hope.

By the time the chamberlain arrived, Gytha had relieved herself of her cape and Isabelle was following suit. Ariana mimicked them, taking off her shoes and inching closer to the bed. She watched as Gytha pulled the covers away from Edmond's body and planted herself on the bed next to him, sitting so she could take his hands as she had done before. Gytha began muttering words that the queen couldn't comprehend.

Gytha incanted as she held the king's hand. The slight heat she felt in her hands told her that the king was still in there somewhere. Pausing, she took the pigeon from the chamberlain, broke its legs, and placed it next to the king's head. Then she turned to Isabelle, who handed her a small knife.

The queen watched with bated breath as Gytha took the blade and nicked each of her husband's wrists, one after the other. Blood flowed from the cuts, and Gytha grabbed the wrists again, directly over the wounds, staining her own hands with the king's blood to create a link to the source of the poison in the king's body. Once again, Gytha began to mutter words of the spell in quick succession, shutting her eyes.

King's Edmond's blood was clearly darker than usual. It barely looked to have come from a living body, had one not seen it. The work of the Egro. Isabelle watched as Gytha's hands slowly began to glow as blue and red arcane threads of enchantment twined from her wrists to weave around the bloodied hands of the king.

"Agurigade – em – impatum."

After Gytha finished the spell, she fell quiet, eyes still shut. Isabelle was held in place, watching.

"Wh – what is it?" Ariana forced herself to ask after a long moment of silence.

"I ... I don't know," Isabelle answered. This was one of the reasons why she hadn't been able to heal the king, and why only a handful, if not a couple, of people in the three kingdoms could. Isabelle could only weave threads of a particular kind of magic, like most mages, and her knowledge of how to fight an Egro spell only went as far as recognizing it.

The air in the room stilled. At first, all three observers were oblivious to what was happening, then they were startled by Gytha's eyes flinging open. Isabelle noticed at once that they had turned black and she met the queen's startled gaze just as the Grand Sorceress spoke again, this time a single word.

"Anioidus!" Gytha said, and immediately the bird next to the king's head stopped writhing and its color changed, pale feathers turning dark and wilting away as the creature withered. The Egro needed another source of life before it could be expelled.

Queen Ariana watched in horror as Edmond moved for the first time in six days. Except it wasn't a gentle wakening. The king twitched and began to jerk violently, so violently that the chamberlain had to grab hold of his legs while Ariana and Isabelle held his shoulders in place. Gytha didn't let go of his hands. Ariana had never seen a human or creature move this way. She feared his bones would break; the bed itself was trembling, and the mantles on the walls shook with the vibrations. The entire room quaked with her husband at the center of it, the veins of his arms darkening as they threaded towards Gytha's strong hold.

***

The scream caused heads to turn towards of the king's bedchamber. Though he was tempted for a heartbeat, Ole remained unmoved, blocking the path of the figures standing in front of him.

"You will remove yourself at once so that we can see the king!" Thorne said fiercely.

"I am here on the order of Her Majesty; no one is to disturb His Majesty while he is being attended."

"Surely you have the sense to know that doesn't extend to the Order of Walrea. Step aside at once so that we may see what is being done to the King of Ravinshore under our watch, Counsel!" Thorne rested his hand near his dagger.

Ole didn't care about the threat; he had a dozen of the King's First Guards standing behind him, and half of the garrison had been deployed to the corridors of the palace. It was almost like he'd know this would happen, as mere minutes after he'd ordered the guards into position, the Order had arrived – Thorne and four other watchers, duly masked and standing threateningly in the corridor of the king's bedchamber. The outer guards had had no choice but to let them through, but Ole didn't care that the Lord Watcher of Walrea with his gauntlet of watchers technically had the power to see the king no matter the chaos.

"You can try whatever you want, but you will have to get past me, and them, to reach that door," Ole said. "The king is not to be disturbed."

"What is that noise coming from the king's bedchamber?" Thorne demanded.

"I have told you already, Lord Watcher. His Majesty is being attended to, and by the queen's command, it is to be none of the Order's concern."

Thorne ground his jaw behind his mask. His eyes glowed red as he drew his dagger, stepped forward and raised it inches from Ole's neck. He was faster than the King's Guards standing to the side, who drew their swords too late. The watchers followed their lord, unsheathing their blades.

Thorne knew he could remove Ole easily; he could do it weaponless without breaking a sweat. He could toss all the guards to the side with a wave of his hand, and have his way if he decided to. He wanted to. The plan depended on what was happening in the king's bedchamber. That wastrel ruler was supposed to be dead by now; he hadn't been supposed to last as long as he had, not long enough to even attempt a cure. No one had been meant to interfere.

The Lord Watcher exhaled, quickly thinking what it would mean if, by some miracle, the king healed. He wasn't prepared to take the chance. He glanced at the guardsmen, who were poised to show their skills. His gaze returned to Ole. Thorne lowered the dagger and balled his left hand into a fist, slowly drawing up the power he would need to push aside the human blockade. No matter that they were in the middle of the corridor of the royal palace, yards away from the king's bedchamber.

Then the sound of the door opening froze his spell. Everyone turned to see the queen step from the room.

The King's Guards stiffened and bowed with the rest of the watchers. Ole and the Lord Watcher were the last to bend a knee.

"What is this?" she asked.

Thorne raised his hand so the queen could see the gauntlet he wore, knowing what it symbolized. "Once again, Your Grace, the Order demands to see the king."

"I should have you buried in the dungeons for days for using those words, Lord Watcher. You seem to forget that even the Order bows to the crown. But I'm in no mood for that right now. I don't intend for your nuisance to continue to disturb the king's peace. If you're so desperate to see my husband, you will have to make yet another trip. He's resting now," the queen said. "But, because you seem so mad for a sight of him, you can come see for yourself."

Ole met the queen's eyes and a furtive nod was enough for him to step aside. The guards behind him followed, allowing passage for the watchers. Thorne stepped through and the watchers stepped right after him.

"Only you," the queen said.

Thorne raised a finger, then proceeded alone. He walked behind Ariana, hoping this was all some elaborate performance to cover up the fact that King Edmond was long expired and his body was rotting on the bed, or that that it had been moved and some other face was hidden under the sheets in some childish endeavor to keep up the lie.

But the Lord Watcher's heart sunk deep into his chest when he saw the bastard lying on his own bed, shirtless and unconscious, but with his chest rising and falling like a bloody babe.

***

Thorne'd had enough. Everything had depended on one thing – Edmond's death. It was what would have allowed them to usher in the next phase of the plan. But with this, everything changed. He might not have seen the king open his eyes, but he knew the king lived, and didn't look to be a man battling death. There was color on his cheeks and a pair of sorceresses he had never seen before flanked each side of his bed. Unforeseen elements.

Thorne hated them. First, it had been the sciff who was still yet to be dealt with, and now the king had somehow survived an Egro that was supposed to be his end. Too many pieces of the plan failing. He couldn't accept it. It was now or never.

The Lord Watcher pulled his horse to a halt at the rise of a hill and turned his gaze towards the palace. Four black horses surrounded him as he huffed in annoyance at the lack of the bell that had been supposed to have rung already, marking the demise of the king.

"Send word to the crows," he said to the closest watcher without turning. "Come dusk tomorrow, they all fly."

TWENTY-EIGHT

"**D**on't worry, this'll be better than the last time you looked for help," Yondi said as they walked through the corners of the new market. He could tell how anxious Olin was as they inched closer to their destination.

"I know you mean well, but it's impossible for me not to be worried," Olin answered. He didn't add his true feelings. He had protested the fact that Yondi had attached himself to this trip and he had said so several times. He'd meant it when he'd told Yondi he didn't want to be the reason anyone else was put at risk. But there was a small rebellious part of him, a part he wanted to deny, that was glad to have company on this trip with Moreen, who he wasn't familiar with. It was at least some form of comfort, being with the only person he truly knew in Queen's Hill.

Yondi exhaled as they walked away from the market, taking the lonely cobblestone path towards the east hills where Moreen said she'd be able to find word about the guardsman. Moreen was walking a couple steps ahead of them. Olin looked at the sky as a bird flew overhead, then continued to walk. But Olin couldn't help but look up again as the bird gave a cry. It appeared to be flying in a circle. Olin couldn't help his body from tensing.

"How long have you known her?" he asked Yondi.

"Moreen?" Yondi asked. "I could say all of my life. Ever since she came to Queen's Hill with her mother, we've been inseparable. If you'd known us as children, you would've thought we were brother and sister, rather than cousins. But I'd take Moreen over any sibling any day. She's my blood."

Olin stared ahead as they walked. "And where's the rest of your family?" he asked.

A cold silence fell. Yondi looked down and hesitated. It was the first time Olin had ever seen him do that. Perhaps he'd asked a question he shouldn't have, taking advantage of Yondi's fondness without considering his feelings.

"I apologize if it's not something you wish to talk about," he said.

"It's not that you've asked a horrible question. It's harmless. It's just been a while since I've gotten to see any of them. Since I left home two years ago. And ..."

"You don't owe me an answer, Yondi," Olin said, partly because he meant it and partly because he'd seen the bird again. It looked to be the same one. Olin was wearing a cloak, as usual, with the hood covering his face. This cloak also had long sleeves, so he didn't have to hide his hands as they inched closer to the sword on his side.

"I know I don't, but ever since I left, it's been difficult to think about them. They're not dead or anything – my parents – but it sometimes feels as though they might be."

Olin didn't feel like prying further. Not simply to pass time when he'd already been an invader in Yondi's life for the better part of two days, making everything about himself and his problems. He'd been oblivious to the fact that Yondi had a life that didn't involve fighting the Order of Walrea. He'd found refuge with Yondi and his master so easily that he'd never considered what could have happened if he hadn't met them.

"I —" Yondi stopped short as Moreen slowed, then stopped completely in the middle of the road. "Moreen?" he said.

Olin's apprehensiveness grew. "Why have we stopped?" he asked.

The silence before she turned. The crowing of the bird above them. The stiffness in his body. The stillness in the air. Olin saw Moreen's eyes. They looked different than when she had first walked through the door. The excitement of seeing Yondi and helping with his quest had been lost somewhere along the road, leaving her eyes bleak, almost cold. Her mouth opened, as if she wanted to attempt to speak, but couldn't quite manage it. Moreen simply stared at her cousin as the crow sounded again.

"Moreen? What is it?" Yondi asked, concern in his voice as he stepped towards her.

"We are there," she said. "I'm sorry, Yondi, I truly had no choice. Believe me."

Yondi frowned at her words. Olin's eyes widened. Footsteps surrounded them from nowhere. Three figures appeared from everywhere and nowhere – the roofs and crevices of the buildings around them. They were all dressed alike, and Olin may have never seen them before, but he knew at once who they were. He spun and unsheathed his sword. Behind him, Yondi was paralyzed with disbelief, staring at his cousin.

Olin, determined not to be idle in this fight, lunged at the nearest masked Watcher of the Red Flame. His swing was blocked by a dagger, but the move allowed Olin to glimpse a mark inscribed in the flesh of the watcher's wrist, and the familiarity struck him with yet another crippling thought. Olin swung for the other side of the watcher, but missed when his attacker seemed to move with the air. He turned to block the watcher's strike to his neck, just as another watcher next to him was thrown against a wall.

Yondi took another stance, arms outstretched and ready to release another pulse. He aimed again at the third watcher and let loose, the same spell that had spilled the barrel of Elm's milk, throwing the watcher a fair distance, even if he didn't shatter like the barrel had.

Olin had managed to keep his own watcher at bay, but then his head jerked to the side at the sound of a scream behind him. Moreen stood, watching with her mouth open and eyes wide. Olin followed her gaze and felt his heart stop at the sight of a watcher's dagger sticking out of Yondi's neck.

As if frozen in time, playing at an inhumanly slow pace, Olin's mind dissolved at the sight. All of the fight in him faltered. The watcher pulled the blade and Yondi dropped to the ground. Olin hardly felt the knife in his own side. He couldn't tear his eyes from the horror forever locked in Yondi's expression. Olin's sword dropped and he fell to his knees as everything went dark.

* * *

Olin's eyes opened moments before he was tossed to the floor. The sharp pain of the wound in his side pulsed as he landed. It took Olin several minutes before he realized that he was on the ground. The pain radiated, feeling as though it was clawing at the rest of his body. He twisted until he came face to face with a pair of boots. Olin followed the legs up to find a pair of eyes, ones he could never forget.

"Wylie's rat. What a sneaky little thing you've been," L said.

Olin wished he could reach up and grab the watcher by the scruff of the neck, choke the life out of him while he watched, and by some chance rip out his throat and feed it to him, but he could barely move his arm or any of his limbs.

There were a hundred questions running through his head, some he couldn't bring himself to process. The main one was: how had a Watcher of Walrea been in Queen's Hill, working with the Order of the Red Flame?

Olin didn't think that was supposed to happen. It was never meant to happen. Each Order was only ever meant to serve the purpose of its own kingdom. If Walrea had a watcher in the Courts of the Red Flame, it could only mean that their goals were aligned. And that meant that one of those goals was the secret he had overheard, the one he hadn't been able to escape – the murder of King Edmond of Ravinshore.

"You might be wondering why you're still alive," the watcher said. "You must believe me, I would have wanted nothing more than for you to be dead already, but I'm forced to think, perhaps, you can save yourself. I have questions for you, but before I ask, I'll let you in on a secret. What you're feeling right now is venom working itself through your body. From the blade. It's certain that you won't see first light. I don't know how many deaths you've seen, if any, but a death from Legian venom doesn't leave much in the way of remains. Your guts are slowly being eaten away. Think carefully about that as you answer me.

"Who sent you to Walrea, and who have you told about what you heard?"

Olin might have wanted to be watcher, once, dreaming of it as he imagined himself serving his kingdom. He may have ended up as only a sciff, but Olin's lack of experience didn't make him fool enough believe there was any way he would escape from the Order alive if he told them what they wanted. There was no chance he would utter any word to the watcher.

Olin swallowed hard and felt the pain pierce through his belly. He forced himself to consciously think about the people he had told his secret to: Wylie, who had died trying to save him; the mage, who had been wary of the trouble Olin brought and was oblivious to the price his apprentice had paid; Moreen, who had betrayed him; and Yondi ...

Yondi.

The image flashed through his mind, of the blade sticking from his neck, blood streaming down and pooling as he dropped to the floor – it felt as though air forsook him. Olin felt the pain grow to an unspeakable proportion. In his chest, it was a needle piercing his heart with every beat. Olin fought back the truth of what had happened, what he had seen – what he had done. He had told himself it wouldn't happen again, that he wouldn't let someone else die in his stead because of his own mess. It was his fault – he'd wandered into this simply because he could never sit still, could never stop seeking adventure. Because he could never stop being curious. Wylie had sacrificed himself for it, and now Olin had gone ahead and sacrificed someone else. Those eyes – Yondi's eyes as he'd laid on the ground suffocating in his own blood – haunted him. Olin would never be free of them; he knew it.

After all, he never forgot a pair of eyes.

TWENTY-NINE

"**I** know you."

Olin opened his eyes from where he lay on the floor of the dark cell. He heard the voice but could see no face. He frowned.

"I've seen you before."

He turned to his left and she appeared from the corner of the small cell, almost as if from the wall itself. The light was nothing but a burning torch in the distance, but he could make out her features clearer than anything else in the cell, and he saw her eyes. He knew those eyes.

"I – I have seen you before too. Who are you? What are you doing here? H – how did you get here?" Olin asked, glancing at the door that was still closed.

"I don't know ... how I'm here," Levyna answered, looking around the strange cell and then at herself. She really had no idea. "But I am here. My name is Levyna." She looked at him. "I saw you on the street, and then I dreamt about you. Who are you? Why are you here?"

Olin wasn't sure what she was, and the fact that she didn't know how she was standing inside a dungeon made no sense. He stared, as if there was a clue hidden on her, but all he saw was a young woman barefoot in a nightdress. He couldn't figure it out, not when he could feel the pain of the poison in his body sucking him in and taking the air from his breath.

Levyna didn't miss the blood on his shirt, or the way he clutched at his side despite the chains. "You're hurt."

"Stay away," he cautioned as she stepped towards him. "I don't know who you are."

Levyna stared at him a moment before she answered, "I have no clue who you are either, but I have dreamt about you and I'm here. I'm worried about what will happen to you."

Olin stared at her. "Do you think I'm that stupid?"

"I normally wouldn't care what you think about me. Except I dreamt about you, just as I dreamt about my father, who is now dead and I'm supposed to be mourning."

Olin's face pinched at her response and he glanced at her again. She looked like she'd been yanked out of bed. "But how can you possibly not know how you got here?"

"If I knew, then perhaps I would have already left," she answered, a hint of annoyance in her voice. "But I cannot help but think it has something to do with you, and why you're dying in a dungeon." The last sentence took a different tone.

What was he supposed to do with this mysterious person? Olin looked around the cell, wondering if he was missing something.

"You are not from Queen's Hill, are you?"

Olin looked back at her. "No. From Ravinshore. And the reason I'm here isn't something you should concern yourself with, not if you care about your life, so please ..."

"My father was the palatine for many years. He traveled to Ravinshore a lot."

Olin's brows rose. "Your father was the palatine?" The palatine that had died the night before in suspicious circumstance? Posdel had been sure of foul play. The palatine that Cyrus was going to replace, Olin remembered. The same Cyrus who had been meeting the watcher that had killed his uncle, killed Yondi, and put him in this cell.

"I'm not supposed to say this, but I dreamt of his death. He never believed it, maybe I didn't either. But it happened. I've been hating myself all day because I didn't try hard enough to make him believe. And then, when I was grieving in my bed, I dreamt of your hand falling. And I don't know who you are or why I dreamt about you, but suddenly here I am. If the reason you're here is something I can help with, then perhaps —"

"You cannot," Olin interrupted. A combination of a fresh wave of pain and a vivid memory of what had happened to the last hand that had reached down to help him forced the words out of him. "You cannot," he said again.

"How can you be sure?" Levyna asked.

"Because you cannot, and you should not, okay? And I'd still say that if you had any idea what you're doing or how you managed to get into this dungeon," he said.

If she knew how she'd gotten here, she could get herself away. But she just walked to the door of the cell and tugged at it hopelessly, then turned back around.

His words were meant to keep her away and she knew it. But still, how could she help someone else if she couldn't even help herself? Despite the frustration gripping her, she had never felt like she wanted to know someone more than she did this stranger who didn't feel like a stranger, who was lying on the dirt and filth of the dungeon floor. Levyna watched as he winced in pain and she didn't hesitate as she walked towards him and knelt by his side.

"I told you to stay away!"

"As it appears, I cannot," she answered. "What happened to you?"

Olin looked at her, at her grey eyes. Though they weren't misty now, she still looked like she was fighting tears, or had been crying all day and was only now snapping out of it.

"Watchers," he said. She froze and he didn't miss it.

"Watchers?"

"The Red Flame," he answered. "And the Order of Walrea."

Levyna's brows pinched. "I – I don't understand."

"I stumbled foolishly into something I shouldn't have, something I had no business knowing. The Watchers of Walrea have been after me since – they found me at my uncle's and he died getting me to Queen's Hill through a portal. I'd been trying to find someone he wanted me to find, with help from a ... friend. But as it appears, the Order is everywhere and even he was betrayed. We were ambushed by Watchers of the Red Flame, but I now know that they did so for the watcher from Ravinshore and most certainly the Order of Walrea."

Levyna frowned as she tried to understand. "How is this possible?"

"It's hardly the most impossible thing I will say to you. But I'm telling you this because you won't know otherwise. Just as Wylie – my uncle – sent me through the portal, he told me to find a man by the name of Cyrus."

Levyna's eyes pinched again.

"I assumed this Cyrus would be able to help after I told him what I knew, and then we came looking for him," Olin said, then paused for his breath, "only for me to find him with a watcher, the same one that had attacked me and my uncle. I didn't wait to meet with Cyrus anymore, and the next I heard of him is that he'll be taking —"

"My father's place as Palatine of the Kingdom," Levyna finished. She fell back to sit on the floor. "Cyrus?" she asked in disbelief.

"Yes. And before you ask how I knew that the man I saw with him was a watcher, I'll tell you that I know because ... because I never forget someone's eyes."

"Are you telling me Cyrus could have had something to do with my father's death?"

"I don't know for sure, but what I have seen and what I know makes me think that there is very little that the Order of Walrea cannot do."

"Why?" Levyna asked. "What did my father have to do with the Order of Walrea?"

Olin shook his head. "Perhaps nothing. Perhaps something – there's a chance that he could have just been in the way."

"Of what?"

Olin looked at her, at the confusion in her expression. He was brutally conscious of what had happened to the last person he'd told the truth to.

"Please, tell me."

"I was a sciff for the Order of Walrea in Ravinshore. I'm quite sure that the Order is responsible for King Edmond's illness. They have poisoned him, and will see him dead," Olin said.

"What?"

"I overheard it. That's why they're after me. And I might not have known it before, but the Order of Walrea has the Red Flame have joined forces."

Levyna had so many questions. She was lost, trying to believe what he was telling her. He had been right –

this was definitely impossible. Everyone knew of the watchers. Their business, however, wasn't something normal people heard so casually. If the story was true, that left one question. "The watchers – they don't keep prisoners."

"And I'm not one, not for long anyway. I'm only alive so I can die from the poison in my body if I don't speak by first light." The mention of the poison seemed to stir the pain, and Olin grunted.

Levyna looked at his side and reached for it.

"No."

"Let me see."

"Unless you're a healer, there's nothing you can do."

Levyna ignored his words and took off his shirt, pulling it up to reveal the blackening wound on his side. A wave of pain stabbed through him again, and Olin twisted to his right, causing Levyna's hand to touch his body. Just like the first touch, both of them felt the jolt. But this time it was interrupted by the sound of a key rattling the cell door.

They both glanced at the door at once, then back to each other, realizing what could be coming through.

"Go!"

"Tell me your name."

"It's Olin. Now go!"

***

Levyna opened her eyes to find her mother sitting by her side. There was no panic in Fiona's expression this time as she turned to her daughter.

"I walked in and you were already asleep, I couldn't bring myself to wake you," Fiona said. "I have spoken with the Lord Guardsman of the palace. Perhaps when you are up for it we can have you write down what else you remember about this young man?"

Levyna sat up on her bed, eyes full again. "Mother, I've met him," she said.

Fiona frowned in confusion. "You have? I thought you said —"

"I had another dream just now, and I saw him. No, I *met* him, Mother," Levyna said. "His name is Olin, he's from Ravinshore, and he's in trouble,"

Levyna didn't let her mother question how she'd managed to see another human while dreaming and began telling her mother everything that Olin had told her, about what he knew, about Cyrus and how he could have had a hand her father's death, and finally about the King of Ravinshore and what could become of him.

Fiona was just as incredulous of the story as Levyna herself had been when she'd first heard it, but the part that made it real for her, for them, was how it involved Fredrik and his role as palatine. The role that Cyrus would now occupy.

"I need to help him, Mother. I need to do something," Levyna said.

But what could they do? If it was all true, they were talking about the watchers, not just of the Order of

Walrea, but also of Red Flame. They were talking about the forces of the three kingdoms that were neither seen nor heard but acted nonetheless as they had for hundreds of years.

There was only one thing Fiona think of to do that could possibly mean something. But even that wouldn't be without consequences.

"I don't doubt you or what you've seen, Levyna. Never. But if there's truth to what you've been told, the only thing we can do is tell His Majesty, in Queen's Hill. If the Red Flame is involved, only the king has the power to question or summon them. But should we decide to go to His Majesty we should be prepared to tell the whole story. *All* of it. We might need to tell him how you came to know this. We might have to disclose that you are ..."

"A dreamer. Yes, Mother, I know. But I don't care about that now. How can I? There's a chance that the Order had a hand in my father's death. There's a chance that the King of Ravinshore is in danger and the only person who knows the truth is going to be killed. I don't think I care what becomes of me now," Levyna said.

Fiona knew from the way her daughter spoke that there would be no stopping her from whatever she wanted to do, even if she didn't know what it would mean. Fiona also knew that nothing her daughter had said was wrong.

***

Mother and daughter walked side by side towards the throne room to meet with King Ranald. They both wore black garments without the hoods. Fiona glanced at her daughter to make sure Levyna hadn't had a change of heart, hoping at least she would agree for Fiona to go alone. As she watched, her daughter's face flushed and she froze. Fiona looked ahead and saw why.

"Lady Fiona, Levyna. I ... did not know I would be seeing you here. Is everything okay? You should be in your quarters, being tended to at this time."

Fiona took her daughter's hand and felt it stiffen around hers as they faced the man that could have had a hand in her husband's death. A man they had once thought to be Fredrik's loyal hand and good friend, who had taken over his position even before his body was cold in the ground. Fiona swallowed hard as Cyrus studied them both.

"Are you going somewhere?" Cyrus asked.

"Yes," Fiona answered. "To see His Majesty."

"At this time? Is everything okay?"

"Yes, but it is a matter of urgency. He is expecting us."

"Oh." Cyrus nodded. "Is that so? Well, then I guess we are headed the same way – I also have an urgent matter to discuss with His Majesty," Cyrus answered. "And could I suggest that perhaps you tell me this matter is so that I may relay it him —"

"No," Fiona said. "I mean, it's better we talk to him in person."

"Yes, of course. I just thought to mention that since you know ... I'm the new Palatine of the Kingdom, His Majesty would confide in me about many things."

Levyna squeezed her mother's hand and Fiona got the message. Before Fiona could respond to Cyrus, she was pulled by the weight of her daughter collapsing by her side.

"Levyna!"

THIRTY

H e had known to expect it. At some point, death would be a part of his mission. And it would be his refuge in the event of capture.

But after getting off the Flea in Edenborough, he hadn't been prepared for what had become of him afterwards. His trip to the city on the other side of the sea hadn't been simply another mission for the Order. When he'd been found and captured by guards in Edenborough for killing a merchant aboard the ship, he had, for the small time his captivity had lasted, basked in the irony of the fact that he was being held for murder, only this time he hadn't committed the crime.

He'd known it would be hard to prove he wasn't guilty. He neither had the time, nor could he risk the possibility of anyone learning his true identity.

Captivity had been unusual, but it had only been a matter of waiting for his chance, and then taking it. Pretending to collapse, dripping blood from his mouth after biting his own lip, and then remaining unresponsive on the ground had been enough to draw the attention of the guards. It had been simple for him to knock the investigating guard to the floor by taking out his legs and then strangle the life out of him.

His path after that had been effortless – wearing the dead guard's clothes and using it to get himself out of the cells. He'd had to knock one more guard unconscious before he'd made it out of the dungeon, but had ended up escaping on same day he'd been captured.

He'd only been able to recover his scarf and his satchel, but he didn't need anything more to resume his journey to the center of the continent, trailing one man.

It took him less than a day to find who he was looking for, and when he did he wasted no time trying to make it look decent or godly. He traced the wastrel to a tavern, where he was boasting about riches he didn't possess and a passion he couldn't give, telling the cheap ladies of the many things he could do for them, if only they knew who he was.

Black Scarf followed him to the back of the tavern where he was taking a piss and, when the good-for-nothing man realized he was there, Black Scarf didn't give him the chance to make a sound before he slashed the man's throat and then cut his face so many times his body would never be identified.

The only thing Black Scarf thought as he returned to the shadows, then moved down the street of Edenborough, was how much he would have loved to tell his sister that the low-life she'd married, the one who'd abandoned her to live a new life in Edenborough, was dead. He would have liked to tell her that the city of Edenborough would talk about him for years, and men and women alike would wonder what crime the man had committed when they learned that it hadn't only been his face and his throat that were slit.

His crime had been taking Black Scarf's sister as a bride, using her, getting her pregnant, and then absconding with all of her money.

Black Scarf's only consolation was that he knew she would find out eventually – in several days, or a fortnight, or a month. She wouldn't know that he'd done it of course, but she was bound to hear of it, of a the man found mutilated behind a tavern with what was left of his manhood stuffed in his mouth. And soon enough she would realize that it was the bastard she had cursed every day for months and vowed to end with her own hands.

Black Scarf returned to Duken on a different ship the day after and headed straight for his sister's house. He wouldn't tell her what he'd done, but he needed to be sure that she was okay. But when he arrived, and opened the door to the house, all he found was a woman holding a bowl and giving him a fearful look before turning away hurriedly.

Black Scarf turned. "Where is she?" he asked, moving his hands to sign his question to the man that had came up behind him. Black Scarf wasn't deaf, but the man said nothing, and then he signed again. "Where. Is. My. Sister?" he demanded.

The man looked uncertain, until Black Scarf grabbed him by the shirt and held him against the door.

"She's dead. I – I'm sorry," the man finally answered.

Black Scarf didn't believe it. He freed the man, looking frantically around the house, then ran to his sister's room. Empty. He went back outside, sinking to the floor as he pulled the scarf from his head.

"What happened to her?"

"She – she was out on a job with the others. I couldn't go because I ate something bad and was unwell all day. But then she came back, alone. Bleeding."

"She went on the road? With those men?"

"You know your sister – they couldn't say no to her. She terrified them, terrified all of us. They all left early, but it was just her, alone, who rode back. She said the others were all dead, that they tried to steal from a couple of travelers from Ravinshore, but didn't know one of them was a crazy sorceress. She said the Maedrian woman killed the rest and tossed her away. She landed on her belly and only managed to get home, blood pooling between her legs. She died before the healer could help. I'm sorry."

The heartbreak was worse than Black Scarf had imagined. He had known something like this would eventually happen, but he'd thought it would be later. Even before his sister had been carrying a child, he'd warned her about of the company of bandits she'd taken up with a few days after she realized that her husband was gone for good. She hadn't ever listened to anything he'd told her about her choice of affairs, not even after she'd grown heavy with child. He'd thought she had finally agreed to take a break, at least until she gave birth, but his sister had gone ahead and done as she pleased, just like she always had.

Black Scarf asked what had happened to the Maedrian sorceress and he was told that she'd escaped with her escort, which allowed his sister to get away too.

He went to her grave after learning where she was buried. Beneath the ground in front of him was the only person he'd ever truly cared about. Though he had never told her what he truly was, he thought she'd always suspected. With both hands, he grabbed the scarf that was an embodiment of who he was, a cloak for his watch, the piece of cloth he'd killed the jailer in Edenborough over, the same cloth his sister had given him the winter he'd lost his voice as a teenager. And it felt as though the ache of the voicelessness came anew.

***

Otto, Lord Watcher of Duken's Order of the Three, was standing in front of a mirror as Black Scarf walked through the door, with no regard for where he was. But after a few steps, Black Scarf stopped midway as he realized his error and swallowed hard, chest heaving as he waited for his Lord Watcher to beckon.

"What is it?" Otto asked without turning.

Black Scarf stepped towards the Lord Watcher, where he signed the rage inside of him. "My Lord, I need to go to Ravinshore, and I need the Order of Walrea's blessing."

"Why? What is your business in Ravinshore?"

"◻There is someone there who has taken something from me, and I need to take the same thing from them," he signed.

"Who is this person? And why can it not wait?" the Lord Watcher asked.

"A bloody Maedrian sorceress who traveled from Ravinshore to Duken. She killed my sister. I will make her pay."

Otto was quiet for a moment. "I am sorry about your sister, but you understand that things are far from quiet at the moment. We are bound to start by dawn —"

"She was pregnant!" Black Scarf signed, placing his hand on his belly. "Seven months with child! And both of them are gone – mother and child! I never ask for anything, but I ask for this – I need to make this right, and I need to do it with my own hands!"

The Lord Watcher exhaled, seeing the watcher's eyes glimmering with the kind of rage he knew had the tendency to bring annihilation to a man's foe, but also to the man himself.

"Did you say a Maedrian sorceress in Ravinshore?" a voice came from the mirror in front of them, and they both turned. The masked face of Walrea's Lord Watcher appeared in the mirror.

"Yes," Black Scarf answered. "There aren't many Maedrians in the three kingdoms, fewer who are sorceresses and even fewer who would dare walk into Duken with magic. She was escorted from Ravinshore, by a King's Guard."

Thorne knew who the watcher was talking about. The Maedrian sorceress had been one of the two strange faces he'd seen at the king's bedside earlier. He was almost certain of it. As the watcher had said: a Maedrian mage was rare in the kingdom. And what other reason would a Maedrian mage have of a King's Guard as an escort, if she wasn't employed by the crown?

"I have your sorceress. I have seen her. I know where she is – in the palace here in Ravinshore. One of the reasons I'm furious now. She and some other sorceress have tried to thwart my plan, but it won't happen. And you are not going to help them by interfering."

"She killed my sister!" Black Scarf signed.

"And you're a Watcher of the Three! Remember that!" Otto said. "It is the Order before anything else, including your own life."

Black Scarf lips pursed tightly under his mask as he stared at the Lord Watcher. He didn't need to be reminded of that. Not by him, not now.

"You will get your revenge, watcher. I promise you that," Thorne said.

"When? How?" Black Scarf demanded.

"When all of this is over, you will be free to hunt her however you choose, wherever she goes. She will have no place to hide in all of the three kingdoms, and there will be no stopping you from doing what you want to her. Nothing. Once we have succeeded and the Order takes power from the crown, you will have no restrictions. But before then, for just a little longer, you must wait. Serve the Order, then serve yourself, watcher," Thorne promised.

Black Scarf looked from the Lord Watcher of Walrea to his own Lord Watcher standing next to him. They had clearly decided. They wouldn't hear anything else of it, and his only choice was to wait. He exhaled, bowed sharply, and walked away.

Once he was out the door, Black Scarf thought about Otto's words again: *the Order before anything else, including your own life.* But not before that of his sister.

THIRTY-ONE

P osdel woke to an empty house. His first thought was how long his apprentice was going to continue serving the sciff from Ravinshore, pretending his life didn't exist. He peeled himself from the bed and walked to the hall to look around. The sword was gone and there was a satchel on the floor close to the hearth.

It took a moment for the words to come back to him, but they did. He had heard the conversation, barely. He knew who the satchel belonged to. Posdel ignored it and turned towards the shelf, searching for some demon rum to awaken his senses. As he reached to grab the bottle of liquor, an odor assaulted his nose. He raised his arm again to sniff, then blinked hard and abandoned the bottle.

"Yond —" Posdel stopped himself. He'd almost forgotten that Yondi wasn't here. He walked back to the room, removed his tunic, and dipped a corner in a small washing basin and wiped each of his armpits. He wiped his neck, his belly, then dipped his hand into the bowl and washed his face. He dried up with the same cloth and found himself another tunic. Finally, he stepped out the room, still struggling to put on his tunic, when he spotted the figure running towards the house from the window. What trouble had Yondi finally managed to get himself into now?

"Master Posdel! Master Posdel!" Giodin shouted, skidding to a stop at the door, hand raised to knock and freezing just as the door opened.

"What is it this time, Giodin?" Posdel asked.

The merchant blinked. "It – it's Yondi, Master."

"I know." Posdel pulled down his shirt as turned towards the house. "What has he gotten himself into now?"

The instant silence from a man who was typically wordy caused Posdel to turn around. He met Giodin's bleak face, his lips pushed up against his mustache and his brows crooked.

"What has happened?" The urgency in the question was prevalent this time, as Posdel realized the true meaning of the merchant's silence.

*

After running all the way from the house, Posdel shoved between the small crowd that had gathered. He slowed and stumbled when he caught sight of of his apprentice lying face down on the floor of the alley in a stream of dark red blood. Posdel could hardly blink as he lowered himself to the ground next to Yondi, kneeling by his body as he placed a hand over his head.

The whispers rained around them and he could hear them all – a quarrel. An accident. Chaos. Obviously. Watchers. That word stung Posdel's ears. He knew. He was conscious of what Yondi's guest had come bearing, that danger that his apprentice had taken as his own problem. Posdel had known of the possibilities and yet he had hoped that ... what had he hoped? That Olin and his problems would disappear? Or that they would find an answer and that would be it? Had he hoped that they would wait for him? Had he hoped Yondi would wait to hear his absent self tell him whether or not he should chase the truth while he ... while he filtered away the images that haunted him by knocking himself out. Images that had been there for years and would continue to be there.

The last thing Posdel had said to his apprentice was that if he was so desperate to help, he should offer to go into the den of the beast on Olin's behalf. Posdel looked up, realizing that his apprentice's body was the only one lying on the road. Olin, the one the watchers wanted, was missing, or dead.

The wagon came and Giodin didn't need to ask for hands. Most of the crowd had known the lively young man, had probably suffered one or two of his harmless shenanigans. Yondi's body was lifted off the street and Posdel watched, still, as his apprentice was laid in the back.

He looked up, above the wagon, and standing not far from the slowly dissipating crowd, he saw a face that caught his attention. Posdel watched as Moreen disappeared.

***

Posdel waited around the corner. When Moreen turned and caught sight of his face, he pinned her to the wall of the building with a wave of his hand before she could run. She groaned but met his eyes, resigned. Her satchel was strapped across her body – she had been to the house and back. Posdel could see from the redness in her eyes that she had been crying, but that wasn't his interest.

"What happened?" he asked.

Moreen shook her head and her breath stuttered as she fumbled the words in her head.

"You came visiting and suddenly he's dead and you're leaving? What the bloody hell happened, Moreen?"

"I – I didn't know. I swear I didn't know."

"You didn't know what?" Posdel stepped closer.

Moreen tried to peel herself away but his spell held firm.

"It wasn't supposed to happen that way. He – he wasn't supposed to get hurt ..."

"You knew about this? You had a hand in it?"

"I had no choice. They told me Yondi was in danger, and that I needed to get the other one – Olin – I needed to get him out so they could get to him. I was promised nothing would happen to Yondi. He was never supposed to get hurt."

"You led them to your cousin? Your own blood? You worked with the watchers? Those vile beings?"

But she couldn't avoid working with the Red Flame. Just like she could never become a member of Duken's King's Guards. Not since she had been taken by the Red Flame and chosen to become part of the Order. This had supposed to have been part of her test, to prove that she was prepared to do anything for the Order. Her cousin had never supposed to have been part of it. She had been ordered to approach and confirm that Olin was indeed in Master Posdel's house. It had been just her luck that she hadn't had to ask him to leave the safety of the house – he'd done that on his own.

"You betrayed your own blood because you were foolish enough to think that an Order could be trusted?" Posdel asked. 'And you thought that would be where it ended?"

Moreen sobbed, realizing she hadn't known as much as she should have when she'd accepted the invitation to join the Red Flame. She thought of everything it had just taken from her, beginning to comprehend Posdel's meaning. Then she realized she was free, the mage's spell had relaxed and she peeled herself from the wall to escape.

Before she could, a knife flew from the shadows and sunk into her neck, and Moreen gripped her throat, dropping to the ground. Posdel did nothing to stop her. His spun towards the building behind them, where a figure was quickly pulling back. Posdel drew threads of enchantment into a ball in his hands, rage in his eyes.

* * *

Levyna felt the earth come alive beneath her feet and her breath heaved as though her chest would collapse. She looked around, realizing she was in an alien place. She didn't recognize it – the walls and the stones of the ground looked different from what she was familiar with. Nothing made sense, until she turned to see a guard walking up to her.

"Who are you and why are you there? No trespassers allowed," the guard said.

Levyna's eyes widened. He was clearly a guard, but he wasn't dressed anything like the guards of the Queen's Hill or the palace she was familiar with. She had no idea what to say to the man, or how to explain how she had ended up wherever she was.

"She's with me," a voice said from behind her and Levyna turned sharply again to find yet another face she didn't know. This time it was a woman, dressed in a mantle just like she was.

The guard's brows furrowed at Gytha, who stopped next to Levyna.

"I am Her Majesty's special emissary and she is with me," Gytha said again.

The guard bowed and turned away.

"Walk with me, now. Don't look back," Gytha said. Levyna turned at once and followed her. The pair walked in silence until Gytha opened a door to an unoccupied room and led them in.

"Who are you?" Gytha asked the terrified girl.

"Levyna, from Queen's Hill," she answered.

"What are you doing here?"

"I – I don't know how I got here. I was in the palace in Queen's Hill a moment ago and then all of a sudden I ..."

"Did you portal?"

Levyna's brows furrowed and she shook her head. "I don't ... know. I didn't do anything."

"So you just appeared here, out of nothing? Have you done this before?" Gytha asked.

Yes, Levyna thought, *less than an hour earlier*. She had been in her bed and then she'd been in the dungeon with a stranger. With Olin. Out loud, she said, "Once, today, while I was asleep. I found myself somewhere in my dream, but it wasn't a dream. I really was there."

Gytha's brows rose as she studied Levyna. She stepped closer and took Levyna's face in her hand, peering into her eyes. "I've only ever heard about your kind in stories, Levyna."

"My kind?"

"Yes. What you are is a marvelous being of magic. You're a traveler, Levyna."

"A traveler?" The question was on her face. Levyna had never heard that term before, except for the normal way as a name for someone who journeyed across a kingdom.

"Yes, your magic is ... unique. It's rare. It allows you to go to places by merely thinking about it. There's much more to learn about it, but that's what it means."

"So I'm not a dreamer?"

Gytha nearly gasped. She frowned as she stared at Levyna. "What makes you think you're a dreamer?"

"Because I've been having dreams of people dying. Ones that have been coming to pass," Levyna answered; her voice was more subdued than when she'd talked about her traveling.

"Goodness." Gytha shook her head, stepped close, and took Levyna's face with both hands again, as if to be sure she was real.

Levyna was here, truly, even if there was some semblance of her somewhere in Queen's Hill at the same moment. Gytha had never met a traveler before, and definitely had never heard of someone who was both a traveler and a dreamer. It wasn't just rare – it never happened. But as much as Gytha wanted to gawk at this unique power, she had a feeling there was a reason Levyna had appeared in Ravinshore's palace without trying.

"Who are you?" Levyna asked.

"My name is Gytha and I am a Grand Sorceress from Duken. I felt you the moment you arrived and I followed the pull to the passage at once."

"Do you sense every person with magic like that?"

"Some, and others that call to me. So why did you call to me, Levyna? Why are you suddenly in the palace in Ravinshore?"

Levyna had apparently not realized where she was; the shock was apparent in her expression as her eyes grew wide. If what the sorceress said was true and she was a traveler moving wherever her mind takes her, then it would make sense that she'd ended up in the place she'd been thinking about ever since her meeting with Olin. This was the palace where King Edmond was, this was where Olin wanted to take the truth of the Order's conspiracy.

Levyna looked into Gytha's eyes, uncertain and cautious. She remembered all too well the reason her and her mother had stopped at the corridor on the way to meet King Ranald. Cyrus. How could she really know who she was talking to?

"Are you going to tell me?" Gytha asked.

"Will you tell me why a Grand Sorceress from Duken is the one who found me here?" Levyna said instead.

Gytha's face might not show it, but she was impressed by Levyna's prudence. It reminded her somewhat of her own self. "I was brought here to help heal the king of something very vile. And it's only by chance that I was the one to find you."

"I – I don't think it's by chance," Levyna said, stuttering in shock. "I would say that it's fate. The king was poisoned, wasn't he?"

"And how do you know that?"

"Someone told me. He's the reason I'm here. He told me he learned something. Heard some people talking about the king's misadventure and how it has to be permanent for their greater cause. He was discovered, and forced to run, lost his uncle and a friend, and now he's trapped in a dungeon where he's dying from a poisoned blade. An injury from the hands of watchers."

Gytha's face went bleak. "Did you say watchers?"

"Yes." Levyna nodded. "The Order of Walrea are after King Edmond's life, and they have somehow gotten to the Red Flame. Even my own father might have died because of it. But they have this young man now, back there in Queen's Hill."

Gytha's went slack with shock as realization hit her – it was no longer difficult to wonder how Egro had found its way to the king. The brash presence of the Lord Watcher in the king's chamber made more sense now. The danger had been totally underestimated.

"Olin is still in Queen's Hill. I – I can somehow ... feel him there still," Levyna said, rubbing at her arm.

Gytha's heart dropped and her eyes pinned the younger woman. "What did you just call him?"

"Olin."

THIRTY-TWO

Olin was expecting it at any moment. He'd fought as long as he could, but it was only a matter of time before his fate caught up to him. There was no denying it.

Even if there was a way to save himself, a part of him would hesitate, wondering if he even deserved to be saved. Regardless of who had held the weapons, Olin knew that it was his fault, because he hadn't been able stop trying to know it all. He had caused everything. His actions had killed his uncle and then a stranger who had become a friend.

On the floor in the dungeon, Olin felt the cold of the night slowly creep in, taking him with the promise of dawn. It was only a matter of time now.

Olin thought about her – the mysterious girl who'd appeared in his cell and then disappeared. She actually disappeared. He'd looked away to the door for a heartbeat, and she had been suddenly gone. He'd thought he must have been dreaming – perhaps the poison in his body making him see things. Perhaps it was a sign he was dying faster than he'd been told. But he couldn't stop thinking about how real it had all felt, how real the conversation had been, and how present she had been when their hands had touched.

But if she was real, what did that mean? Help? He would prefer to let the silence and cold consume him before one other person died because he'd been nothing but a snoopy bastard. The other part of him, the part that didn't want to die on the dungeon floor, was trying to remind him that the fate of Ravinshore still depended on him. The kingdom would die with him if help didn't come. If the young woman in the nightdress didn't come back.

At the Bastion of the Flame, which had been the Red Flame's stronghold for centuries, a watcher saw a pair of his comrades patrolling the passageway when they suddenly dropped to their knees, gasping before they were thrown against opposite walls. The watcher pulled his knives, caution on his masked face as he stepped surreptitiously around a bend in the corridor. He peered from where he was pressed against the side of the wall, blade held close to his chest. His face twisted when he couldn't find anything. The corridor was lit by the torches on the walls, but there was no one in sight. Then the torch flames' danced aggressively, disturbed by something passing by. The watcher turned swiftly, only to stiffen and fall to his knees as his insides were crushed by an unseen hand.

Gytha manifested from nothing as the watcher fell to the ground, lifeless. On the Grand Sorceress's face was a storm that couldn't be quenched; in her eyes was a fire prepared to consume whatever wandered into her path.

"Exionis!" she said as she walked away, and behind her the bodies of the watchers caught fire.

Before she got far, a half a dozen masked watchers appeared in her path, poised for an attack. The sorceress released a concussive pulse, but it was quickly shielded by a mage watcher prepared to match her, grunting as he thwarted Gytha's attempt. The mage stepped in front of the group, hands poised. The watchers behind him watched in horror as those arms suddenly fell limp at the elbows, then his knees followed suit. They heard the sound of the mage's bones breaking as he landed face-down, body bent grotesquely.

While Gytha dealt with the wayward mage, the watchers took advantage, sending three daggers flying in her direction. Gytha's hands didn't leave her side, but all the knives stopped midflight, then turned and darted back at the unsuspecting watchers. The watchers remaining didn't get the chance to decide whether or not to engage, as each of their daggers suddenly unsheathed and buried themselves in their own throats.

An arrow flew through a nearby door, missing her by inches. Gytha glanced up. The wooden slab around the door shattered into pieces, flying to hit the bowmen, a masked archer who wasn't in uniform standing inside the room.

Gytha heard the sound of someone hitting the wall behind her and she turned to see a scraggly-looking man with the residue of enchantment thread in his hands. It appeared he'd stoned a watcher against a pillar. Their eyes met before Gytha vanished.

Posdel followed suit towards the dungeons, arriving in time to see Gytha breaking the first door down, still without raising a hand.

Behind the door, several yards inside, stood a watcher, much taller than the diminutive ones Gytha had disposed of in the hall. He was guarding a cell door. Gytha saw what he was holding, and knew he was the one she was here to destroy. She watched as he lifted the sword in his right hand, and glanced into the cell.

"I will have his head before you —"

Posdel stood by as the sorceress disappeared, only to manifest behind L, whose eyes hadn't even been quick enough to follow the attack. Before he could turn, his head slid off his body and he dropped.

Gytha stood above his remains, gripping Wylie's sword, which she had taken from him, in her hand. She moved quickly into the cell to collapse by Olin's side.

Olin had been waiting for the silence to take him, but had been woken by the sound his tormentor being decapitated by a figure in a cloak. His vision blurred, and he frowned as the figure slowly knelt by his side. He squinted in the barely lit cell. It wasn't the girl in the nightdress – this woman had different hair. He heard her let out a breath, then she took his face in warm hands that felt like life. Olin blinked, and her eyes came into focus as his breath faded.

"Olinander ..." she called in a soft, teary voice.

It couldn't be. Was this the silence?

"M – Mother?"

* * *

Ilda watched a man who'd had too much to drink wave his hands, beginning to wander towards the young woman serving his table. Ilda prayed he would make the mistake of touching her, so she could have a reason to do something fun tonight. She pierced the man with her gaze. His friends noticed the murderous intent in her eyes, as they began cautioning him quickly, pointing to the bar where she was waiting. It was good they knew to not misbehave in her presence, but Ilda wished that she'd gotten the chance to break the bones of the man's hand.

The serving girl returned to the bar just as Ilda felt a breeze sneak in from the kitchen. She stepped away to the back, to find that the door was still locked but the window had found its way open. She stared at the ominous sight for a moment before she closed it.

Ilda turned to leave, but stopped short, staring at the floor in front of her. She bent to pick up a crow's black feather. She swallowed hard. She knew what it meant. But for it to be on the floor so suddenly made her think it could be simply a coincidence.

Undecided, Ilda returned to the bar, where the serving girl handed her coins from a customer. This time Ilda didn't doubt the crow emblem on the side of one of the silver pieces. She looked up, catching sight of the customer disappearing outside into the approaching dusk. Ilda glanced at her daughter, asleep behind the bar, and sighed, knowing she would leave soon. The mark had been sent for the crows to fly in Ravinshore.

* * *

Edmond was no longer ghostly pale and his breathing had returned to the rhythm of life, but he was still asleep. His eyes had yet to open.

Queen Ariana grasped her husband's hand, clinging to the hope that Gytha was right and Edmond had been healed. Ariana had hoped, after the shaking had passed, that terrifying moment where the entire palace had felt his spasms, that he would open his eyes and she would be relieved. But Gytha had urged a little more patience. Hopefully not as much as she'd had to endure before. Gytha had said the king was free of the Egro, and that all that remained was for his life force to take back his body. This sleep was a good thing, Ariana had been told. In time he would wake. He hadn't broken any bones. Ariana had been tempted to demand why Gytha couldn't simply make him wake, but despite how desperate the queen had grown, she knew that the Grand Sorceress would have done so, had she thought it wise, or had it been possible.

Edmond was no longer dying, but it was still hard. The sun had set on yet on another day where Ariana hadn't seen him open his eyes and look at her. She consoled herself that his life force had returned to his body because he had survived, because the king was made of something special and had been able to hold off the Egro until help arrived. All Ariana had to do now was to believe completely that he was coming back to her, to his children. To his kingdom.

Darkness had fallen. Ariana could almost hear the howling of the Urlyin wolves in the distance, waiting, even if they couldn't see their faces. She thought of her children, guarded and safe in their chambers. She thought of the chance that there was another enemy stalking the shadows of the palace.

The Queen of Ravinshore heard a creak from the window of the chamber.

* * *

If Ole could keep watch by the king's door, he would. But the entire corridor was already lined with guardsmen who wouldn't blink an eye all day. Ole downed the rest of the wine in his hand, setting the cup on the table and walking to the window of his bedchamber. He opened it and peered out into the evening. The grounds surrounding the palace were dead quiet and barren of wanderers, save for the guardsmen standing at their posts. He could see a few from here and Ole breathed deep, only it didn't seem to help.

The air was cold but Ole didn't mind. If there was a chance the chill would keep the image of what he'd seen away from his mind, then he would take it. But Ole doubted it would do anything but remind him to keep the window shut before he fell asleep tonight.

The palace was the quietest he could remember it being in a while. Not that nuisances roamed often, but this silence held the weight of something looming.

The poisoner taking his own life had carried the message with his act rather than with his words. The Order's intent had been thwarted today, but it seemed very much to still linger in the air. And with the chill, it saturated the walls of the palace, as if to remind them all that stillness didn't always mean peace. Stillness and quiet could usher in chaos.

Ole jerked his head to the side as the wind whistled and the cup dropped from the table behind him.

* * *

Thunderclaps seasoned the sky and the winds came heavy. A storm was on the horizon. Rain followed and soon, the sound of the windows slapping against the wall concurred with the rhythm of an eventful night. The old guardsman stepped out his bedchamber towards the hall, where he called out to the servant. Silence answered. He moved to shut the windows as harsh winds battered the walls. He pulled the first shut and reached for the second, but drew his hand away seeing the stain on his palm. It wasn't just rain. He lifted it to his face and it shimmered in the faltering flame of the lamp behind him.

He turned, eyes widening with the realization of what it was. Too late. A masked figure stood in front of him. There was a swift slash before he could defend himself. The blow split his neck open, and the Queen's Hill Commander of the King's Guards grabbed his throat with his already bloodied hand as he fell back against the window. He gargled futility till he went quiet against the wall. The rain pummeled his body.

* * *

Ariana watched the chamberlain leave after locking the windows. He closed the door to the king's chamber and she returned her attention to her husband. Then she saw the figure standing in the middle of the room. With a gasp, Ariana sprung to her feet, a scream at the tip of her tongue.

"Please, I'm terribly sorry for intruding, Your Grace. But there is something you need to know," Levyna said.

THIRTY-THREE

"The ones you have to be wary of are the same ones meant to protect His Majesty and your kingdom. I've brought this to you because the young man who discovered it days ago has been hunted across Ravinshore and Queen's Hill and has now been captured. The Order of Walrea is responsible for the king's illness, Your Grace, and I believe it will not end there."

Levyna went on to tell Queen Ariana about Olin and his quest to deliver the truth to Ravinshore, including the trouble he was now facing. She hoped Gytha would be able to reach him in time. Before she'd vanished suddenly, Gytha had asked Levyna to make sure that the queen knew the truth.

A thunderclap sounded. Levyna flung open her eyes. She knew at once that she was back in her bed chamber, as if she'd merely been asleep.

Levyna turned to see her mother talking to a healer. The healer noticed she was awake, and nudged Fiona. Fiona held her daughter, moving her hands to her face, thankful that her daughter was well. In a routine she had become familiar with, Fiona dismissed the healer and the maid.

"You had me scared to death, Levyna," she said, the panic almost drowning the relief in her voice. "I half lost my mind even before the healer told me she couldn't be sure what had happened to you besides being faint from the strain about your father."

"I'm sorry for the trouble, Mother. But I'm as fine as I can possibly be with everything going on."

"What happened? You must tell me."

"I was in Ravinshore this time, Mother. It appears I am a traveler," Levyna said as her mother settled on the bed next to her. "I found myself at the palace in Ravinshore, where I met a Grand Sorceress who felt my power. I told her what had happened and she told me what I was. She said I'm a traveler, that I'm able to move to wherever my mind wants."

"Wherever?"

"Yes. I don't know for sure what else there is to it. Both times it's happened has been when I felt the need to help Olin."

"So this could happen again?" Fiona asked.

"I don't know. She didn't get the chance to tell me how it works truly or how I can control it. After I told her about Olin being in danger, she left at once to find him and I ..."

"What is it, Levyna?"

"I think I need to find him too, Mother," Levyna said.

Fiona's face pulled and she shook her head slowly. "Why? Even after everything you know, and the kind of danger that surrounds him, even with everything you're going through?"

"I wouldn't have known the truth of what happened Father had I not met Olin. And if I hadn't wandered to Ravinshore on his behalf, I wouldn't know what I am. I know I'm grieving, Mother, but finding answers seems to be the best thing I can do to keep myself together right now. Otherwise I would force myself to wilt away in this chamber while the enemy roams free. To be truthful, Mother, I don't know how I could sit here, not when a part of me can leave whenever I feel like it. Not when I feel a burning urge to find Olin," Levyna answered, looking down at her hands.

Fiona stared at her daughter. This was all linked to her husband's death. Perhaps this was all a different form of grieving for Levyna. Fiona still felt guilty for taking the dreams for granted and the consequences that had befallen them because of that. But the reality was that her daughter was caught in the middle of the affairs of the Red Flame and Walrea. Fiona felt like a mother who was being asked to listen to the impossible.

"I have told Queen Ariana of Ravinshore."

"You have?"

"She knows. About Walrea and whatever plan they might have. She knows everything I know, everything Olin could tell me. King Edmond is no longer dying, but he's not awake yet. She knows to prepare herself and her children."

"Perhaps in the morning we could tell His Majesty. I couldn't bring myself to it after you fell."

Levyna nodded. "Perhaps. But if I'm not able to, then it will be your burden to bear, Mother. Because I need to find Olin."

***

Olin was sure he had died. What he'd seen in the dungeon before falling unconscious was even more unbelievable than Levyna appearing again.

He opened his eyes to a familiar sight, one that dug up a fresh ache. His hands were free of the shackles. It took him only a moment to realize that the pain in his side had eased and he no longer felt like choking on his breath. He stirred and sat up.

"You will do well to remain resting."

Olin turned to where a seemingly sober Posdel was standing by a table, busy with a mortar and pestle. A familiar jar of oro sat next to him. Olin swallowed hard. He was lost. He didn't know how to begin to explain, and simply silently watched as Posdel abandoned the pestle, picked up a small bottle from the shelf, and poured its contents in a small cup.

"Take, drink," he said, walking over and handing him the cup.

Olin took it, glanced at the contents for a moment, but asked no questions as he downed it. It tasted awful but he didn't feel like he any right to complain. Posdel returned to the table and silence ensued for a long moment before Olin heard his voice again.

"If you wish to throw up, don't do it on the bed or you'll have to clean it yourself."

"I don't."

"Good."

"I ... It was my fault."

"No, it was not."

"If I hadn't forced him to help me at the river, if he hadn't brought me here. If I hadn't involved him at all, he would still be alive. He would still be here."

Posdel scoffed. "You give yourself too much of a credit, sciff. To think that you made Yondi do anything. You did not. He was my apprentice for years. I've known him since he was a scruffy little boy on the street and there was never anyone who could make him do anything he didn't want to. Yondi had been taken by something, by you or by the idea of you, by the mystery and adventure you brought. That was what sold him, otherwise he would have abandoned you by the river if he wasn't interested.

"Yondi was a piece of work. You might not have noticed, but he had a way of getting what he wanted. There was nothing you could have done once he decided to help you. Not you." Posdel shook his head. "I, on the other hand ... I could perhaps have done something. When you came, I knew where this was headed." He turned to Olin. "I knew it was a matter of time before the Order found what they were after. I just ... I was too distracted to realize the extent of it. I thought they would get to you, because Yondi was always going to be harder to kill. But then I reckon they found the one weakness he had – his damn heart – and they used her to get to him."

"Why did she betray him?"

"She was one of them, or at least she thought she was. They wanted you, and Yondi was never going to abandon the adventure."

"I should have insisted on going with her alone."

"If you are so desperate to torture yourself, then by all means continue trying to argue about a boy I've known for years. You only knew him for a few days. He was my responsibility, if anything. I was the one who should have realized the moment she walked into the house." Posdel began grinding more of a black substance Olin didn't recognize. Then he cocked his head. "She merely dragged him down with her. Foolish – thinking she could ever trust the Order."

The mention of the Order made Olin remember. With a jolt, he got on his feet.

"The Order – how did you get me here? Why even am I back here?" Olin asked.

Posdel looked up from what he was doing and glanced Olin, who was already standing on his feet. "You were wrong, do you know?"

"W – what?"

"There's no way you should be able to talk, let alone stand on your feet, if you truly have nothing to do with magic."

Olin sighed. "Why are you talking about this again?"

"Because you're on your feet, even after you've been healed from a wound that should have put you down for a day. Instead you're walking. And what I saw today explains much. I had help getting you here, very powerful help. She healed you and enchanted the house. No one is getting in unless I say so."

Olin's heart thudded. *She.* He hadn't been dreaming after all. The woman had really come into the cell. But how could he know it had really been who he thought?

"You've never mentioned that your mother was a Grand Sorceress."

It was exactly who he'd thought.

"I didn't know I had a mother who was a Grand Sorceress," Olin answered. "I didn't know I still had a mother."

Posdel didn't look interested in the details. "Well, whatever happened, she tore through the Bastion of the Red Flame to reach you. I didn't quite know what would become of me if I couldn't prove I wasn't in her way."

"Where is she?" Olin asked the obvious question as if to challenge to the man's praise of her.

"She did what she had to, but couldn't stay. I didn't argue with her."

Olin's expression grew grave as he turned away. Feeling a wave of dizziness, he slowly lowered himself to the bed. She was gone again, just like that. Like a storm that pulled things apart and left in silence. "Did she tell you how she ... how did she find me?"

"A traveler."

"Traveler?"

"Yes. She said a traveler appeared in Ravinshore's palace and told her about you. She'd said she found you and you were in trouble, and told your mother everything about the Orders and the watchers."

Was that what she had been? A traveler? The girl in the nightdress. Levyna. She had found a way to help him after all.

"I will admit, even I didn't know travelers still existed."

"What are they?"

"Mages who are able to move across distances with the power of their mind."

"Can't everyone?"

Posdel shook his head. "Oh no, not this way. Normal people don't move wherever they wish in an instant, casting their mind across kingdoms while their body remains in place. Normal mages don't find their way into dreams. Mages create portals to move across distances, but a traveler could take themselves just about anywhere. Even though a traveler's specter is more of an essence outside their true body, they still feel just as real. They haven't existed for centuries or more. I've never seen one. But one found her way to the Ravinshore palace and told the Grand Sorceress about you."

"She was in the dungeon. It felt like a dream."

"It could have been one. Reality is the one you know. It happened outside consciousness; it doesn't make it unreal."

Olin had more questions that he couldn't put into words at the moment. The most important thing was the fact that the Order was still out there and their intentions hadn't been thwarted. Risking abandonment, scorn, and a whole lot of other consequences, Olin said, "I need to get to Ravinshore, tell the crown what the watchers have done and what they have planned."

Posdel turned back to his table and continued grinding his powder. "A few days ago those words were foolish. Now, not so much. But the Grand Sorceress knows, and she was at the palace with the traveler."

"Levyna."

"Who?"

"The traveler, her name is Levyna," Olin said.

"Well, Levyna told the Grand Sorceress, and I have a feeling that didn't end with her decapitating your captor," Posdel answered. "The crown must know by now."

"How can you be sure? Did she tell you?"

"She told me she asked Levyna to make certain that Queen Ariana of Ravinshore knew everything, seeing as the king was still yet to wake."

Olin's brows raised. "Is he ..."

"No, he's not dead. Not yet anyway, and he's no longer on the verge. The Grand Sorceress extracted the Egro in time. He's healed of it, but he has yet to wake. Perhaps if he had magic, he would be on his feet too," Posdel said, with a nod to Olin's defiance of death.

"Is that why she was in Ravinshore? Gytha?" Olin asked, his voice almost whispery, as if he didn't want the question to be heard. As if he didn't really want to know.

Posdel glanced at him. "I'm the wrong person to ask that. All I know is that she saved King Edmond and not long after found the traveler, or rather Levyna found her."

"So Queen Ariana knows what the Order did?"

"I believe so, yes. Which means you don't have to hurry yourself into the hearth with the flames alight."

"Still, there's more. Walrea isn't alone, they have the Red Flame and maybe even the Order of the Three. They killed the Palatine to replace him, they've attempted to take the life of the King of Ravinshore, and they most likely don't plan to stop there."

Posdel scooped the contents of the mortar into a small bottle. "The Red Flame doing Walrea's bidding is no longer a mad thing to say."

"There's a plan, and I think I saw it."

Posdel turned to Olin. "What?"

"Back at Walrea, when I overheard the Lord Watcher, I was hiding in a secret chamber in the hall. Before they came, I saw something. A scroll on the table. There were others but that was the only one open and ... I didn't know what it was at that time, but I think I might now. Do you have something I could draw with?"

Posdel's brow raised. The shelf in front of him held nothing but bottles, pots, and jars of potions. He walked across the hall to another table, where he pulled charcoal from a drawer. Then he moved into the bedchamber, and rattled inside a coffer for an empty scroll. He took it to the nearest table, and Olin got to his feet and joined him. Posdel brought the lantern closer so they could see. As he did, he noticed that the oro in the jar nearby began glowing as Olin got closer.

Olin seemed oblivious to it as he began drawing from memory what he'd seen on the scroll that day. The sea, the line, the mountains, with the lands and the markings. He drew the markings as he remembered from seeing them again on the Red Flame watchers that had captured him. The flame symbols, the tridents, and the circle with three lines. He placed the symbols on each part of the scroll. When Olin was done, it came together precisely as he had seen it.

"It looks like a map," he said.

"It is, but it's also more." Posdel leaned in. "This is a map of the three kingdoms. There's the city of Edenborough, on the other side of the sea from Duken."

"You can read this?"

"Yes, it's Yetrik, an ancient language mages used, thought to be dead or dying. Not many people in the three kingdoms can understand it, and certainly not many can write it."

"The Lord Watcher of Walrea could." Olin studied what he had drawn. "It's more than just a map of the three kingdoms." He pointed at a part of the map.

"Ravinshore," Posdel said.

"There are three symbols on it, just like the rest. If that belongs to the Lord Watcher of Walrea. If Ravinshore has those, then Queen's Hill has —"

"The flames. The Red Flame."

Olin stared, his brows furrowed. Then he picked up the charcoal, and as though he was finishing up the details, he crossed out a mark on Ravinshore and one from Queen's Hill.

Posdel frowned. "Why did you do that?"

Olin frowned. "I don't know. It feels incomplete. Like it has been altered since ... the last time I saw it."

"Do you mean to tell me that you can see what has been done to that scroll even after you left it behind?"

Olin ran his hand through his hair. "That would be ...- impossible. Would it not?"

"Not if the scroll was enchanted, not if you have the magic you're still trying to deny. The Orders of the Three Kingdoms are working together, and a traveler exists. I think I've crossed into the realm of believing impossible things for today." Posdel peered at the drawing. His eyes widened. "And perhaps whoever crossed those out didn't do so out of boredom."

"What do you mean?"

"Because, not long ago the commander of Ravinshore's army died in a whorehouse." Posdel pointed to Ravinshore, where one mark had been crossed out.

"How ..."

"Were you not born in Ravinshore? You talk as if you don't know the winds carry every fart to the rest of the three kingdoms before it even leaves the ass of the person," Posdel said. "We know that the Palatine of Queen's Hill is dead."

"He was Levyna's father," Olin said.

Posdel glanced at Olin, thinking of the odds that fate had managed to weave the thread of misery connecting them. He watched as the sciff leaned in again.

"And I would assume with that second mark you've just crossed out on Queen's Hill, even without hearing the bells in this storm, that someone important to the kingdom has died."

"You mean to say ..."

"The king might be the only one with power over the Order, but a king's source of power comes from his allies and his army. Take that away and you already have control of the kingdom."

"The commanders, the palatines."

"And the kings themselves."

"The Order of Walrea wants to take the kingdoms," Olin said.

THIRTY-FOUR

The storm lasted through the night. Dawn had not yet parried the darkness when they heard the knock on the door. Olin sat up at once, and Posdel slowly stirred. They shared a glance. Whoever it was, they weren't expected. The was a chance it could be someone wanting to finish what they'd started.

Olin pulled the sheet off and got on his feet; Posdel was right beside him.

"They cannot enter unless I want them to."

"You trust what Gytha did?"

"You're standing here, are you not?"

Olin quieted and nodded as Posdel moved to the door. "I have nothing but foes who know better than to come at this time. Who will you be?"

"A friend," a voice answered. It was a woman, and at once sounded familiar to Olin. "Please, it's Levyna. I wish to see Olin."

Olin's eyes widened as Posdel turned to him sharply. "Your traveler?"

Olin didn't know what answer to give. Posdel turned away from his dumbfounded face and unlocked the door. He raised his right hand, glowing like a torch to illuminate the face on the threshold. The faces. Beside the younger woman was another who looked like an older version of the girl, even from what little they could see from beneath their cloaks.

Levyna pulled down her hood, as did her mother. She looked beyond the light in her face to see Olin, a step behind Posdel. "You're alive," she said, relief evident in her voice.

"So it appears," Olin answered.

"This is my mother, Fiona. I could hardly rest all night worrying about you. I had to come."

Posdel stepped aside. "Please, come in," he said, in a courteous manner Olin didn't know the man capable of.

Levyna and her mother stepped into the house; as they entered, the veil of the spell Gytha had enchanted glowed around them.

"I apologize for the abrupt visit. Levyna was bent on finding him. She's been frantic since last night, was prepared to enter the storm even," Fiona said.

"And you knew he was here?" Posdel asked.

"I don't know how to explain it, but I sensed him the same way I found him in the dungeon, only this time it was stronger and I actually knew where to go."

Olin stared at her, taking in the fact that he was seeing her yet again. He hadn't prepared for this. "Is everything okay? Why are you here?"

"I just couldn't shake the feeling that I needed to find you. I'm sorry if it sounds silly, but I can't explain it," Levyna said. Behind them Posdel offered Fiona a seat.

Olin tried to figure out what to say next.

"Take the lady's cloak," Posdel said, as if suddenly embarrassed by his rudeness.

Olin glanced at him and then back at Levyna, holding his hands out. Levyna undid her mantle and slipped it off her shoulders as Olin stepped behind her to hang on the wall like Posdel had done with her mother's.

Levyna took her own seat on the other available chair. Olin could hardly bring himself to look away from her even as he sat on a stool nearby. "I have to ask, are you really here or ..."

"I would hope that she is, seeing as I am too," Fiona answered. "We came by portal, because apparently she can create those now."

Olin looked from Fiona to Posdel and back to Levyna.

"It's one more thing I can't explain," Levyna said. "And I don't suppose Grand Sorceress Gytha is here now? Perhaps she would have an answer. She knew I'm a traveler, after all."

"No, she's not," Posdel answered before Olin could.

"I'm relieved you're okay. I kept remembering how you looked when I left, before I ended up in Ravinshore. I wouldn't leave me be. Are you healed?" Levyna asked, eyes falling to Olin's side, remembering the sight of it before.

"Better by the moment." Olin nodded. "You were at the palace in Ravinshore. Did you see the queen? His Majesty?"

"I saw them both, in the king's bedchamber while he was unconscious. But I did as you intended. I told Queen Ariana what you learned about the Order, and about your troubles," Levyna answered.

"If only you'd known what else he knows now," Posdel said.

Fiona turned to him. "And what is that?"

Posdel glanced at Olin before he stood and fetched the scroll. He didn't bother carrying the lantern as he his hand was still glowing bright enough that they could see. He showed them the drawing. Levyna rose to her feet with Olin and they moved closer to Fiona and Posdel, who was explaining what Olin had managed to recreate and what it most likely meant, including the fact that Fredrik had been in the way, if the plan was what they believed.

"He would not have yielded," Levyna said.

"No, he certainly wouldn't have," Fiona answered. They both knew the kind of man her husband was, even in the face of death.

Levyna turned to Olin. "It makes sense that they've hunted you across kingdoms. You didn't just hear about the plot to kill the king, you saw their entire plan."

"But I didn't even know it was that at the time. Not till the pieces came together."

Posdel watched them and his brows slowly rose.

"What is it?" Fiona asked.

"Pieces. Missing pieces," he said. "One can be one and not even know it."

"You're speaking in riddles again," Olin said.

Posdel moved to the table, where he picked up the jar of oro, then grabbed the bottle he'd just fixed. "There's something of a legend. Though most mages are born with magic, realizing their powers from a very young age and growing into them, some don't know of their magic until it's completely awakened. The legend says these mages, though rare, are Pertes."

"Pertes?" Fiona asked.

"Yes." Posdel set the jar of oros on the ground and took Olin's hand, pulling him in front of the jar. "It's Yetrik for 'pieces of one.' " He took Levyna's hand to have her stand on the opposite side of the jar. "The one comes alive, when they find the other."

"What are you talking about?" Olin asked, confused.

Posdel removed the stopper from the bottle. "Your magic, Olin! If I'm wrong, this oro will die once I pour this in this jar."

"You still won't give this up?" Olin said. Fiona stood to see.

"And what if you're right?" Levyna asked.

Posdel decided to find out, rather than answer. He opened the jar and poured the contents of the bottle on the slug. He watched with Fiona as the oro's glow threaded out of the jar, intertwining as it wrapped itself around Olin and Levyna. The thread continued to glow, but the creature remained alive and stayed the same size in its jar.

Olin looked at Levyna. Both felt the same jolt as before, this time at full strength even though they weren't touching and the oro served as buffer. Olin felt his entire body tremble and then seize, and he saw the same mix of confusion and thrill in Levyna's eyes. But soon, Olin's trembling was no longer only internal, as he began to shake violently.

Before Posdel and Fiona could react, Levyna specter split from her body to take Olin's hands. He stopped trembling. Her body fell to the ground and her mother rushed to her side. Levyna's specter set Olin on the ground until he stopped trembling.

"I told him he had magic. Look at his hands," Posdel said.

Olin's hands had burst into flames.

***

Olin opened his eyes to find Levyna's specter by his side. Her true self was unconscious. But that was hardly the only thing that had him questioning reality, as he stared at his own hands, and the flames surrounding them.

They were on fire but he felt nothing, no heat. His body had no idea it was burning. But Olin did feel lighter, as though he would float when he got to his feet.

"You have magic," Posdel said, with a hint of what would have been excitement, had the circumstances been different. Levyna chose that moment to jolt back awake causing everyone to jump.

"Sorry," Levyna said.

Olin could see it for himself, now. He couldn't deny it. This wasn't a simple coincidence, not like before when the Master had insisted he had magic. Olin stared at his hands as the flame burned. He clenched his fists and watched them extinguish. He opened them again. The flame was gone, but reappeared as soon as he wished it.

"Olin, you will find out more about your magic in time. Many of your powers could come at the will of your essence," Posdel said.

Olin thought about his mother, even though he didn't want to. He had magic after all, and there was a chance it was because of his mother's blood, running through his veins. The Grand Sorceress.

Learning she had an actual role to play in Olin's magic was a revelation for Levyna, as she listened to Posdel explain the connection between them. It wasn't nothing. It was thrilling to see Olin came alive, turning from the stranger she had met days ago and becoming someone she could feel across the room.

Posdel was asking Fiona about King Ranald. Meanwhile, Levyna looked over Olin in a long glance, wondering what fate had brought this boy with a headful of brown hair into her life.

Olin turned to her and their eyes met and held for a moment before she looked away, exhaled and everything went quiet.

Levyna blinked into nothingness.

She opened her eyes. This time it wasn't her mother leaning over her. It was Olin. She turned to find her mother. Though Fiona had seen it enough times to know not to be worried, it couldn't be easy, seeing her daughter peel away from consciousness so effortlessly.

"Are – are you alright?" Olin asked.

"I'm fine," Levyna answered, but her face betrayed her worry. "But I'm afraid someone else might not be."

"What did you see?" Fiona asked, dread in her voice.

"A little girl crying over a dead stag," Levyna answered.

***

Isabelle arrived at the house at dawn. When the door opened to a small face, she found herself speechless for a moment.

"Who are you?" the young girl asked.

"Hello. I'm Isabelle."

The girl frowned and she tilted her head. "Isabelle? What kind of name is that?"

"It's Maedrian. You must be Maria."

"I must be. Have you come to sell us something?"

Isabelle shook her head. "No, no. I came to say hello to your father."

Alden appeared behind his daughter, brushing his hair away from his face as he pulled down his shirt. Then he blinked, surprised. "Isabelle? Is all well?"

"Yes, all is well. I apologize if I've called too early. I only wanted to check that you are doing well, and say thank you for everything."

Alden glanced at his daughter, placed a hand on her shoulder and looked back up. "You didn't need to, but it's kind of you and I appreciate it.

"It was the least I could do for someone who made certain I returned to Ravinshore as I'd left," Isabelle said.

"Was she the one you went to protect?" Maria asked.

Alden's face twisted with chagrin, seeing as they had protected each other fairly evenly, and it had been Isabelle who had protected him when the actual trouble came.

"I am," Isabelle answered, looking at Maria. "Your father was one of the bravest men I have ever met. And, all through the journey, he wouldn't stop talking about you. He told me he missed your birthday."

Maria shrugged. "He has promised me a blue ferret instead."

Isabelle nodded. "Well I didn't bring you a ferret, but this is yours," she said, kneeling to child's level to hold out a bracelet on her palm.

Maria's eyes bugged at the gift as she looked up to her father, who nodded. "It's beautiful!" she said as she stepped to take it.

"It's made of tiny pebbles from the shores of Maedro. They glow in the dead of the night and bring good health." Isabelle clasped the bracelet around the little girl's wrist and watched as she touched it.

"I like it a lot. Thank you!" Maria said.

Isabelle hadn't been expecting the little girl to lunge at her with a tight embrace. Holding her, Isabelle felt herself smile; it was mirrored by Alden.

***

"It's funny how the one who stays home gets a gift and the one who endured you for days gets nothing," Alden said as he walked the sorceress to her horse.

"Knowing how much she means to you, I was sure it would mean just the same thing, if not more," Isabelle said.

Alden nodded and then shrugged. "You are very wise, Sorceress." He glanced at the house, where he could see his daughter through a slit of an open window.

"She's as beautiful as you described."

"Yes. And all of the credit goes to her mama," Alden answered.

His smile seemed to strain for a moment at the mention of his dead wife. Isabelle tugged at the lead of her horse as she prepared to mount.

"Will Ravinshore be seeing you anytime soon?"

It was her turn to shrug. "Perhaps. Perhaps I could come by to see a friend," she said, ending her gaze on the house.

Alden chuckled. "That would be —"

Blood splashed across her face, and Isabelle's eyes widened in horror. Alden's final words were lost in another spurt of blood from the knife sticking out the back of his head. Another dagger hit his back before Isabelle could do anything, and Alden dropped in front of her.

"No!" Isabelle raised her hand to form a shield as she fell by his side. This time, however, she realized there was nothing she could do. Frantically, she looked up. Her eyes darted to the door of the house as it opened and she saw the look Maria's face as the girl stared with lost eyes at the horror on the ground.

Realizing the little girl could be the next target, Isabelle sprinted to the house before Maria could run to her father's body. She scooped the girl off the ground just as she felt the sharp pain of blade bury in her side. Isabelle grunted as she took shelter in the house, waving her hand to slam the door shut. She turned her wrist to lock it.

Isabelle held on tight. Maria could only manage a broken, "Father," as her breath stuttered in the Isabelle's arms.

Black Scarf waited outside the door in stillness. For once, he wished he had his voice so he could tell the woman why he was there, why he was going to kill her and anyone else he found with her. He wished he could scream loud enough so that woman would hear his sister's name before she died. He wanted her last memory to be that of the family she had taken from. Black Scarf wished the Maedrian woman to know that this had nothing to do with the Order of the Three. He was not hunting her as a Watcher of the Kingdom of Duken. He bore his loyalty to the Order second to that of his sister.

Black Scarf had killed in his life as a watcher. He had taken lives without question in service to the Order of the Three and the name of the Lord Watcher and for the Kingdom of Duken. He was a weapon beaten and created to have no mind of his own when it came to his duty, and he did as he was told, he did as he was ordered. Excerpt when it came to his sister. He'd found himself a mage to send him through the portal because Thorne's plan and Otto's words were never going to be able to able to keep him from her a moment longer. Even if she vanished into the realm of the unknown, he would hunt her down.

Black Scarf had been a monster long before he'd been tamed to bear needles and stab darlings for his kingdom. Before he carved out this woman's heart she would know that. He hoped she would be able to see it in his eyes.

Black Scarf pulled more knives from sheathes at his side and walked towards the window, only to the duck as fist-sized stones pelted in his direction. He rolled out of the way to catch sight of the attacker – some white-haired stranger he'd never seen before.

The watcher moved quickly as William threw more stones in his direction, blocking his path to the door. But the watcher only cared about reaching his goal, and had forsaken the subterfuge his kind were known for.

William's hand raised in the air and he released a pulse that would be strong enough to knock Black Scarf back a few paces while still keeping the building standing. After it released, he looked and saw that his strike had done nothing. The watcher was no longer there.

Conscious of his surroundings, with his senses heightened, William jerked his head to the side, summoning a shield to stop the blade piercing through the air towards him. The knife battered against the shield he'd created and dropped on the floor. William yanked with a spell and the weapon flew into his hand. He gripped the knife in one hand and placed the other hand over it.

Black Scarf stirred from where he was crouching behind the house. Finding the backdoor, he rattled it, but it didn't open. He prepared to batter it open, but was distracted by a gust of wind. He shielded his eyes, but the dust settled quickly – too quickly. Black Scarf spun sharply, knife raised, but not before the mage found the back of his neck with his own knife.

William emerged from behind his cloak, standing over the watcher as he bled out on the floor.

Death was always a given, as far as Black Scarf knew. It was the constant that was always coming, the shadow he could never escape. Death was the cloud he would forever have over him, even in the deepest holes he'd tried to crawl into since he had become a Watcher of the Three, but it didn't stop it from aching.

His only regret, as his breath succumbed to the flood of blood in his throat, was that he had failed his one mission. He couldn't have cared less about his own death, if that was the only thing he was leaving undone – but he had not yet seen the sorceress's face and she wouldn't know that he was dying for the one person whom he served before his Order.

Though he didn't have a voice, Black Scarf signed with final strength so the mage towering over his body would see.

A fist with a thumb pointing up. An index finger raised with the thumb touching the other fingertips. A fist with a thumb pointing up. A thumb poking out between the middle and ring fingers with the other fingers curled. And a fist with a thumb pointing up.

"Adana."

THIRTY-FIVE

Ole ran. The torches lining the corridor walls danced as he breezed past. He didn't care that he felt old and his knees could stiffen and land him on his face, or that he'd barely had time to even throw on a robe, he hurried from his quarters towards the king's bedchamber. He had to see for himself.

Behind him, a young messenger was trailing by a few steps. Ole ignored the guards densely lining the walls. Finally, he arrived, and brought himself to a stop and pushed the door open.

Queen Ariana turned at the sound of the door opening. The sight of the Court's Counsel didn't lighten her grip on her husband's hand as he sat up on the bed. She and Ole shared a look. Ariana had a wide smile on her face; her eyes were still teary from how much she hadn't been able to hold back. The queen sniffled, even in the presence of the Grand Sorceress Gytha, standing by on her command. Ariana had summoned both her and Ole in the same breath after she'd recovered from her surprise.

It had been his touch that had woken Ariana from where she'd lain by his side. A gentle rub at the back of her hand that had jolted her out of her slumber and nearly thrown her into delirium. She had held his face, stared into his eyes and kissed him, mindless of his title now that she could see those pale blue eyes of his peering back at her.

Now Ole gasped and had to keep himself from dropping to his knees at the sight. "Oh. Oh, Your Majesty!" He bowed once and then again, and then a third time in his flood of emotions.

"Ole." King Edmond's deep, riveting voice almost brought the older man to tears.

"My Lord."

"It's good to see your face again. When I said I was growing tired of it, I didn't know what I was wishing for," the king said.

Ole chuckled, feeling like he had to keep himself from bouncing on his feet. "And I don't think there could be a more gracious delight than seeing your face filled with life again, My Lord."

"He would never know, would he?" Queen Ariana said from next to her husband, still holding his hand.

"I heard there has been much going on?"

"Yes, Your Majesty. But nothing beats the news of your return to us, nothing! Everything else is far tertiary at best," Ole answered.

"Yes. Nevertheless, I'm sure there are other concerns as well, like the matter of how I was sent into an endless slumber in the first place." The king made to get on his feet and Ole instinctively moved forward, but Edmond slowly placed his foot on the ground and stood, not without feeling the effects of being horizontal for close to eight days. The wave of dizziness struck him, but his wife's hand was by his side.

"You have just awakened," Ariana said sternly.

"I have slept for too long."

"But you did not really asleep."

"And that is exactly what I'm saying," Edmond said to his wife, before he turned to the unknown face in his bedchamber.

Gytha's expression hardly betrayed the fact that she was standing in the king's most intimate room, though her confidence made sense. After all, she had been the one to fish him out from the Egro he had been drowning in.

Each of them knew the truth now, that the attack was the work of the same Order that had been meant to protect him. There were some things that a kingdom needed believe to bind it together, keep it safe. One of them was the Order. The Order of Walrea had been meant to be the King of Ravinshore's wall of invincibility against outside forces. That it had turned against him instead wasn't something the king could sit casually pondering.

"How did it happen? Who was it?" King Edmond demanded.

Ole's eyes met Queen Ariana's before he answered. "It was a chamber servant, Your Majesty. For one of the younger princes. He had been here for a year before being taken to the palace. His name was Eshra. He'd taken the role of a Ravinshore commoner, though we have since found that he had no true claims to a family here."

"How did it happen?" the king asked again, as he moved gingerly from his bed to a chair.

Ole blinked at the queen again and then at Gytha. "It was through a robe, My Lord. Your favorite one."

The king glanced at his counsel. "A robe?"

"Yes, Your Majesty. That was one of three ways to get the poison inside you – through something that would cling to your skin, or your meal," Gytha answered.

"And which is the third?" Edmond asked.

"You would have had to come in contact with a dark sorcerer who would cast the Egro on you in person."

"So this poisoner had access to my clothes?"

"Yes, he took a chance with one he knew you would at least touch, even if you didn't wear it. And he had to have watched enough to know where he would strike," Gytha answered.

King Edmond looked from the Grand Sorceress to his wife. "And Ole refers to the man in past tense."

"Yes, he is gone, though by his own hands and not nearly as pleasing as it would have been had I been the one to slit his throat," Ariana answered.

There was no one in the room that doubted her. But something greater than the poisoning was on the horizon and they knew it.

The first light slowly rose above the palace in Ravinshore. A surreptitious dullness fell over the king's bedchamber as Gytha made to depart – she felt the chill and her brows furrowed. From where she stood, she heard a thud that the rest were oblivious to. It came from outside the king's bedchamber. Outside the palace.

"Something is happening," Gytha announced. She turned, her back to the king as she faced the windows.

"What do you mean?" Ariana asked, glancing at Ole and stepping away from her husband's side for the first time.

Gytha heard another thud. She didn't need to open the shutters to know what it was. She let out a breath.

"They're here," she said.

In the next moment the windows of the king's bedchamber blew open and two watchers flew in. Ariana stepped back at once and the king sprung to his feet. Gytha glanced at the first watcher and a vine shot in from the window, grabbing him by the torso and pulling him back outside, where he was split it two. The second watcher balled his hands into fists and wove a shield against Gytha as he lunged towards the king. The Grand Sorceress moved her right hand in a wave and clenched her fingers. The watcher stopped in his tracks, woven shield in his hand. Gytha turned her fist over and the watcher dropped to his knees. She opened them and swiped her hand to the side, and King Edmond, Queen Ariana, and Ole watched in terror as the watcher's own shield was rammed into the side of his neck by his own hand. The watcher dropped to the floor and blood pooled around him. Gytha turned away and raised her hand.

"Aberrenis, ed-yedoim con-tria," the sorceress chanted the spell and the shutters slammed shut. She turned to the face Ole and King Edmond, who had drawn swords. "You will need to stay in this room. They won't be able to enter unless you allow them to," she said.

"I am not cowering in my bedchamber while my kingdom is under attack!" the king said.

"You are not cowering. You are being wise, knowing that if they reach you, your kingdom will fall. I will see this through, Your Majesty. Stay here."

"You cannot tell me what to do!" Edmond moved towards her, but stopped as Ariana grabbed his arm.

"Your Majesty, I didn't save your life to watch you die now trying to prove that you're a warrior. Your people need you alive. If you do not heed your queen, I will not hesitate to send you back to sleep if that's what it takes. Let me handle this," Gytha said.

"Edmond," Ariana called her husband's name as she tugged his arm. Her voice held the panic of a woman who would take the sword from his hand and do whatever was needed to protect her kingdom, her king, her castle, and her children. The memory of seeing him unconscious at the jaws of death was fresh in her mind. She couldn't stand to watch him now as he ran towards their enemies who had come to eliminate him for good. No matter how much she wanted those enemies crushed, no matter how defiant she wanted to be.

This was why she'd asked Gytha to stay, because she'd known it would only been a matter of time before Thorne and his Order decided they could no longer wait.

"Please, listen to the sorceress," she said.

King Edmond, still dressed in his bed shirt and trousers, barefooted and furious with a sword in his grip, stared into his wife's eyes and exhaled. He turned in time to see the Grand Sorceress vanish from the room.

Outside the king's bedchamber, the King's Guard faced off against watchers targeting the king. As one after the other fell, the battle inched towards the corridors of King Edmond's chamber. Standing among his men, Thorne wove an enchanted thread, then threw his hands forward and pulled them back, bringing down the huge door leading to the passage to the king's room on top of a wave of guards. The Lord Watcher stood with a single pair of watchers against the six guardsmen.

"Step aside now and live," he said.

"You are not to set a foot further, Watcher!"

The guards remained unwavering, each with swords drawn, even as the Lord Watcher's hands glowed red with threads. Thorne wasted no time, waving his hand towards the guards. All of them rose into the air. Thorne then threw them against the walls, three apiece, and the watchers behind him moved to finish off each grounded guard before they could free themselves of the Lord Watcher's enchantment.

Four were killed, each ended swiftly with blades from the watchers as Thorne proceeded, walking between the slaughter to the door of the king's chamber up ahead.

The watchers were about to kill the last pair of guards when they were thrown all the way to the end of the main passage, so hard their skulls could be heard breaking as they hit the walls.

Thorne jerked to see what had become of his watchers, but after turning, he couldn't see an attacker. He didn't move, standing on the spot as the air grew colder and then thinned. The Lord Watcher clasped his hands at once, collecting the air around him and sending a wave through the path ahead. It bounced off a figure before she manifested from the air.

Gytha stood, grey mantle cloaking her body as she stared at the watcher.

"You. Who are you and what business of yours is this?" Thorne asked.

"It was not my business until I realized what you did to someone I care about."

Throne frowned behind his mask. "What?"

"You killed Wylie and then you tried to kill my son," Gytha said.

The Lord Watcher chuckled. "That old bastard and his rat? You're the one who mothered that —"

Thorne held up his hand and formed a shield with his thread, blocking the Grand Sorceress's gaze as Gytha waved her hand. Thorne struggled, but managed to keep

356

grounded as Gytha's attempted to blow him away as she had done to his watchers. He held firm, using most of his energy to keep the thread woven around the shield.

The moment he felt the pulse falter, the Lord Watcher brought down his shield, pulled out his knife and sliced his palm. The blood seeped and Thorne called to it. His eyes glowed and the thread around his hands burned. He pointed his hands at the floor and the thread at once flung towards the Grand Sorceress.

Thorne wanted to watch her vanish. He needed to see. But his face pulled into a frown as Gytha reached down and grabbed the power he'd released, yanking it up and then pulling him towards her, hard enough that Thorne couldn't stop himself from falling on his face in front of her.

Thorne watched in utter horror as the Grand Sorceress yanked again at the thread, ripping it from his essence. Before he could do anything, Gytha raised her hand and he felt the bone of his arm shatter. Thorne's breath seemed to stop and his heart raced in his chest as he felt his head pulse with the weight of Gytha's stare.

Gytha could break his brain through his skull without laying a hand on him, but she wanted it slow and torturous. It was only right, after what he had done. Before she could, she was forced to lift her head to stop a knife inches away from the center of her chest. A second knife found her shoulder. Gytha looked down the hall and saw a watcher standing by the remains of the guard they'd finished off.

Gytha pulled the blade from her shoulder and the one stuck on her shield and threw them at Thorne on the floor. The Lord Watcher grunted in pain. Then she raised her left hand towards the closed window, tossing Thorne out, shattering the window as he was flung all the way down to the grounds of the castle.

Gytha could already feel the sting of the poison that had been laced in the enchanted blade, but she placed her left hand over her shoulder, locking it in place with a freezing spell that would keep the right side of her body dead, and the poison with it.

The watcher tried again with another knife, but Gytha thwarted it before she vanished in air. Then Gytha appeared behind the watcher, who spun quickly to stab at her again, but with a wave Gytha threw them against the wall. This watcher wasn't dressed quite like the rest. The mask and the hood covered the face, but the vest was grey instead of black. The watcher got back up, quicker than any other had, ready to lunge with their knives. Gytha sighed, beginning to feel exhausted, but she pointed her arm at the watcher, throwing them back against the wall. She was prepared to set this one afire for the burning sensation in her arm.

"Exor —"

Gytha stopped mid-spell, noticing the scar just above the gauntlet on the watcher's right arm. She looked up at the masked face, peering at the eyes. Those hazel eyes. She bloody knew them.

"Ilda?"

THIRTY-SIX

If she'd had her way, Fiona would prefer to have stayed home, if it wasn't for the fact that they knew the Order's plans and couldn't sit idle.

Olin still desired to return to Ravinshore, though it didn't burn as brightly, as he knew that the crown was unaware of the extent of what the Order of Walrea was planning. But they had been told now. Olin expected that once the queen learned the truth, Black Castle and the king would be protected. Ravinshore would not fall; Ravinshore could not fall.

When Levyna and her mother had left the palace, the news of this new death hadn't reached them, but after they arrived at Posdel's house and learned that the Red Flame was planning to seize the kingdom, the news was worse than they feared. If indeed the Commander of Queen's Hill's army had been killed, then the king was surely next.

Levyna's couldn't tell for sure from her new dream. It had bothered her, though. The child crying over a dead stag. Posdel's translation was a child was crying over her dead father. Levyna didn't know who the child or the father was, but the one thing she did know was that she wanted – needed – to return to the palace in Queen's Hill. Olin had agreed.

While the grief of the loved ones they had both lost hadn't gone away by any means, neither of them felt the need to question the newfound connection beyond what Posdel had said about fate. Pertes. The thought was there, in the back of their minds as first light rose.

And Olin was still alive, despite what the watcher had boasted when he'd been captured the day before.

The palace was quiet as they made their way in, not littered with the forces of the King's Guards as expected. The plan was that Fiona would go to the king concerning their suspicions. It would ultimately be her words, and those of her daughter, the family of a dead palatine, speaking against the newly appointed Cyrus.

There was a chance, however small, that the king wouldn't believe them. But if it was true that the commander was also dead, then King Ranald had to see that his forces in the kingdom were being manipulated. Olin had said that, if the need arose, Levyna could show the king her power, and Olin would narrate everything he had gone through at the hands of the Red Flame and Walrea.

As they passed through the hallway by the old palatine quarters, a pair of guards stationed by the door greeted Fiona. Levyna glanced back at the one on the right and Olin followed her gaze. He saw the guard's eyes dart in their direction. Olin heard a thudding: the guard's heart was racing in his chest. The guard tightened his grip around his weapon, even though they posed no threat. All the signs Wylie had taught him to spot someone who was either lying, hiding something, or worried about something.

Olin slowed down and thought, *He's hiding something.*

I think so too.

Levyna's eyes bugged. They froze in the middle of the hall, staring at each other.

Fiona turned to see why her daughter had stopped, and found Olin and Levyna staring in silence.

"What's happening?" she asked, wondering if Levyna had gone somewhere or seen something. As a mother, she was trying to get used to the signs of her daughter's power. The addition of Olin hadn't made it as simple as Posdel had tried to explain it.

Posdel stopped too. Olin and Levyna were in a realm of their own. He scoffed. "You wouldn't believe it," he said to Fiona. "They are talking – with their minds."

They were indeed in a realm of their own.

What do you think this is? Olin thought.

I don't know, but I have a feeling it has to do with me – with us, Levyna answered.

We need to know. Olin looked towards the guard and Levyna followed his gaze.

How?

I think I ... might need to touch him.

"Will you be involving the rest of us in this conversation?" Fiona asked.

Levyna looked away from Olin to her mother. "You will find out soon, Mother. Olin needs to touch that guard."

Fiona frowned and Posdel's brow perked. "What?"

"I cannot explain, but I feel like I need to touch him. He's hiding something," Olin answered.

"Which?" Posdel asked.

"The one with the scar," Levyna said.

Fiona broke away from the group and Olin followed. Levyna and Posdel hung back.

"Guard, this might seem silly but I must trouble you for something," Fiona said.

The guard looked from Fiona to Olin and back.

"My son here would like to see your gauntlet."

"Oh," the guard said.

"You don't have to take it off," Olin said.

The guard blinked at them both, passed his spear to his left hand and raised his arm to Olin, who took it. He immediately saw the reason for the guard – Vernon's – panic.

Olin saw through the Vernon's eyes. What he had done two nights before as he'd slipped into the palatine's washroom and drowned him in his bathtub. Olin pulled away swiftly, dropping the guard's hand in shock. Vernon stared at Olin, confused as to why the boy's eyes were fixing him in place.

"What is it?" Fiona asked.

"It's him," Olin said.

"What?"

"He ... he did it."

Levyna gasped as she heard the words Olin didn't say. "He killed ... Father," she said, voice whispery, but loud enough for Posdel to hear, for Fiona to hear, and for Vernon to know that he was no longer safe.

Vernon spun the spear in his hand, lunging at Olin. He was a second too late. It was though Olin disappeared. Posdel stepped to intervene, but was left to watch as the sciff moved like someone else he'd seen recently.

Lacking a target, Vernon's spear swerved towards Fiona, but Olin swiftly pulled her back. The watcher, seeing an opening for an escape, took it, pushing past the other palace guard, who was blinking and confused.

Levyna's rage at the man's escape burned through her, flaming with the ache in her heart and Olin found himself feeling it. Olin barely gave it a second thought as he moved, appearing just ahead of the escaping watcher. Olin opened his hands and pointed them at Vernon, giving the Watcher of the Red Flame no mercy as the fire consumed him.

Fiona moved to her daughter's side, with Posdel a step behind, watching as the man was reduced to ash on the ground.

"Oh," Posdel said.

Olin stared at his hands as the flames died. He looked up, uncertainty in his gaze as he met Levyna's eyes as more guards arrived. Olin hardly noticed them as he hurried towards Levyna, who grabbed her mother's hand and then Olin's, who in turn took Posdel's. Together, they disappeared.

***

The guards in the throne room stirred and rushed to protect King Ranald as the group suddenly appeared out of nowhere.

It had been Olin's magic, but he had followed Levyna's instinct. They let go of each other's hands, lingering a moment longer than the others.

"What is this?" King Ranald demanded, getting to his feet.

Fiona stepped forward. "Your Majesty, we are sorry for the intrusion, but it was important to reach you at once."

"What could be so urgent that you impose yourself on the King's Court?" Cyrus said, not moving from his spot a step below the throne.

Fiona's eyes darted to her daughter's as they registered the man's presence. It was practically inevitable. "A matter that involves the safety of His Majesty, the Kingdom of Queen's Hill, and the safety of the three kingdoms," Fiona answered.

"And you barge into His Majesty's presence to demand he listen. That will not happen. You will leave at once or risk the wrath of the throne, Lady Fiona!" Cyrus barked.

"It is a matter His Majesty must hear!" Levyna spoke before her mother could answer.

"Fiona, you and your daughter have only been granted grace for your husband's memory, and mercy due to the fact that you are currently grieving, but this will not be allowed!"

"Enough!" King Ranald said. "What is this matter that has caused you to appear in my presence, Fiona?"

"It's about my husband's death, your former palatine, and the death of the commander of this kingdom's army, Your Majesty," Fiona said.

King Ranald's face pinched. He had only recently been informed of the commander's death. "What about them?"

"They were both murdered, Your Majesty, and the Order of Red Flame is responsible for it. And they are not alone."

Cyrus scoffed. "What madness are you spewing?" he said, taking a step down.

"No more words from you, Cyrus!" The king ordered and Cyrus fell quiet.

"It is far from madness, Your Majesty, I have heard it and seen it with my own eyes. My name is Olin from the Kingdom of Ravinshore where the Order of Walrea poisoned King Edmond and killed his commander. They hunted me to Queen's Hill, where I thought I would find help with Lord Cyrus, like my Uncle Wylie told me before the watchers killed him. But he didn't know that Lord Cyrus eats with the Order of Walrea and Red Flame, who had Palatine Fredrik killed and murdered the commander," Olin said.

Cyrus's face pulled into a frown at at the words. "Hold on, y – you're Olin? Wylie's —"

Realization dawned on Olin as the room burst into chaos. He could only watch as the guard closest to Cyrus moved behind him and slit his throat.

Fiona screamed, and Olin moved to the king at once, opening his hand towards the first guard that pulled his dagger and snapping the neck of the other before his blade could cause any harm to King Ranald. At the same time, Posdel released a pulse that threw the guard who'd killed Cyrus against the wall. Levyna glanced at Olin and immediately set free her specter, dropping her body to the ground just as the last guard tried to attack from behind. Levyna's specter grabbed the guard and he collapsed. She pulled the guard's blade and stabbed him with it.

King Ranald stood, trembling as all of the guards in his throne room laid dead on the floor. They had been ghost watchers.

Olin looked at Cyrus's body and wondered what else he had been wrong about.

* * *

Duken was quiet.

While Ravinshore and Queen's Hill slipped towards chaos, the kingdom with its back to the sea remained undisturbed as the morning grew with the day in its infancy. Otto stood by the window in the wide hall of the Fort of the Three, feeling the cool breeze from the sea as it made its way to the kingdom.

He glanced up as crows flocked through the sky. And he let out a deep breath as he felt the energy in the room shift. He glanced at the mirror behind him and stepped towards it. A familiar face appeared, without the mask. It looked as if hell had danced with the Lord Watcher of Walrea, but he was alive, still.

"Thorne."

"Otto."

"You look ..."

"Things —" he coughed hard and his face pinched as he wiped blood from his lips "— things have not gone as planned here."

"I can see that," Otto said, studying the man's appearance.

"What is happening in Duken? Why have you not struck?" Thorne asked. "Did you not get the message? The Three were meant to strike with the rest. What do you wait for?"

"Nothing," Otto said.

"I do not understand."

Otto shook his head. "Duken and its Order of the Three wait for nothing, Thorne. There will be nothing happening in Duken today or any other day. The Order of the Three will not go against its king."

Thorne frowned. "What nonsense do you speak, Watcher? This plan has taken years to prepare. The Orders are to be the one true power of the three kingdoms! Have you lost your sanity?"

"My senses are perfectly adequate, Thorne, and it is Lord Watcher."

"Do you seek to humor yourself, is that it?" Thorne said, the condescension saturating his voice.

"I don't need to. You said you had a plan, but it was *your* plan. Dreamt up by you for the rest of the Order to fulfill. You wish for the Order to take power from the crowns, so that we can then become one. One Order – Walrea – ruled by you, over the rest of the kingdoms. Is that not it?" It was a question, but Otto didn't give Thorne a chance to respond. "Do you think me stupid? I know that Liaton found out and that was why you had him killed. You killed the Lord Watcher of Queen's Hill so the watchers could serve you instead, and you expect that the Three will do as you please. Lay waste to our king and siege our kingdom, all for a plan you created and have let fester for almost a decade?"

"Otto!"

"You know the saying, 'Burn yourself before the thunder strikes?' The Three chose to let you believe that we would do as planned. I let everything you did pass. But your appearance shows that you've met the unexpected. That the three kingdoms are more than the plot you hatched on the back of greed." Otto looked towards the window. "You probably cannot hear from the blood seeping from your ears, but it's still here. Quiet and peaceful, and it will continue to remain so. The Order of the Three will continue to make sure of it."

"You will pay for this, Otto. I promise you! You will regret this betrayal!" Thorne yelled, struggling for breath with the ache wrecking his body.

"You speak of betrayal as you talk from a hole. You have more to be worried about if whoever did that to you is still standing. For your own sake, don't consider Duken refuge, or you will be flayed in the streets and tossed as chum into the sea."

Thorne's face grew bitter and red. Otto just chuckled at the face of Walrea's supposed mastermind, and the mirror went dark.

THIRTY-SEVEN

I t had been fifteen years since the last time Gytha had seen her. They had been friends who were going to become family. Wylie had taken a liking to Ilda the very day he'd set his eyes on her. He'd wished for her to become his. It had seemed like it would happen, until the day Ilda disappeared. She was never seen in Ravinshore again, until Gytha herself was exiled.

"You disappeared," Gytha said, speaking from outside the gates of the dungeon cell beneath Ravinshore's Black Castle. "You left no word. Not a sign, nothing. You just left."

"And you're one to judge me?" Ilda scoffed from inside the cell, hands chained to the wall.

"I had a reason to leave! It was hardly a choice for me!"

"Does that make you feel better? Did you think I had a choice either?" Ilda said, looking up.

"What was the reason for your choice? What made you disappear and turn a good man into a miserable one?" Gytha stepped closer to the cell.

Ilda broke into a hysterical laughter. "You really don't see how wrong it is that you're the one accusing me of this? At least I didn't leave a child in the cold, dark hands of a heartbroken man."

Gytha couldn't hide how that stung. Silence fell for a seemingly long moment before she finally spoke. "Is this why you disappeared? Is this what you chose?"

Ilda was quiet.

"You chose something that killed the man you used to love and hunted and almost killed the boy he carried in his cold, heartbroken hands."

Ilda looked up at her slowly. There was a question in her eyes as she stared at Gytha.

"How is it possible that you don't know? You must have heard about Wylie. You really never wondered who they were after? I never abandoned my child. He had a guardian that your Order took away from him. My son was inches away from losing his life. I might forgive you for trying to kill me, Ilda. But there is nothing you say that can excuse what happened to Wylie and what you almost did to my son." Gytha turned to leave but stopped as Ilda called.

"Please, I must beg you. Whatever you do with me, don't let my daughter be abandoned. Please."

Gytha eyed the ghost watcher one more time before she walked away.

* * *

Olin wasn't sure he wanted to hear what she had to say, but Levyna had been the literal voice in his head telling him to give his mother a chance to explain. And that was after Posdel had laid the foundation for the conversation, leaving the house just as Gytha arrived. Levyna had wandered off, pretending as if she wouldn't hear all about it afterwards.

Gytha took off her mantle. Olin stared at her, as though searching her appearance for something to remember beyond her face. Beyond those eyes that never left his.

"Are you going to say something, or do you intend for us to just sit here?" As he asked the question, she brushed her hair to the left side, just like he did.

"I was a little younger than you are now when I started showing signs of my powers, but I didn't understand them. And I hid them. Not long after, I met your father on a merchant trip to Duken. He was with his brother, and Wylie made him talk to me when we reached Duken. They were both good men, kind men. Your father was ... an incredible person. He was funny and witty and stubborn and adventurous and curious. He was a merchant who traded mostly wheat across the three kingdoms, but he wanted to travel more than anything. He wanted to see the world, to Edenborough and beyond. He imagined that he would someday become the most famous in the history of the three kingdoms. I loved him." As Gytha talked, she looked to be seeing the memories afresh.

"Not long after we met, we married and I became pregnant with you. I remember the day he found out I was with child – Wylie had to lock him in the house because couldn't contain his excitement. We were preparing to have you when my powers returned. I started to notice that things died when I touched them – plants withered, animals shriveled and died. It lasted for days and it was terrifying. I still didn't tell your father or Wylie. It stopped, but other parts of my magic slowly awakened. When Wylie found out, he tried to help me control them.

"Then you came, and you were the most perfect thing I had ever held in my hands." Gytha turned her hands up as though she could see the image. "If your father acted crazy when I was pregnant, you can probably imagine how he was when you were born, when you were handed to him. He was unstoppable. Bathlom wanted to give you the world. He wanted you to have everything you ever wanted. He talked endlessly about the adventures you would have when you grew older. He cherished you so much, I would have been jealous if I hadn't loved you even more than he did.

"You had everything. I had everything with you and your father. My life – our life – was perfect. Until the day my magic returned. You were only a year and half old. It was night. I felt it take over my body and I woke in the middle of the night. You were asleep in your bed. Bathlom had been sleeping next to me, and my hand on his body felt cold. I took the lantern and was paralyzed with the horror at what I had done –my hand had been on your father all through the night and I don't know how it happened, but Bathlom never woke up, Olin. I had taken his life while we slept and I didn't even realize."

Olin swallowed hard as he pictured it.

"I lost my mind. I couldn't bring myself to touch you. The idea that I would to do the same thing wasn't something I could live with. Wylie carried you and fed you for days while I watched in fear and considered chopping off my hands if it would do any good. Time passed and I couldn't take it anymore. I needed to know what was wrong with me and how to stop it. To do that, I needed to find someone who knew more about magic than anyone else, and that meant leaving Ravinshore. Leaving you, Olinander.

"I didn't know when I'd be able to return. It was the hardest thing I have ever had to do in my life," Gytha said. "I told Wylie and he begged me, he begged me not to go, offered to come with me, even, but I knew that you would need him and I wouldn't be able to cope with merely watching you from a distance and not being able to do anything. Even if that was what I ended up doing later. For years."

Olin's brows furrowed. "You were watching me?"

"I was. I came back a couple of years after I left. I watched you from corners and the sides of the road. I watched you from across Wylie's old house. I was there the day you almost nailed your hand to the wall," she said.

"And you never said anything. You never came close? You didn't think to let me know."

"I hadn't found the answer to my magic, then. I was still too terrified to have you too close to me, couldn't risk harming you like I'd harmed your father."

"You could have waved. Said a word. Left a message."

Gytha raised her hand to her eyes, to the tears that were falling. "I could have. I thought to, but I was ... I was scared."

Olin scoffed. "Scared?"

"Yes. You looked happy, you were growing. I was scared I would come and start something that would make all of that go away. I know it doesn't make sense, but I could never stop being terrified, even from a distance."

"So what changed?" Olin asked.

"Wylie found me and told me to stop coming. He asked if I would stay instead, and when I gave excuses, he told me that I had my wish. He told me to stay away until I was ready to face what I had done – leaving you. He was protecting you, just like he always had, even before you were born. You might have been born of his brother's seed, but you are, by every account, Wylie's son.

"Seven years passed before I realized that the death had been caused by my magic being crossed. The sorcerer who told me uncrossed them. I spent years learning to use it, finding out just how powerful I was. All the while I never stopped thinking about you. I have thought about this day in my head a million times since I uncrossed my magic and became sure I wouldn't kill unconsciously. But with every year that passed, as I grew even more powerful and became a Grand Sorceress, I also grew increasingly scared of what would happen if I walked myself back into your life.

"And then I received the emissary from Ravinshore, and followed the queen's summons, and with every step you were in the back of my mind. And then Levyna mentioned your name."

* * *

The boatswain called warning. The last passengers, a pair of brothers, made their way towards him and handed him the money as nonchalantly as he had had ever seen anyone do in his life. He watched as they walked to the main deck like they owned the vessel. The boatswain glanced at his captain, who shook his head. The boatswain started to turn, but was stopped by a man dumping money in his arms and walking aboard. More coins than necessary for a single passenger for twice the trip. The boatswain swallowed his protest, watched the man hurry below deck, and he turned and called for the ship's departure from the waters of Duken.

The captain wasn't trembling. The sea was calm and this time he was confident a storm wasn't hiding beyond the horizon. His bones didn't ache, bringing him to the edge of the roaring sea as she held his ship. The Flea set sail to the excitement of a hopefully uneventful journey.

In the common deck of the ship, a small boy with a wooden horse looked away from his mother in the direction of the man sitting opposite him with a thick scar on his wrist. The man glanced at the boy with scary eyes as he pulled the hood of his cape even lower.

Edenborough would be his stepping stone. That was the only way survival would be assured. Yes, he had an army who would still fight at his command, but if he was ever going to accomplish anything, he would need to live first. Let the chaos die down, however long it took. He would be back. He was far from done yet.

Ravinshore was the Order's.

Queen's Hill was the Order's.

Duken belonged to the Order.

They all belonged to the Order of Walrea. They all belonged to him, and he was going to come back for them.

Thorne only regretting that he hadn't squashed Wylie's sciff when he'd had the chance. That had been left it to no-good L. And L. Thorne regretted his patience with the wayward watcher while waiting for Edmond to die. Thorne regretted leaving Duken without taking Otto's head with him to toss in the sea as chum for the fishes. He hoped, dearly in his heart, that Otto remained alive so he could return and bury him headfirst into the ground for his betrayal.

Thorne rested against the hull, his breath calm as the thought of a bit of distance from the three kingdoms comforted him. He glanced at the scars in his wrists, where his threads had been yanked out of his arms. He wasn't running; he was merely retreating.

At the back of the deck, disguised as an old woman with grey hair, Gytha watched as the man who had almost taken her son's life dreamt of sanctuary. She stared at him.

EPILOGUE

W illiam had followed her.

After they'd left and he'd returned to his house, he'd realized he couldn't get her out of his mind as easily as he'd imagined. He'd told himself that she had all the help she needed and he would only be a distraction. And Isabelle hated distractions. She'd left them by the riverside so she wouldn't be distracted from the quest.

But the conversations they'd had that night came to him and her absence had suddenly weighed on him, again. When he'd finally given in and gone to check if she was alright, he'd found her leaving the palace and he had turned around, second guessing his actions and about to return home. Until he'd found himself on her heels once again. And then she'd been stabbed.

Now, he found himself glancing to the side every few moments to see her face, sunken but still striking; she gave him a painful smile even as she wrapped her arms around the little girl who would become her world as they rode to Duken. And hopefully a part of his.

* * *

Levyna opened her eyes to a different ceiling. She turned her head to the side and found a new face offering her a look she didn't recognize. Olin had taken the role of caregiver from her mother. Levyna preferred him, even if she would never let her mother know.

You're right. She might finally have a reason to hate me if you tell her that, Olin thought. He was sitting in a chair next to the small bed in Posdel's house.

"She cannot hate you."

"Even when it looks as if I've stolen you away from her?"

Levyna smiled, dimples forming on the sides of her flushed cheeks. But they fell away too quickly.

"What was the dream about?" Olin asked.

She looked at him. "A phoenix," she answered.

"Rebirth," Olin said as he looked down at the scroll he held, leaning to take her hand.

Levyna picked up the scroll he'd drawn and stared at a face she was familiar with. It looked just as she remembered Yondi, the one and last time she'd seen him.

ACKNOWLEDGMENTS

Thank you to all those who helped throughout the writing and editing process. Without you, this book wouldn't be here today.

Thank you to the beta readers who helped refine the story and pick up on some plot holes that I missed; oops.

The editors that I had a pleasure of working with helped me trim up and refine the story to what it is today. Thank you so much.

ABOUT AUTHOR

Originally from Alice Springs, Australia, A.M. Dyer currently resides in Broken Hill with his spouse and biggest fan, Buddy the Kelpie cross. Dyer works in the Broken Hill mines as an Electrician and volunteers with St. John Ambulance to provide medical aid at events. Though Dyer is passionate about helping others, he always felt the urge to pursue the creative outlet of writing as well. With the drive to craft his stories pushing him and the knowledge that there was never a perfect time, Dyer saw no reason to procrastinate on his dream. He set to work. The culmination of his efforts, a debut Young Adult fantasy novel, released in May 2022.

Son of the Flame, Book 2 in The Ash and Stone series will be in stores soon.